PASSION'S AWAKENING

Leaning back for one breathless moment, Aurelia looked adoringly up into the face of the man she had come to love so well in such a short span of time.

Slowly and with deliberate intent, Lord Dalton bent his mouth to Aurelia's, drawing her still nearer in his embrace. She could feel his frame shake with emotions barely suppressed, and his eyes spoke more eloquently than any voiced declaration. With an unexpected gentleness, their lips met, and Aurelia experienced such a moment of utter bliss that it seemed to elevate her to some other existence. . . .

Now that Lord Dalton had expressed his love, Aurelia knew she must warn him of the terrible threat to his life. But if she disclosed her dangerous knowledge, she could lose him forever!

I10635501

THE
Signet Ring

Adora Sheridan

BALLANTINE BOOKS • NEW YORK

Copyright © 1979 by E. M. Pavlik and J. F. Hong

All rights reserved under International and Pan-American Copyright Conventions. Published in the United States by Ballantine Books, a division of Random House, Inc., New York, and simultaneously in Canada by Ballantine Books of Canada, Ltd., Toronto, Canada.

Library of Congress Catalog Card Number: 78-61843

ISBN: 0-345-27785-6

Manufactured in the United States of America

First Edition: April 1979

Dedicated to
JOSEPH LAWRENCE PAVLIK

All the events and characters portrayed in this book are purely fictitious.

~~~~~ CHAPTER 1

THERE ARE individuals who are able to take command
of any situation that may arise in life, and then there are
those who tend to run back and forth in a frenzy of
indecision if the slightest change in routine occurs. Faye
Courtenay, Duchess of Harcourt, was of the latter category. At the moment she was attempting to organize
her household for the impending departure of her
daughter, Lady Aurelia, and herself to London for the
start of the Season.

"Why did I ever decide to bring you out into polite
society *this* spring?" wailed the duchess as she struggled
to pack a portmanteau for the journey.

The bedroom, to an uninformed observer, appeared
to have been struck by a hurricane. Mounds of clothing
were strewn about the room, and the three ladies occupying the area sought to sort through the satins and
laces in order to select appropriate apparel for a young
lady about to be presented to the world.

"Now, Mama, you know that it is high time I had my
coming-out at Almack's. It should have been last
year, but as Aunt Philippa was ill, we could not go.
There is simply no reason not to go this spring, so do
be sensible and fetch me the blue silk on the dresser."

These words were uttered by a lovely vision garbed
in pale lilac, the Lady Aurelia Courtenay. She was perfection itself to behold; with her golden hair and spar-
kling blue-gray eyes, she appeared to have stepped

1

from the pages of a fairy tale—the princess from *Sleeping Beauty*, perhaps.

Her Grace turned to the third person present, Lady Standen, and asked, "Gabrielle, do you think the blue silk gown is too young for Aurelia?"

"Perhaps it is a bit, madam," remarked the dark-haired beauty. Lady Standen turned to Aurelia, her face serious but her eyes holding ill-disguised amusement as she said, "You will undoubtedly want to purchase some clothes when we arrive in London, Aurelia, for I know you hope to be all the rage and cut a dash. And you will, my dear, you will!"

This statement, delivered with such mocking sincerity and such an earnest expression, caused Lady Aurelia to shoot back banteringly, "As do we all, my dear Gabrielle. However, while some may only aspire to the heights, others succeed!"

Lady Faye shook her head at such talk, but this was a normal mode of conversation for the two young ladies who, having been friends since childhood, were to be presented at the same time by Lady Faye. Lady Standen's parents were both deceased, so the duchess thought it was perfectly natural for Gabrielle to come along.

The Standen name was well known in the Huntington area, as was that of Courtenay. The two vast estates bordered each other, and before Gabrielle's birth there had been hopes for a male heir to the Standen fortune, and a suitor for the hand of Lady Faye's new-born daughter. This was not to be, but the two girls had become fast friends.

Lady Standen was an ideal foil for Aurelia's gold and rose tints. Her raven tresses and warm brown eyes could not subtract from Aurelia's beauty, nor could the opposite occur. Following the loss of her parents, it was no wonder that Gabrielle's guardian, an elderly uncle, had depended on Lady Faye for advice on how best to introduce his niece to society.

Out of sympathy for the orphan, Lady Faye had proposed that Gabrielle accompany Aurelia and herself to London. She also hoped that Gabrielle's presence would help to avert any mischief that Aurelia could possibly get into, for it was well known about the countryside that Aurelia could fall into more scrapes than the devil himself. True, Gabrielle had often been a party to Aurelia's shocking coils, but, her Grace reflected, it could have been much worse had she not been present. All in all, the best possible course had been taken.

Glancing around the room, the duchess moaned inwardly. There was so much to do and so little time in which to do it all. She felt a migraine coming on.

"Mama, do hurry! We must finish all the packing this evening, and you are simply standing there holding your forehead!" Aurelia exclaimed.

The ladies continued their sorting and folding until it appeared that all was in order. By dinner, the three women were completely exhausted. The last bandbox finally sealed, Lady Faye collapsed in a heap onto one of the plush chairs in the sitting room.

"Aurelia, please tell Crane to have the cook serve dinner in half an hour. I need time to rest my aching muscles."

"You will stay to dine with us, of course, Gabrielle," Lady Courtenay said as they descended the staircase in search of Crane, the family butler.

Lady Standen replied in the affirmative, since it was much too late for her to go home.

As the young women reached the foyer, Crane appeared as if by magic. Lady Courtenay relayed her mother's instructions.

"Very good, Lady Courtenay. Will Lady Standen be staying?"

"Yes, she will be dining with us," she replied. "Oh, and, Crane, I hope you have finished your packing. We leave for London at dawn, and I wouldn't want you to forget anything."

Assuring Aurelia that he was completely packed and ready, Crane departed to deliver her Grace's wishes to the cook.

"Davis has all of my things loaded into the family carriage and will be here early tomorrow, so we won't lose a moment of traveling time," Gabrielle said. "A most efficient butler, but for his peculiar habit of sniffing when he disapproves of something."

"Yes," Aurelia agreed, "he does tend to do that overmuch, but he is rather a snob, so I suppose there is nothing for it."

It was a peculiarity of both ladies that they were disinclined to travel with maidservants of any kind. They considered them more in the way than a help, and had refused to have a maid accompany them on the trip to London. This was a sore trial to Lady Faye, who would have preferred to be attended and waited upon; however, knowing that her daughter was adamant, and reflecting that she could employ a girl when they arrived in London, the duchess had given way.

The girls chatted together in the drawing room until Lady Faye descended for dinner, having changed into a gown of purple silk with the aid of her personal maid. As there were only the three of them that evening, the meal was rather light. A poached salmon with almond sauce, a roast pheasant, and tiny game hens stuffed with mushrooms were sufficient for their purposes. After a game of piquet, the ladies retired to their respective rooms to await the dawn's coming.

The next morning Lady Courtenay and Lady Standen went over a list of things that were essential for the trip, to be sure they had missed nothing. Aurelia read off the objects as Gabrielle checked them off.

"Foot warmer?"

"Check."

"Riding saddles?"

"Also present."

"Well, that is the entire list. It seems we have everything," Aurelia concluded.

"I can't think of anything else myself, but then I'm constantly forgetting something when I go on a trip," Gabrielle said.

Aurelia had a thoughtful look on her fair face as she

tried to recall what could be missing, for she felt as if something were indeed amiss.

"I have it!" she exclaimed suddenly, and turning on her heel, she strode to the library, Lady Standen following in her wake.

Opening the library door, she walked over to the enormous marble fireplace that dominated the room. Above the mantel were several sets of dueling foils and pistols, which she proceeded to examine with care and then handed each one to Lady Standen.

"I knew we had forgotten something," Gabrielle remarked, "but it hadn't occured to me that we were about to set out without any means of protection. You are very clever for remembering, Aurelia. These are magnificent weapons. Where did you get them? I don't remember ever seeing them before."

Aurelia hesitated a moment before replying. "They were my father's, and Mama preferred that they not be displayed. I just put them up only recently, after I took them down from the attic room."

As she turned one exquisitely carved pistol over in her hands, a look of disturbance crossed her countenance, for it reminded her of her own deceased father.

Lady Courtenay was aware that the marriage between her mother and father had been arranged. They had been very ill-matched because their personalities were almost directly opposite. While her father had been emotional and opinionated, her mother was rather stolid and scatterbrained. The differences between them had been a source of much friction, and theirs could not be said to have been the happiest of marriages.

The relationship between the duke and the duchess had gone from bad to worse as the years went by, so it was no surprise to Aurelia that, when her father passed away, the duchess had had no qualms about cleaning out the gunroom completely and putting her husband's weapons away. Lady Faye considered the numerous pistols and foils so much clutter; besides, she disliked and feared weaponry of any kind.

At first Aurelia had complied with her mother's wishes, but later, because she was much more her father's daughter than her mother's, she had insisted on letting them be seen again. She was proud of the skill her father had possessed, as well as admiring of the instruments' artistry.

The duchess, who was not half as strong-willed as her daughter, had complained minimally about the arms being put up but had not really interfered.

Rousing herself from her reverie, Lady Courtenay asked Gabrielle, "Which do you think we should take?"

Gabrielle was about to answer when Lady Faye walked in.

"There you are. I have been searching for you. It's almost time to leave."

Seeing the array of weapons being inspected by the girls, the duchess became most dismayed. "Aurelia! Never tell me you intend to take those along? You know Davis and Crane will be armed for our journey."

Aurelia gave her mother a look that was very descriptive of how competent she felt Davis and Crane were with pistol and foil.

"Upon my soul, Mama," Aurelia sighed with exasperation, "you know full well that I would not trust our safety to those two. Why, Crane fences as if he were clearing bushes, and Davis cannot shoot to save his life. Why do you think father taught me to handle a foil and a gun? He was not one to trust his safety to others, either."

Lady Standen agreed, and faced with the combined persuasion of both ladies, the duchess was induced to consent to the idea.

"I know the two of you will have your own way whatever I say, so you may bring weapons, but for heaven's sake, don't brandish them about for all to see," Lady Faye pleaded. With that admonition, her Grace hurried off in her characteristic manner to supervise the loading of the trunks onto the carriages.

Lady Courtenay, after much reflection, chose a pair of engraved, gold dueling pistols and a foil of French design that possessed a handle set with pearls and sapphires, having previously tested for aim and balance. Unlike most young ladies of fashion, Aurelia could both shoot and fence like an expert. Her forte was the French dueling foil, in which she excelled even beyond the prowess of her father, a noted swordsman in his time.

It had been he who had placed a miniature foil in her hand at the age of six and taught her to fence. As Lady Standen had been Aurelia's constant companion from birth, she too had been taught to defend herself. Her passion, however, was the pistol, and she was generally held to be an excellent shot. Gabrielle chose for herself a pair of ivory-handled dueling pistols and a small foil of local origin.

Thus armed with what the duchess described as "an arsenal," the ladies proceeded to clear away the last-minute details that always spring up when one takes a trip. Finally, when everything was ready, all three ladies entered the carriage, made themselves as comfortable as possible, and settled down for the journey ahead of them. As they watched the house grow small in the distance, Lady Faye, eyes raised briefly heavenward, expressed a fervent desire for a quiet trip.

"No doubt you shall have your wish fulfilled, Mama," commented Aurelia placidly as she arranged a foot warmer about her feet.

The duchess frowned. "If there is any mischief to be had, you will certainly get into the thick of it, for a more gadabout child I have yet to meet. You will be in some scrape or other before we have reached London, so I suppose it is futile to ask for a peaceful journey," she snorted.

There was nothing to be said to this statement, as it was quite possible, if past behavior were any indication, that Lady Courtenay would indeed find one or more diversions to become involved in as the trip progressed.

For the most part, the ride to their first rest stop was uneventful. The roads were clear, the weather mild. Lady Faye could find no fault with any aspect of the trip so far. Even the coachmen were driving better than usual, and when they arrived at the Boar's Head Inn, her Grace was unusually relaxed.

The proprietor rushed out to meet them as the coaches ground to a halt before his modest establishment. He was a pleasant-looking man, for an innkeeper. His inn was renowned for its good food and comfortable accommodations. While Crane and Davis helped the ladies to alight from the coach, he hurried forward, his face all smiles.

"Your Grace?" he inquired as Lady Faye gave the area an appraising glance.

"Yes, I am the Duchess of Harcourt. And who are you, sir?" she asked as she inspected him through a raised quizzing glass.

Many an upstart had been cowed into submission by one of the duchess's inspections, but seeing that he was only the owner, she was merciful and gave him but a cursory glance.

"I am Mr. Barnes. Your rooms are ready, and luncheon will be in an hour's time," he informed her.

Eyeing him once again through her glass, her Grace frowned.

"I require more than an hour's rest before eating, to be sure, sir! You will serve lunch in an hour and a half, and not before. Is that quite clear?"

Mr. Barnes's reply was apologetic, and he assured Lady Faye that luncheon would be at the time she wished. With that, the man nervously showed the women to their rooms.

Upon reaching her immediate destination, her Grace collapsed onto the feather bed.

"It is so good to lie down after riding in that stuffy carriage for so long," she sighed, removing her gloves.

"Mama, it has only been a short while, really. I can't see why you are so tired. I'm not at all. Are you, Gabrielle?"

Gabrielle shook her head. "Not in the slightest. As a matter of fact, I would like to take a ride around here to pass the time while you are napping, your Grace."

Aurelia was agreeable, but the duchess nearly started from her bed at this idea.

"You simply cannot go riding around the countryside unescorted!" she exclaimed in horror. "It simply is not done. Young ladies of quality simply do not ride alone. It doesn't signify what you do at home, for we are not there! If you wish to ride, you must have Crane or Davis accompany you, since we have no groom with us." Lady Faye was most emphatic on this point.

This did not appeal to either young lady, however, as neither one had a very good opinion of the riding abilities of the butlers.

Aurelia regarded her mother with dismay. "Mama, we couldn't possibly take them along. They are no fun whatsoever. They ride abominably, and you know that is true."

No amount of cajoling could dissuade her Grace, so the girls left her room crestfallen. Or at least Lady Standen did. Aurelia, on the other hand, had a very different attitude. Looking at her friend, Gabrielle could see the wheels turning in Aurelia's head.

"I know that look," she said as she followed Aurelia into their room. "You are planning something again, and I'll wager you aren't going to tell your mother about it, either."

"Gabrielle," Aurelia announced mischievously, "you know me all too well. I have an idea how we can go riding together without Davis and Crane. No one will ever know that we have even left the inn."

Gabrielle was all ears as Aurelia disclosed her plan in a conspiratorial whisper.

"It's quite simple, of course. That is what convinces me we shall certainly succeed," Aurelia began confidently. "We have only to borrow some clothing from Crane and Davis, tuck our hair up under our hats, and voilà, we are transformed! We need not concern ourselves with attendants, and we will never be missed."

Gabrielle asked uncertainly, "But how can we at--
tempt this? Crane and Davis would never allow us to
borrow their clothing, and I know they would tell your
mama about the escapade."

"They needn't know," Aurelia replied quickly. "I
saw them go down to the kitchen to attend to their
needs. If we act with haste and you have the heart for
it, we can obtain the articles we will need while they
are below."

There was only a moment's hesitation, then Gabrielle replied, "Done! It is worth the risk, I think."

"Then let us be quick. We haven't much time and
we must go about it carefully," Aurelia said excitedly,
relishing the thrill of a small adventure as she led the
way cautiously into the deserted hallway.

Walking softly on the worn wood planks, Aurelia
winced as one loose board creaked, protesting even her
light weight. Mindful of the danger, Gabrielle stepped
gingerly over the spot, drawing close behind her friend
as Aurelia halted before the room shared by their butlers. Turning the knob of the door, Aurelia opened it a
crack, peering discreetly within for signs of occupancy.
There was no movement evident, and she opened the
door wide enough to step inside. Gabrielle would have
followed, but with a swift motion Aurelia indicated that
she should stand guard at the door. With great trepidation Gabrielle obeyed, every nerve alert for signs of an
approach as Aurelia disappeared within the room.

Closing the door gently behind her, Aurelia quickly
scanned the room's contents, only faintly aware of the
strong scent of lilac powder in which the butlers had
packed their starched and lye-permeated linen prior to
the trip. The sweet and astringent smell prickled her
nose as she sought out her prize.

Aurelia's eyes rested at last on the large leather
cases in a corner of the room that sufficed to hold
Crane's attire, and she moved swiftly toward them, her
fingers eagerly reaching for the buckles and clasps se-
curing them.

Once opened, the bags revealed some intriguing

little parcels wrapped in brown paper, neatly arranged among the clothing. Aurelia would have liked to open one up, but the thought of discovery and propriety prevented her. No doubt they were presents for relatives in London, she reflected, hurriedly removing apparel from the bags.

Outside, Gabrielle was aware of every nerve strung taut as she listened for footsteps, so it was with great relief that she greeted Aurelia's emergence, a large bundle of clothing tucked beneath one arm. Looking about suspiciously, the two women headed back to their room. Gabrielle feeling distinctly like a criminal fleeing the law as they skulked stealthily toward sanctuary with their booty.

Approximately twenty-five minutes later, two young gentlemen descended the stairs of the Boar's Head Inn. Mr. Barnes did not recall having met them, but they looked vaguely familiar. Although they were dressed relatively conservatively, their rather delicate features and aristocratic bearing indicated they were of excellent breeding. Also, they sported quite a large quantity of jewels, attesting to their wealth. It did not occur to this good man that the young gentlemen were rather undersized for their attire and that, except for the profusion of ornate rings, their garments could have been that of any well-paid butler.

Walking up to the gentlemen, the proprietor asked, "Can I be of assistance to you, my lords?"

The blond-haired gentleman spoke first, in a rather odd voice.

"Yes, my companion and I would like to take a ride before luncheon. Do you have any available horses?"

"Why, as a matter of fact, I do have some horses I can place at your disposal, sir, but do you think you should go riding in your condition?" the innkeeper wondered with concern.

A look of surprise crossed the young man's face.

"My condition?" he repeated, searching for an explanation. He glanced at his dark-haired friend, who inquired: "What condition are you speaking of? There is nothing at all wrong with my friend."

The proprietor now looked doubly surprised.

"Why, both of you must have it!" he exclaimed. Seeing that the gentlemen were still puzzled, he explained, "You both seem to me to have a bad cold. It is affecting your voices. Do you think it wise to ride with such a condition?"

The gentlemen assured the innkeeper of their good health, and ten minutes later the two were riding along on a pair of black horses provided by Mr. Barnes, laughing uproariously at the success of their ploy. Had the innkeeper been more perceptive, or their acting a bit less believable, the two young "gentlemen" would have been found to be in actuality Lady Standen and Lady Courtenay. Having each "borrowed" a set of clothing from their butlers, the ladies had, in their inimitable style, pulled off an extremely tricky feat. One which, if discovered, would most certainly lead to an enormous scandal for their families.

They were not concerned with this thought, however, as they rode, enjoying the fresh air and the feel of a good horse beneath them. Both ladies had taken the precaution of bringing along a pistol, tucked in the waist of their breeches, for protection. One could not be too cautious in unfamiliar territory, but they did not anticipate that they would actually put them to use. The weapons were there more for reassurance than for anything else.

Having ridden for some minutes, the women slowed their mounts to allow them to rest. They decided to go off the road and walk the animals through the surrounding wooded area, as Aurelia had a particular fondness for the green serenity of the woods.

"I hope your mother doesn't decide to look for us before we have a chance to change back into our dresses," said Gabrielle as she swept a low-hanging branch from her path.

Aurelia, who was slightly ahead of her friend, answered, "There is little chance that she will, since she took one of her pills to calm her nerves before she went to sleep."

At that moment they thought they heard what sounded like people talking. Gabrielle motioned Aurelia to dismount, and this they both did, tying their horses to a bush and proceeding quietly on foot toward the sounds. As they neared, they could tell that the voices were coming from the direction of the main road, but in a section that was densely covered on both sides by thick trees so as to be a perfect area for highwaymen to waylay their victims. At this point, more prudent and perhaps cowardly girls would have turned back from fear or indecision. However, Lady Courtenay and Lady Standen were neither cowardly nor too terribly prudent, so they continued to walk closer and closer to the road. Finally they reached a spot from which they could observe all that occurred below them on the byway. What they saw was hardly unexpected. Just as they had supposed, there was indeed a coach halted on the road, with five highwaymen surrounding it, their drawn pistols aimed at the driver and at the doors of the vehicle.

The leader of the ruffians appeared to be a rough fellow of less than average height and more than average weight. He looked as if the population of vermin on his person must be of enormous proportions indeed, and he evidently did not believe in shaving or bathing regularly.

The doors to the coach opened, and two well-dressed young men descended with their arms raised.

"Gabrielle," Aurelia whispered, "we must get closer so we can hear clearly what is being said."

Gabrielle nodded. "Yes, I agree, but I think I will circle around them. That way we can catch them in a crossfire if need be."

So saying, she drew her pistol and began to creep cautiously to the opposite side of the road.

Aurelia waited until Gabrielle was in position, then she moved herself closer to the coach and tried to decipher what was being said. She had been correct in her assumption that the fat creature was the leader of the group, since she could now make out that he was instructing three of his henchmen to search the vacated coach.

"'Urry up," he growled at one of them. "We ain't got all bloody day."

The men hurried to comply with his wishes and continued to search as he commanded.

Aurelia was able to discern the features of the two gentlemen who had alighted. One of them wore a most vicious and threatening expression that marred his otherwise attractive face.

He looks like the very devil himself, Aurelia said to herself, as she studied him.

It was to this gentleman whom the highwayman directed his next words:

"Well, it would seem that ye 'ave found a right clever 'idin' place fer yer riches. Me men can't find a thing."

His men had indeed come up empty-handed, though they had searched the vehicle quite thoroughly.

The fiery young man's dark eyebrows knitted even more tightly than they had before. "You will never lay hands upon that money if I have anything to do about it, you scoundrel!" he snarled.

He bore the utmost contempt for his captor and did not attempt to hide that fact. Whether this individual was extremely brave or just foolhardy was debatable, Aurelia thought.

Her reflections were interrupted by the second young gentleman, who said, "My friend is correct, you know. You will never get that money because it isn't here. We sent the blunt ahead of us by special messenger to London." The speaker was a good-looking man who appeared to be better-natured than his friend, though still naturally displeased at the turn of events.

His companion had a look of savage satisfaction on his face as he again vented his feelings. "Did you really think we would be stupid enough to travel with such a large sum on our persons for scum like you to attempt to take from us?"

This question, delivered with vitriolic disdain, had a disastrous effect on the villain's temper. Pulling his pistol from his waistband, he pointed it at the two gentlemen.

"Do ye know, do ye 'ave any notion, who Oi be?" he roared as he waved his pistol from man to man. "Oi kill ten o' yer kind afor' lunch. Oi be Scurvy Joe, th' most feared o' all 'ighwaymen. Oi'm wanted fer murder already, so two more gentry coves won't matter to me," he threatened. "If yer lyin' 'bout th' money, Oi'll cut out yer livers!"

The two men didn't say anything further, though the dark one's face did not alter at all. Noting the sataniclooking gentleman's expression, Scurvy Joe was sorely tempted to use his weapon.

"Oi've been paid to kill ye, and Oi've only waited this long 'cause o' th' money. Oi'll ask ye again. Where be that money?"

Just then there was a commotion in the bushes across from where Aurelia was hidden. That would be Gabrielle, she thought as she drew her pistol and cocked the trigger.

Startled by the sound, Scurvy Joe ordered his men to search the area while he kept an eye on the captives. Aurelia waited in her hiding place as one of the ruffians came toward her, unaware of her presence. Just as he was almost upon her, she leaped up from behind and struck him on the temple with the butt of her gun. He fell to the ground as if dead, but on checking his pulse, she found him to be only unconscious.

Scurvy Joe was beginning to look very uneasy, and when he heard the thud from his man's fall, he called out frantically, "Andy! Where be ye? 'Ave ye found anythin'?"

Aurelia heard a similar sound from across the road and knew Gabrielle had succeeded in downing another henchman.

Scurvy Joe began to sweat visibly. "Answer me, someone!" he shouted.

Two of his men ran back onto the road, fear being the dominant expression on their faces.

"Let's go, Joe," said one. "There be nothin' 'ere, and Oi can't find Andy anywhere."

Looking nervously about, Scurvy Joe seemed to make up his mind.

"Mount up, boys! We're leavin' right now!"

They did as they were bade while Scurvy Joe pointed his gun at the two gentlemen again.

"If ye 'ave any last words, say 'em now," he ordered, cocking the trigger.

The two men said nothing.

Aiming his pistol straight at the vitriolic young man's heart, Scurvy Joe prepared to fire. This was too much for Aurelia. She sighted and fired at the offending ruffian. Scurvy Joe suddenly felt a searing pain on his hand, the impact of the shot flinging wide his pistol.

There was instant pandemonium, and Aurelia moved off to find a better position.

"We're surrounded," one of the highwaymen wailed as he turned his horse in a circle, gun in hand, searching for some target.

Gabrielle shot him, hitting his left shoulder. This was the last straw for Scurvy Joe and his band. They rode off as quickly as possible and did not look back.

Not quickly enough, however, for the splenetic young man now had possession of Scurvy Joe's pistol and fired with great deliberation at the retreating figures. The man that Gabrielle had injured previously was hit by the shot and fell from his horse, his other arm now incapacitated as well. Scurvy Joe and the remaining ruffian made good their escape.

Suddenly Aurelia felt a presence behind her. She whirled, her gun at the ready, but it was only Gabrielle. Aurelia sighed with relief.

I've tied up my man with his shirt so he won't get away. What about yours?" she asked.

"The same."

"Let's get away from here before those two come

looking to find out who we are," Aurelia said, glancing about nervously.

"Too late! They are approaching."

The women hid hastily behind a bush as the two recent captives came up to investigate. Then Aurelia had a thought and produced a handkerchief from her pocket. She tied the cloth around her mouth to disguise herself and motioned her friend to do likewise. Gabrielle found a cloth in her own pocket and did the same, grasping Aurelia's intent entirely.

It was one thing to help these gentlemen in their hour of need, but it was quite another to be discovered in men's clothing, shooting guns, and, in general, not behaving in a socially acceptable manner. They could not risk the scandal. Now the two young ladies were motionless as the men searched the area about them.

"See anything, Brett?" asked the baleful gentleman.

"No, nothing at all, Philip. They must be gone by now," replied the other, peering behind a large shrub.

The man called Philip scowled. "That simply can't be. They must be here somewhere," he insisted.

He continued to look for them avidly, but his friend did not share his enthusiasm for the search.

"If they wanted to be found, Philip, they would have presented themselves before this. We should just leave it at that."

There was evidently no reasoning with this Philip fellow, however. Aurelia and Gabrielle could see that he would not desist until he had found them, so they decided to make themselves known rather than to be discovered cowering behind the bushes. Drawing their pistols, they waited until the men had their backs to the bush in which they were hiding, and rose up, guns in hand.

Aurelia cleared her throat and spoke through the mask covering her face. "If you are looking for us, gentlemen, look no further."

Both young men halted in their tracks.

"Please raise your hands and drop your weapons," she instructed. Philip released his gun.

"Turn around, please, slowly," she ordered.

They did so, and the girls had their first chance to inspect the lords at close quarters.

The scowl was back on Philip's face, and Aurelia thought it better not to aggravate him, having seen a sample of his shooting ability.

"You may lower your hands," Gabrielle said.

As they did so, Aurelia continued: "We have no desire to rob you, I assure you, but for reasons I cannot explain, it would be most inconvenient for you to know our identities."

Her voice, through the mask and spoken at a lower pitch than usual, passed for masculine. Or at least Brett thought so.

"Sir, we were only looking to thank you for your assistance, nothing more. I am Viscount Sheringham, and if I can ever be of assistance to you, you have only to ask." So saying, he bowed to his rescuers.

Lady Standen looked at Lord Sheringham closely and was pleased with him, all told. He seemed more appealing than ever as he rose from his bow. Lord Sheringham was a very good-natured, handsome young man of twenty-four who possessed dark brown hair and brown eyes that eloquently expressed his every mood. His tall, athletically built figure did justice to the perfectly tailored coat of blue bath cloth he wore.

As Gabrielle examined Lord Sheringham, Aurelia indulged in a closer inspection of Philip.

Seeing that Aurelia was staring pointedly at his friend, Brett deduced it was time for an introduction.

"And this is my good friend Philip, the Earl of Dalton."

Philip made a bow, but it was not in the best of grace. Rising, he said, a touch of sarcasm in his voice, "Charmed."

Aurelia was obviously unimpressed by this remark, so Lord Dalton tried another tactic: "We would not reveal your identities, I assure you."

He said this in as sincere a tone as he could muster, but the effect was little, if any. It was then that he noticed a ring on Aurelia's finger. He leaned forward slightly in an attempt to get a better look at it, but Aurelia moved the hand behind her to keep it from his sight. She did not trust this man, and no one who was even remotely acquainted with Lord Dalton would have blamed her.

Lord Dalton's features were not those conducive to good fellowship. With his black hair and icy blue eyes, he could be extremely handsome, but for his tendency to scowl. Depending on his mood, he could resemble Lucifer before or after his fall from grace.

Fortunately, at that moment Philip Dalton's features had eased up considerably from their former state so that he looked almost friendly. At least Gabrielle thought it fortunate. Aurelia, on the other hand, felt as if he had discovered something about them that she preferred he did not know. She could see that Lord Dalton was now gazing at Gabrielle in the same thorough manner in which he had scrutinized her, and she decided that this had gone far enough.

"If you gentlemen would be so good as to turn around again and give us your word of honor not to move from this spot for the next ten minutes, we will take our leave of you," Aurelia said.

Lord Sheringham gave his promise willingly, Lord Dalton, more reluctantly.

As they turned around, Lord Dalton spoke again.

"We may not know who you are now, but I have ways of finding out what I want to know."

This was stated with the total assurance of a man used to completing what he sets out to do. It was not said in anger, but there was no gratitude in it, either. Somehow Aurelia knew that expressions of gratitude would be rare from this man, and thus she was not offended.

The women left quickly, making sure that they were not followed as they went. Arriving at the spot where they had tethered their horses, they mounted rapidly and rode away.

Pulling the cloth from her face, Aurelia queried, "Do you think they suspected that we were women?"

Gabrielle shook her head as she tried to undo the knot in her scarf with one hand, the other being engaged with the reins of her horse. Finally managing to untie it, she turned to her friend.

"I really don't think so, Aurelia. At least I don't think Lord Sheringham did."

"It is that Philip who worries me, not Lord Sheringham."

"He was staring at us very hard," Gabrielle noted thoughtfully. "He seemed to notice your ring in particular. Which one is it?"

For the first time Aurelia looked down at her hand to identify which ring he might have seen. She gasped, and Gabrielle looked at her in alarm.

"What is it?" Gabrielle asked anxiously.

Aurelia was speechless. Gabrielle brought both mounts to a standstill and took Aurelia's hand. She inspected the rings and discovered the reason for her friend's reaction. On Lady Courtenay's third finger was a ring her father had given her that bore the family crest.

"Do you think he knows whose crest it is?" Aurelia asked, worry creeping into her voice.

Gabrielle reflected for a moment. "He may have a vague picture of it, but I don't think he saw enough to be sure."

Aurelia thought over Gabrielle's assessment, and it made good sense to her. From what she had seen of Lord Dalton, she was sure he would have made some comment about it had he recognized it. Nonetheless, she decided not to wear her signet ring, for awhile at least.

The two women encountered no trouble when, after arriving at the inn, they left their horses to be cared for and made the exchange of clothes. Obviously no one had discovered anything missing. With a sigh of relief, both girls collapsed into chairs and awaited the knock on their door that would tell them luncheon was ready.

They were tired, and it was mutually agreed that they would discuss the episode after they had eaten and rested.

So it was that Lady Standen and Lady Courtenay descended to luncheon, each thinking her own respective thoughts about their adventure of that day. Lady Faye joined them, believing her charges to have indulged in a long, restful nap, as she herself had done.

CHAPTER 2

LORD DALTON and Lord Sheringham had stood as if transfixed for the requested ten minutes, during which they felt extremely silly. Their coachman, having been ordered to remain by the carriage, had done so dutifully, spending the time binding up the wounded robber's injuries until he was instructed to assist the lords in searching the surrounding area for the missing bandits. He did not ask either gentleman where they had been, and by the look on Lord Dalton's phiz, it was a matter better left fallow. It had taken half an hour to ferret out the missing highwaymen, and as they both were in a state of unconsciousness, Lord Dalton was unable to question either one. Lord Sheringham observed, with no little amusement, with what poor grace Lord Dalton accepted his fate.

"We will simply have to question them later," Philip said tersely, motioning the coachman to help load the bodies onto the carriage.

Lifting the wounded man's inert form last, Brett remarked, "Don't think this one will be able to say much in any case. In a bad way, you know."

With a despising glance, Philip Dalton noted the blood-soaked bandages and the man's pasty complexion. He could almost be persuaded to consider it a pity that the man had not expired on the spot, such was his disgust for the creature before him.

"We can turn them in at the next village," Brett suggested.

Philip nodded to this in an absent manner, his mind occupied with other matters. Having completed the loading, he and Brett entered the carriage and instructed their coachman to proceed to the nearest town. The preoccupied look on Lord Dalton's face was familiar to his friend, who waited patiently until such time as Philip would be moved to speak to him. He did not have long to wait. Glancing up from his contemplation of a dark corner of the coach, Lord Dalton smiled at his friend.

"Ah, the sphinx is about to speak," Brett said funningly.

"Correct as usual, Brett. Your perspicacity is amazing on occasion. Really!" Philip commented wryly. "I was just thinking that there was something awfully unusual about those two men who came to our aid."

Brett looked at his friend, puzzled. "How unusual?"

"Well, they were rather short, don't you think?"

"No more than usual," Lord Sheringham replied after a moment's consideration.

"Well," Philip continued, "I would say, by their size and by the way they were obviously disguising their voices, that they must be the sons of some local squire gone adventuring, and very youthful at that."

"Perhaps we can make inquiries about them in the next town," Brett said, "for I know you wish to repay them."

A dry smile appeared briefly on Lord Dalton's face.

"Most certainly I do," he answered. "I find it maddening to be beholden to a pair of green 'uns barely out of the lesson room."

Regarding his friend for a moment, Lord Sheringham knew the truth in this statement. Ever since he had first met Philip at school years ago, he had noted his almost fanatical aversion to accept assistance or to acknowledge a kind act on his behalf. To be indebted to a pair of bantlings for his life would be unendurable.

I can hardly blame him for being reluctant, Brett thought. Considering his home life, I suppose it is inevitable for him to distrust everyone.

As he thought this, Lord Sheringham realized he did not really know all the facts about Philip Dalton's childhood, since he was more conversant with Philip after he had come to live at school.

He smiled as he recalled his first day at Harrow, the occasion on which he had met Philip. He himself had been quite young and unsure. Having been educated previously at home by a tutor, he was not used to so many strange faces at one time, but since he was by his very nature a likable individual, he had found no difficulty in presenting an amiable figure. As he had stood by the playing field, he had noticed another boy sitting alone on the grass. It had been Philip, of course, and Brett had been fascinated by him.

Through the memories of a much younger Brett he recalled how even then Philip had seemed to possess his own personal thundercloud that followed him around, tempering the very atmosphere about him, so that anybody looking at him must surely feel uneasy. His features had been softer in those days, but the piercing blue eyes had been there, as had been the arrogant posture and the cool, assured way of walking and speaking. Brett had made a mental note on the spot to avoid raising that particular individual's ire at all cost, and might never have become involved with Philip had not circumstances thrown them together.

Brett had been watching some second-year students playing on the field when he noticed something rather odd. One of the largest boys, who had been eyeing the boy in the corner with a look that bespoke malicious intent, had kicked the ball toward the sitting figure.

Philip had risen to retrieve the ball with his back turned, so he did not see three of the older boys detach themselves from the crowd and advance. The other youths vanished as if on cue, and Brett realized that the moment had been prearranged. He could not stand by and watch a trio of stronger individuals attack that solitary boy. Shouting a warning, he had rushed boldly into the fray, a tendency that showed more bottom than sense. He could remember little of the ensuing melee, but as he recollected, he had been less than skilled in the pugilistic arts. The fight had been brief, Philip having quickly dispatched two of his opponents and assisting a downed Brett.

What an odd fellow he was in those days, Brett thought. He remembered how Philip had remained aloof to him for some time even after the skirmish. But, he mused, we managed to be friends in spite of his damnable pride.

He was roused from his reverie as they appeared to be approaching the town.

Constable Larken, a man of ruddy complexion and remarkable bulk, relieved the two men of their unconscious cargo. The constable assigned a couple of his men to deliver the injured bandit to the physician's offices.

Lord Sheringham would have preferred to report the attempt on Philip's life to the constable, but Lord Dalton withheld the information, since there was no real proof of what they both suspected—that Philip's stepfather, Lord Chandler, had hired the ruffians.

As they reentered the coach, Brett could contain himself no longer.

"Dash it, Philip! You should have told the man about the murder attempt. We both know that Lord Chandler was behind the effort. He has been a thorn in your side ever since he married your mother, God rest her soul, twenty years ago."

Immediately Brett regretted having mentioned Philip's mother, as the pain became evident on his friend's face. Just as quickly, Brett saw Philip's features revert to the urbane expression he habitually adopted in public.

"My mother's poor taste is not in question here," Philip replied smoothly.

At the abashed look on Brett's face, Philip relented slightly.

"I would simply rather not indulge in speculation without solid proof. Let's leave off until we have occasion to question those who are in custody."

Brett nodded. "All right, but you're going to have to face this situation sooner or later."

Seeing that his friend was still reluctant to talk about it, and that they had just arrived at the inn, Lord Sheringham let the matter drop.

Conversation was at a minumum during the meal that evening, which consisted of roast duck with orange sauce, several pigeons garnished with garden-fresh asparagus, and a kidney pie that was indeed delicious.

Lord Dalton was apparently still brooding about Lord Chandler or his mother or both, and Lord Sheringham knew it was best not to bother him when he was in this condition. After their port Brett left him to contemplate the matter alone in his room.

Philip lit a lamp and prepared for bed. The soft light illuminated the old-fashioned furnishings, bringing back memories that he had tried, almost forcibly, to forget. His ancestral mansion possessed the same faded but comfortable quality, and for a moment he was overwhelmed by past images. He could see in his mind's eye his mother, a lovely woman with soft brown hair and blue eyes, always smelling of perfume and powder. She had been a child bride and, by all accounts, his father had been the perfect groom. Philip knew nothing of him other than a portrait he had once seen and the gossip of the servants. His father had been killed in a riding accident, a circumstance fraught with irony since he was considered a bruising rider. His mother had been left a widow after only three years of marriage, with the burden of a child and the management of the vast estate.

Philip had known even at an early age that his mother was very weak and helpless, and though he loved her, he had harbored resentment toward her for her lack of strength and especially because she had succumbed to Lord Chandler's dubious charm, a scant two years after his father's demise. It had been for the money, of course, that Lord Chandler had married his mother, and when they had wed, he had obtained almost complete control over the property.

"Or at least he thought he did," Philip murmured through clenched teeth.

The marriage had been a farce from the beginning, Lord Chandler never bothering to hide his disgusting liaisons with various and sundry women. Philip had seen his mother grow ever weaker under Lord Chandler's dominating presence, and he had developed an abiding hatred for his stepfather.

Philip had been aware almost from the beginning what the result of such harsh, unfeeling treatment would be, and his fears were confirmed as he had watched his mother gradually deteriorate before his eyes. She had finally succumbed to pneumonia after ten years, not possessing the strength to overcome the disease after years of being racked by coughs and other ills. She died only a shadow of the woman he had remembered in his childhood, her fragile, wasted condition forbidding him entrance to her rooms more often than not. Philip's conviction that Lord Chandler had, in essence, murdered his mother only deepened his already virulent loathing.

The chilling eyes, which Brett had so often seen trained on hapless individuals who had raised Philip's ire, were an acquired trait. The incident that marked this acquisition had first occurred when Philip was ten years old.

Lord Chandler had met with opposition from his youthful adversary when he had attempted to establish his then current mistress in the house. Lord Chandler had beaten the child into insensibility, and Philip had remained unconscious for three days, delirious throughout and almost dying of fever. On the morning of the fourth day he had regained consciousness, and it was on that morning that his eyes had first held their look of cold animosity. The look never left him, though the rest of his face might appear calm.

The mistress had not stayed long; she could not bear up under those scathing eyes. Though Philip was obedient to Lord Chandler after that day, he had been beaten many times because his eyes betrayed his inner feelings. After a year, Lord Chandler had sent him away to school to escape his ever-present surveillance, but found he was haunted still by those eyes, so unnatural were they in their portentiousness.

School had been a new episode in his life, but memories of home still lurked in the shadows of Philip's mind. He knew that he cut an intimidating figure at Harrow and made a great many enemies with little or no effort. His superior attitude and his visible scorn of others had pitched him headlong into trouble. He knew well how to antagonize people, but did not know the first thing about making friends.

He reflected that Brett had been his only friend and wondered at his tenacity. He had rebuffed Brett countless times, but Brett had been ever pleasant to him in return. Slowly but surely, Brett had gotten to know Philip and was not repulsed by what he found. He did not fear or disdain Philip, and they had become inseparable friends. Brett was the one person whom Philip trusted irrefutably, and they had total understanding of one another. Brett cheerfully bore Lord Dalton's company in London, Philip holding his country estate in aversion since his mother's death.

Thinking of how Brett had let him alone at dinner, keeping the conversation light and frivolous, Philip realized that he had been very poor company. He made a mental note to be extra pleasant to Brett tomorrow at breakfast. Breakfast! he thought. I won't be able to greet the morning if I don't get some sleep. Climbing into bed, he attempted to block the thoughts that crowded his mind and rest.

As Philip struggled for sleep, Brett was in the process of completing his perusal of the town's local tabloid. Reading the day's news every evening before retiring was a habit he had acquired as a child, and it usually assured him of an undisturbed repose. Folding the paper neatly, he placed it on the top of the bureau for the next occupant of the room to enjoy. Then, rising from the overstuffed chair in which he had been seated, he stretched his body, catlike, trying to loosen his muscles in preparation for bed. He winced at a twinge of pain in his lower back.

That's what comes of sitting in a coach all day, he thought, rubbing at the sore spot. This was an unwise move, as it only served to allow his shoulder muscles to register a similar complaint. "I must be getting old," he mused aloud as he rubbed the offending area. This did nothing to ease his condition. "Nothing for it but to get a good night's sleep and hope it goes away tomorrow."

He proceeded to undress, carefully hanging his clothes in the prescribed fashion to preserve their crisp appearance. Though no dandy, he would be considered by most individuals in the know to be a very well-dressed young man. He made a striking contrast to Philip's usually oppressive but opulent mode of attire. Whereas his friend would clothe himself almost entirely in black, decorated perhaps with embroidery upon the waistcoat, Brett would wear bright colors with a profusion of jewelry. His powder-blue traveling suit with gold and blue edging was an excellent example of his taste. Appropriately adorned with a diamond stickpin and several rings and fobs, Lord Sheringham was more than merely presentable. He accepted the inconvenience of traveling *sans* valet for the sake of simplicity and because Philip preferred to travel light.

Pulling the bedclothes up to his chin, Brett reached over and snuffed out the candle. Closing his eyes, he attempted to relax but felt uneasy, as if something were out of place. He shook himself mentally. Dash it, getting as bad as Philip now, he told himself.

Pushing the uneasy awareness from his mind, he finally fell asleep. His was not to be a peaceful night, however.

In his room down the hall, Philip was slumbering fitfully. He awoke with a start to a sound at the window, a faint scratching. Someone's trying to get in, he thought.

Slowly rising from bed, he continued to listen for the slightest movement. Someone was definitely trying the window to his room, but he had locked the shutters tightly before retiring for the night. Silently Lord Dalton moved toward his open trunk to get the pistol that lay beneath his clothing. He had a fair idea who might be out there.

"Persistent devils, I'll grant them that," Philip muttered as he finally reached his goal.

His hand quickly burrowed underneath the clothes and found the smooth barrel of his gun. As he pulled the weapon out and held it at the ready, he heard the shutters abruptly cease their previous activity. He walked to the window being sure to stay out of range should the intruder decide to shoot through it. He listened intently and then realized that the scraping noises were moving away from his room and along the outside wall.

Where the devil is he going now? Philip wondered as the scraping grew fainter.

Suddenly he knew where the intruder was going. Brett habitually slept with his windows open to admit what he considered to be the invigorating night air. Running across the room, Philip shot back the bolt to his door and dashed down the corridor.

Reaching Brett's door, he pounded on it, praying that for once his friend had closed the shutters.

From within he heard the sounds of Brett getting out of bed, then his footsteps approaching the door and his voice inquiring what the din was about. Just as Brett opened the door, there was an enormous crash as the intruder kicked open the shutters that Brett had left slightly ajar. Stepping into the dark room, Philip could see the silhouette of a person in the window, a knife upraised and glinting in the moonlight. He hesitated an instant, decided against using his pistol, and rushed forward as the figure leaped to the floor. Hurtling toward the intruder with great force, Philip caught him with a solid blow, but the interloper was not fazed. Philip attempted to wrest the knife from the man, and eventually the constant, irresistible pressure that Philip exerted on the muscular wrist had its effect. The knife came clattering to the floor, and Philip threw the man against the wall with the intention of questioning him.

Brett had not interfered up to this point, unsure if his assistance would help or hinder his friend, but now he came forward. As he did, the culprit gave a swift movement, wrenching himself free of Philip's grip, and made a mad dash for the open window. Brett and Philip, running toward the window, heard the sudden slip, the desperate but brief clawing as the man attempted to find a purchase, then the sickening thud on the ground below.

"My God, Philip, what the devil was that?" Brett asked as they peered out. They could just barely distinguish the body of a figure, illuminated by the moon's rays, lying lifelessly on the grass. It was one of the remaining men who had stopped them on the road that day.

"Well, I've got my answer now," Brett said. "Your stepfather doesn't give up the hunt easily, Philip."

As the two gentlemen turned to go down and view the body, they heard footsteps approaching the room, and the sound of the proprietor's voice.

"Oh, dear! Oh, dear! What has happened here?" the innkeeper cried, wringing his hands. Seeing the decimated shutters, he groaned loudly and seemed about to indulge in another outburst of "Oh, dears."

In his most soothing voice, Brett attempted to halt what appeared to be a case of extreme nerves. "Don't worry about that. We will, of course, pay for the damage. We are going downstairs to see if the man who fell while trying to get in through my window is dead, so I would suggest that you go back to sleep."

During this speech Philip had grown impatient and had already descended. Pushing the innkeeper gently toward the open door of his room, Brett quickly followed suit.

Though a number of individuals had peered into the hall at the start of the commotion, they soon lost interest when it proved there was nothing to see.

Lord Sheringham finally approached his friend's side, to find Philip examining the body for identification. As he searched, Lord Dalton frowned.

"There do not seem to be any papers on him at all. Wait, here's something."

Reaching down into the dead man's vest pocket, he fished out a crumpled piece of paper. He tried to discern the writing on it, but he couldn't, though he held it up to the moonlight.

"Let's go back inside. I can't make out what it says out here," Philip said as he rose.

In the inn, Brett stepped over to the wall on which a lamp was hanging, found a match, and lit it.

"You know, Philip, I won't have a moment's rest until Scurvy Joe is under lock and key or swinging from the end of a rope. If we could connect him with Lord Chandler, we could effectively spike Chandler's guns for good. As it is, Chandler could strike at any time and we would have no proof."

Philip nodded while he read the note in the dim light. Then he handed it to Brett.

"Very informative," he said as Brett scanned the paper. "Apparently this man was supposed to have disposed of us, then delivered that note to my stepfather confirming our demise."

"He obviously wasn't up to the task," Brett remarked dryly.

"Well, there is nothing more to be done this evening," Philip commented wearily. "We can send for the constable in the morning to remove the body. Wouldn't do to shock the other boarders," he quipped wryly.

As the two men started back upstairs, they were met at the top of the steps by the innkeeper, who could not sleep after the commotion. Seeing him, Lord Dalton paused.

"Perhaps you should cover the body with a cloth so the guests won't be exposed to such a sight," he suggested.

"Of course, my lord," the man replied, gulping convulsively at the prospect of having to view the body himself.

The two friends began to settle in for the rest of the night, cramped as they would be in one room. Several minutes later the proprietor of the inn knocked on their door softly, but with persistence. With a groan Brett admitted the man.

Padding quietly into the room in stocking feet, the innkeeper seemed very excited.

"My lord, you will never guess—"

"I am in no mood for guessing games. If you have something to say, then do so," Philip retorted sharply, his temper wearing thin.

"Well, your lordship, it is only that the man below is the same man who was here earlier in the day asking a lot of questions about a robbery on the road. Of course, at the time, we didn't know it was anything to do with you, Lord Dalton."

This information did not seem either to please or to enrage the earl, who only nodded.

"Fine. You have done quite well, but now I think what we all need is a little sleep," he said, guiding the proprietor out the door. "We will deal with all the details in the morning, and thank you for your assistance in the matter."

Closing the door, Philip turned and examined the arrangements Brett had made for retiring.

"You had best fetch a blanket from your room and sleep on my couch," Philip suggested.

Brett agreed to this and made his way back to his room. Walking over to the bed, he became aware of something glittering on the floor in the moonlight. He bent to examine it and found it to be a long and razor-sharp knife. Uttering a low whistle, he walked back to Philip's room, dagger in hand.

Observing the weapon, Philip asked, "His?"

"To be sure," Brett replied. "It fell from his hand, remember? Wicked-looking thing, isn't it?"

He gave it to Philip and watched him heft it in his hand for a moment, then place it on the tabletop.

"It's well balanced in any case," Philip commented nonchalantly as he slid into bed.

"Well balanced!" Brett exclaimed incredulously. "That could have been sticking in your back had things turned out differently, or in mine for that matter, and all you can say is that it is well balanced? You definitely do not realize the gravity of this situation, Philip," Brett asserted as he tried to make himself comfortable on the couch.

Lord Dalton did not take exception to this and merely snuffed out the candle.

"Good night, Brett," he said, no trace of concern in his voice.

Seeing that there was no use in pursuing the matter further, Lord Sheringham settled himself down for a well-earned night's rest.

The next morning, after a hearty breakfast provided by the ever-attentive innkeeper, Lord Dalton and Lord Sheringham paid a visit to the constable in hope of questioning the bandits they had turned in.

Constable Larken was waiting for the two men outside the jail house as they rode up.

"Good day to you, my lords," he called out as they dismounted and walked toward him.

"Are those men conscious?" Philip inquired, pulling off his gloves.

"They came around about four this morning," he replied. "You must have really given them something to remember you by. I've never seen two men stay under for such a long time."

After a short pause he added, "The other one passed on to his reward earlier this morning. Confessed to trying to rob you on the road. He mumbled something else, but I couldn't make it out. Robbery is not the sort of thing a dying man wants to take with him, if you know what I mean, your lordships."

Lord Dalton did not feel up to explaining the affair to Constable Larken, so he merely nodded.

"Yes. Well, may we see them now?"

"Of course, my lords. Come right this way," he said, leading them inside the dark recesses of the jail house.

There were only two cells, since this was a relatively small town, and they were barren except for a cot and a washbasin. The prisoners occupied one of the cells, and by the sorry look on their faces, they seemed to be regretting their participation in the previous day's activities.

One of the men had a black eye that looked quite painful, and it was he who spoke first, directing his statement to Lord Dalton, since he appeared to be the individual with whom to deal.

"Oi know ye've come to ask us questions, guv'nor, and me friend and Oi 'ave talked it over, and we be willin' to tell ye everythin' we knows, in return, that is, fer a break."

Philip considered this for a moment. Looking at Brett, he indicated they should leave the cell.

"I think I should dicker with them, Brett. They may know something of value. In the meantime, perhaps you could ask around town about those young men who helped us the other day. Someone around here should know who they are." Then he added ruefully, "People are much more likely to tell you than me."

Brett accepted the task, and agreed to meet back at the jail in half an hour.

Returning to the cell, Lord Dalton found himself drawn aside by the constable.

"You'll have to talk through the bars, my lord," Larken insisted. "I wouldn't trust anybody in there alone with that pair."

Philip conceded the point, and soon was left in privacy with the two men.

"Well guv'nor, do ye agree to deal wit' us?" asked the man with the black eye.

"Are you going to be the spokesman for the two of you?" Philip asked, looking at the other prisoner.

"Aye guv'nor. Ye see, Tim 'ere be a mute. 'E can't speak a'tall. Oi kind of takes care of 'im."

The mute, who had been watching attentively, nodded his agreement, and Lord Dalton could tell his silence was not feigned.

"Well, let's get on with it then. I will let you go on the condition that your information is of use to me. I have that much influence at least. Is that clear?" he asked, staring straight into the highwayman's eyes.

The man appeared to be sizing Lord Dalton up.

"Ye look to me to be a man o' yer word, so it's a deal."

"All right. Who hired you to rob our coach yesterday?"

"Well, guv'nor, Scurvy Joe didn't tell us who sported the blunt fer th' job. 'E said it was 'is own idea."

Lord Dalton was evidently displeased at this, and the man went on hurriedly.

"But we knowed 'e warn't tellin' it true, 'cause 'e knowed which road ye'd be on and what time, and 'e even knowed yer names. Now that ought to be worth somethin' to yer," the man said hopefully.

Philip motioned him to continue.

"Well, we just thought we was goin' to rob ye. It came to us as a surprise that Joe was goin' to kill th' two o' ye. We wouldn't 'ave gone along wit' it if we'da knowed. Me and Tim, we never pulled the cork on no one, and don't mean to never."

"What about the man who escaped with Scurvy Joe?" Lord Dalton asked. "What do you know of him?"

The highwayman hesitated a moment, rubbing his chin contemplatively.

" 'E might 'ave knowed more than us. 'E be a friend o' Joe's. 'Is name be Leper Sam." He laughed. "That's 'cause all th' women stayed away from 'im like th' plague."

He had a good guffaw over this, but it died on his lips when he observed that Lord Dalton was far from amused.

"Your friend Leper Sam is no longer among the living. He tried to assassinate my friend and me last night. Needless to say, he failed in that endeavor," Philip said, his voice implying what he did not say aloud.

The robber shuddered at this bit of news, and miraculously his memory improved.

"Oi seems to remember somethin' now," he muttered nervously.

"I thought you might," Philip purred.

Glancing nervously at the earl's face, the captive continued cautiously. "Well, Oi remembers that Joe said th' cove what wanted th' deed was some city swell. A lord or some such."

Philip digested this information and was lost in thought when the highwayman interrupted him to put him in mind of their agreement.

" 'Ave we got a deal, guv'nor?" he asked hesitantly.

Looking at the man as if he had just remembered his presence, Philip answered, "Yes, I'll have the constable release you on the condition that neither of you attempt to contact Scurvy Joe and that you leave the area immediately."

To this the two robbers agreed, being reminded that Lord Dalton would not take favorably to any diversion from the set course.

Though the constable was reluctant to release the bandits, he had no choice, for Philip dropped his charges against them.

As Lord Dalton emerged into the daylight, he saw Brett walking toward him with an expression that revealed his lack of success.

"Did you find out anything?" Philip asked, though he knew in advance what the answer would be.

"No. Nothing. No one here in town to whom I have

spoken recalls anyone answering their description. Perhaps you should just forget them," Brett suggested.

Philip was disinclined to accept his friend's hopeless attitude on the matter, but put off discussing it for the time being.

"Well, how did you fare?" Brett sighed.

"Not much better than you did," Philip replied. "One of the blokes made a reference to a 'city swell' who hired Scurvy Joe, but there is no direct connection between the highwaymen and Lord Chandler. Oh, yes. They did say he was a lord."

"Well, it must be Chandler," Brett declared, certainty in his voice. "If only we could prove it . . . but we're no closer to that than before."

Philip smiled grimly. "I am certain we will think of some way to deal with him," he said, his face bearing no hint of mercy.

Brett shuddered at the smile as he mounted his horse.

"I wouldn't be Chandler for all the money in Christendom when you finally get hold of him."

Philip, who was skilled in all manner of weaponry, could make short work of almost anyone, Brett thought. Lord Sheringham was sure he had never seen anybody faster or more expert with a foil, which was Lord Dalton's specialty.

"To be honest, Brett, I don't blame you in the least. It will not be pleasant," Philip confirmed, spurring his horse toward the inn.

They arrived at that establishment just as a coach pulled in. The two gentlemen dismounted, and Brett looked on as three ladies stepped down from the halted vehicle. One was a rather elderly dowager, but the other two were young.

Must be going to London for the start of the Season, he thought.

A strong impulse to walk over and introduce himself to them overcame him, especially regarding the dark-haired beauty, who, from this distance, appeared to be quite out of the common way. However, even if propriety had not forbidden such an act, the circumstances compelled Lord Sheringham to observe the social niceties.

"Come along now, Brett, we must leave immediately," Lord Dalton said, motioning him away from temptation. Brett was still hesitant, and as Philip entered their waiting coach, he called out to his friend impatiently:

"Brett, we've lost enough time as it is."

Lord Sheringham took one last, longing gaze at the ladies, who had not yet noticed him, and then climbed in behind Philip.

"No need to fret. Just wanted to take another look at the ladies who just arrived. I suppose it would be a mistake to simply walk up and introduce myself," Brett said wistfully.

"Most certainly a mistake," Philip agreed. "If the mother wouldn't cut you dead, the daughters would. Simply isn't done, bantling."

Seeing that his friend was truly put out, Philip added cheerfully, "You will see them in London, I am sure. Besides, they are probably just a pair of whey-faced ingenues. Better off without them."

Brett shook his head at this. "Philip, they might be very pleasant people, you know. Not everyone is the same; besides, they were far from 'whey-faced,' I can tell you that."

This did not seem to penetrate Lord Dalton's look of calm conviction, so Brett simply sighed and leaned back in his seat.

I suppose Philip was right, he thought. We'll meet them in London, and it would be rather improprietous of me to introduce myself, in any case. He shuddered slightly at the mental image he conjured up of the older female giving him a set-down for his impertinence. A steady gaze through her quizzing glass would have been sufficient.

Even so, as the coach began to leave, Brett looked out yearningly at the ladies, who were about to enter the inn that he and Philip themselves had so recently vacated.

"The blonde is a dasher, too," he murmured admiringly. Then the vehicle turned, and the inn was no longer visible. He sighed audibly, which drew an amused look from his companion.

CHAPTER 3

THE PROPRIETOR ran out to meet his new guests as the coach containing Aurelia, Gabrielle, and the duchess stopped in front of his establishment.

He saw young Lady Courtenay descend first, a beautiful sight in rose-pink. Then Lady Standen alighted, a vision in celadon and gold. Lastly, her Grace stepped down with the assistance of Davis's hand on one side and Crane's on the other. She was not looking her best, though her maroon carriage dress usually became her. The lady was obviously unwell.

The proprietor rushed forward to offer his services but her Grace, seeing a rather common-looking individual coming toward her, arms outstretched, waved him away with the lace handkerchief she held in one feeble hand.

"Sir, my men shall aid me, if you please," she said weakly.

"We will need a room for my mother, who is ill as you can see, and one for Lady Standen and myself," Aurelia told the innkeeper, who appeared to be at a loss as to what to do.

"Of course, my lady. Come this way. Shall I call for a physician?" he asked.

Aurelia followed after him and the butlers, who were lifting Lady Faye off the ground and carrying her in. Gabrielle remained behind to supervise the unloading of a few boxes that they would be utilizing for the evening's stay.

"We will be needing the striped bandbox and the two black ones," Gabrielle said to the boy who was bringing down the requested parcels. Looking at them, she realized there was one other thing they would require that was inside the coach.

Her Grace's pills must be in her reticule, Gabrielle reasoned to herself as she searched the coach for the illusive object.

"Will that be all, my lady?" the stableboy asked.

He was holding the boxes in his arms, and Gabrielle saw that he was but a young lad of ten years. The packages completely blocked his view.

"Don't you think you should take the packages in separately?"

The boy shook his head vigorously. "I can do it, my lady," he asserted. "Besides, I have my other chores to attend to, if you please."

"All right, but don't hurt yourself," Gabrielle replied with a smile.

She resumed her searching, and the boy turned carefully to deliver his packages upstairs. He had not gone half a dozen paces when Gabrielle heard a horse approaching at a fast clip.

The rider is certainly in a hurry, she thought. She then found the purse she had been looking for, secreted behind a corner cushion.

"Found it!" she cried triumphantly.

Almost at the same instant she heard a yell outside the coach and the sound of a horse whinnying in terror. Looking up, she saw a man trying to control his mount, which had obviously panicked. The horseman was swearing profusely, and Gabrielle was horrified to see that the stableboy was on the ground, frozen with fear as the animal's hooves reared above him.

Dashing from the coach, she ran to the prostrate child, nearly becoming trodden into the ground herself as she pulled the boy out of danger.

The innkeeper came running out at the commotion. "What has happened here, sir?" he asked anxiously.

With barely controlled rage, the rider said, "That little mongrel got in the way of my horse as I rode in, and scared the animal into a fit."

The man cast a caustic look at the child, who was crying into Gabrielle's shoulder.

"You odious creature!" she spat. "You might have killed him with that ridiculous manner of riding into a place!"

The proprietor was flabbergasted as to what should be done. He was not often faced with the prospect of intervening in matters of quality, and did not relish the idea in the least.

Finally he said in his most placating manner, "Well, the boy's not hurt and your horse has calmed down now, sir. Why don't we leave it at that and allow me to show you to your room?"

The gentleman seemed to have had enough. "All right, but keep that little ruffian from my sight!" he snarled.

He brushed by them and made for the entrance. As he passed through, Aurelia tried to exit at the same moment. Pushing her rudely aside, he continued on. Aurelia was indignant for a second, but the feeling waned quickly when she saw Lady Standen and the boy on the ground and the bandboxes strew about in several directions.

"Gabrielle, what happened?" she cried, running to help them up.

The youth, having regained his voice, said, "That man tried to run me down with his horse, then he tried to have his horse crush me, but the lady here wouldn't let him." He gave Lady Standen a grateful look.

Gabrielle nodded in agreement. "That's the story,

more or less. Perhaps a little more intent was read into the man's actions than was actually there, but even so, he is a horrid man to speak as if the whole affair were the child's fault, for it most certainly was not."

Aurelia could see that her friend's ire was raised, but they had more important things to discuss. Making sure that the boy was unharmed, the two women went into the inn. They had not yet spoken of the previous day's experience, because they had not had a moment alone since their return from the adventure. After lunch Lady Faye had insisted on continuing the trip, having deemed that the hour's rest that she imagined the girls to have taken before luncheon was sufficient to last them until they reached the next stopping place. The duchess had estimated that they would reach the hostelry by nightfall, but she had not reckoned with the occurrence of a broken axle halfway to the town. It had taken hours to find someone to repair it, and the women had slept in the coach until nearly dawn. Once the vehicle was finally fixed, they had continued on their way to the second stop of their journey, arriving much later than planned.

The innkeeper met the girls in the foyer, and by the cool way in which Gabrielle eyed him, Aurelia knew that he had displeased her friend in some way.

She decided to take the lead and asked, "Are our rooms ready?"

"Yes, my lady. They are ready now," he replied, leading them upstairs. "I am sorry for the delay, but we have been busy repairing some damage."

"Oh?" said Aurelia in her offhand manner, which, to a brighter individual, would have signaled her disinterest in the problems attached to the running of an inn. However, the proprietor was not too astute, and remained undaunted.

"Yes, my lady. We had quite a night here. Two lords were attacked by a thief, and one of them, a most disturbing-looking gentleman, I must say, scuffled with the intruder. Quite a row, really," he declared as he reached the top of the steps.

It was fortunate that his back was turned to the girls or he might have seen them look sharply at each other at the mention of the "disturbing-looking gentleman."

"You did not say what became of them," Gabrielle prodded anxiously.

"Well, the gentleman struggled with the stranger, as I said, and when the thief tried to escape out the window, he slipped and fell."

Stopping before a small door, the innkeeper gave the dull brass doorknob a swipe with his cloth.

"I am afraid that this room is all we have at the moment. We are quite full at this time of the year," he apologized.

Lady Courtenay nodded. "It is fine." Then, as the man turned to leave, she asked, "By the way, who did you say the two gentlemen were?"

The proprietor stopped and scratched his head. "Oh, yes. Now it comes to me. Their names were Lord Dalton and Lord Sheringham. You are acquainted?" he inquired curiously.

"Vaguely," she answered. "That is all, thank you." With that Aurelia closed the door and looked at her friend.

"They must be the ones who were driving away as we pulled in," Gabrielle said, sitting on the edge of one of the beds occupying the chamber.

"Do you suppose they were looking for us?"

"I don't know. If they were, we must find out why."

A thought struck Lady Courtenay. "We can send that little boy around town to gather information."

"Not a soul would suspect him, I suppose."

So it was that Jeremy, the stableboy, was seen about the town asking quite a few questions, most of the townspeople freely answering them, as he could be a rather persuasive child at times.

In the meantime, Lady Courtenay and Lady Standen at last had a moment to themselves to discuss what had happened. It was difficult to decide what, if anything, should be done. If the gentlemen were indeed trying to discover their identities, the ladies would most certainly be faced with the danger of exposure.

"What we should do is to make their acquaintance in London, see just what type of people they are," Gabrielle suggested, picking at the coverlet on the bed.

Aurelia considered the idea, turning over in her mind other possible solutions.

"Well, that sounds better than doing nothing and waiting for them to discover us for themselves if they can," Aurelia acknowledged as she pulled on her dinner dress. "They might not even reveal our little peccadillo . . . There is something else we haven't discussed."

"What is that, Aurelia?"

"If you will recall, that brute Scurvy Joe mentioned that he had been hired to assassinate Lord Dalton. We have to do something about that, too."

"I suppose so," Gabrielle replied, "but what? We don't know who hired them."

Aurelia gave a small shrug and sat down on the bed.

"Well, that gives us another reason to make their acquaintance—to keep them alive if we can! I'm sure the monsters will try again, and though I am not terribly fond of Lord Dalton, I feel responsible for him now that I've saved his life."

Gabrielle smiled. "Why, I thought he wasn't so bad. Don't you think he is attractive at times?"

Aurelia glanced up at her friend through her lashes.

"I suppose he has a good face in general, but he has a rather surly disposition, to be sure, and I think it will be attempting the impossible to get to know him. I shall try my best, however," she replied. Then, looking mischievously at her friend, she added, "I am sure you would not deny that it wasn't Lord Dalton whose features appealed to you the better. I would say you have a decided preference for Lord Sheringham."

Lady Standen would have made an objection, but stopped short when she heard hoofbeats approaching the inn. Aurelia rose from the bed and walked to the window to see who was arriving. She gave a small gasp of surprise as she looked into the yard. Her curiosity having been aroused, Lady Standen moved to the window to see what was happening. What she saw gave her disagreeable shock. There, tying his horse to the rail, was Scurvy Joe.

The proprietor rushed out to greet yet another guest but stopped short when he caught sight of the unkempt ruffian. Aurelia could not make out what was being said, but the innkeeper eventually, if reluctantly, let Scurvy Joe in.

"What can he be doing here?" wondered Gabrielle.

"Couldn't be in search of us," Aurelia decided. "He has no way of knowing who we are, so he must be here for some other reason. We should ask the proprietor about him when we go down for dinner."

"I agree, but we must be very discreet."

There was a knock on the door that made Gabrielle jump. Through the wood frame they heard the voice of the innkeeper informing them that it was time for supper. Shamefacedly, Gabrielle opened the door.

"Tell me," Aurelia asked, "will we be dining alone?"

The man seemed taken aback at the question. "Well, no, my lady. We usually seat the guests together for supper. More congenial."

"My friend was just wondering, because we observed a rather bizarre-looking man riding up, and I must say I would leifer not dine with such an individual," Gabrielle informed him.

Aurelia nodded her agreement with this statement. "Yes. He looks exceedingly filthy and quite disreputable."

The proprietor shook his head vigorously. "No, no, I assure you, my lady, that he will not be dining with you. He was allowed in only because he is to meet someone here on business."

"Oh? Who?" Aurelia asked innocently.

"I believe he said he was to meet a Lord Chandler, my lady. The gentleman who rode in earlier."

Gabrielle's eyebrows shot up. "You mean that—that creature who nearly killed the stableboy?"

"Yes, my lady," he replied nervously.

Seeing that they had no further questions, he withdrew hurriedly, spurred on by the look of distaste on both ladies' faces.

"Well, now we know why he's here," Aurelia said. "I wonder who this Lord Chandler is and what his business is with such a deplorable man."

"I wonder, too," Gabrielle agreed. "But at the moment I am starving to death, so do let's go down to supper and talk about it later."

They left their chamber and descended to the dining room. Since dinner was still being prepared, the two lovely women seated themselves on a sofa in the sitting room to wait. While they were making small talk, Jeremy arrived and conveyed to them the news he had obtained during his foray.

Looking uneasily about, he leaned forward slightly and in a conspiratorial whisper said, "I asked around like you wanted me to."

"Sit down here and tell us," Aurelia offered, making room for him on the couch.

A few minutes later the proprietor looked in and saw his guests conversing with the child.

How nice of the ladies to talk to him, the innkeeper thought. I suppose they are listening to some foolish story of his.

If he could have heard what they were discussing, he would have been surprised to discover young Jeremy relating yesterday's events to the ladies in detail—not only what had transpired at the inn, but what had happened at the jail as well.

"That was a good job, Jeremy," Gabrielle said, handing him a coin.

Holding fast to the money, he dashed off for home.

Watching him leave, Gabrielle asked, "Well, what do you think of that? The constable was listening at the door during Lord Dalton's entire conversation with the felons."

"Yes, it would seem that he has an insatiable curiosity," Aurelia remarked. "I wonder who else the good constable told."

"Lord Chandler might have asked if he has dealings with Scurvy Joe. And just where is Lord Chandler at this moment, I wonder?" Gabrielle asked.

Aurjela would have answered her friend, but another person entered the room. He could best be described as a very young schoolteacher.

He was a guest at the inn, as were they, and he seemed to be very unsure of himself socially. Making an awkward bow before the ladies, he introduced himself as Mr. Tome. The two women nodded coolly in response, amazed at his presumption in speaking to them without first having been introduced. They had no desire for an intruder, but this small acknowledgment on their part sent the young man into such a state as to strike pity into their hearts.

Stammering and blushing, he made his greeting. "Honored to ma-make your ac-acquaintance, madams."

Aurelia decided that he meant no harm and was truly ignorant of social propriety. Extending her hand, she attempted to be as nice as possible. The young man saluted that dainty member with a great deal of solemnity. As he rose from his bow, an elderly couple entered the room. They took no notice of Aurelia and Gabrielle but seemed deep in a conversation of their own.

"Why, Tristan," the matron said in apparent distress, "I should know Alecia Dalton's little boy anywhere. Philip has always had that same look, even as a child."

At the mention of Lord Dalton's name the ladies pricked up their ears. These people evidently knew him and had been present the night before. Aurelia could barely hear what the couple was saying since Mr. Tome was at this point attempting to make light conversation and failing miserably, as might have been predicted. Finding himself in the company of women who might be expected to indulge in the literary pursuits, Mr. Tome was endeavoring to strike up a discussion of works they might have read.

"And what do you think of that satiric poem 'The Rape of the Lock'?" he asked earnestly.

Finally fed up with the man, Lady Courtenay replied, "I do not approve of *any* sort of rape, sir."

Feigning offense at his choice of words, she moved away from the sofa with Lady Standen in tow, leaving Mr. Tome gaping after them much in the manner of a beached fish. The two women seemed to wander aimlessly, but their goal was to come within earshot of the elderly couple again. As they walked over to the window, they recaught the drift of their conversation.

"You know, Tristan, I have never liked Lord Chandler. When Alecia's first husband died and she married him, I knew he was marrying her only for the money. I think it served him up right that Alecia left everything to Philip when she passed away, poor dear."

Her husband regarded his wife indulgently. "Yes, my dear, I quite agree. Chandler has always been an outsider and a bounder, even if his family tree is one of the oldest. He is the last of the line, as I recall, but, if I do say so myself, I'll be glad when this particular branch of the family dies off," he declared with some vehemence.

"You know, dear," his wife said in a near whisper, "there were quite a few rumors about the circumstances leading to Alecia's decision to leave all her money to Philip."

Her husband looked astonished. "Why, what rumors are those, dear? I had heard none."

"There was talk that Alecia had to have the legal documents smuggled into her room as she lay on her deathbed so that Lord Chandler would not prevent her from changing them. It was the lawyer of the estate, Caruthers, who brought them under the cover of wanting her signature for a few small bills."

Tristan thought for a moment before asking "Caruthers . . . wasn't he in charge of the fortune until Philip reached his majority?"

"Yes. He had Chandler ushered from the estate directly after Alecia passed away. Some say Lord Chandler swore to kill Caruthers someday. Imagine that! Making such a threat, and before witnesses. Of course, when Caruthers died last year there was an inquiry into the possibility of foul play, but they found no proof of it."

"Well, he *was* an old man, dear," her husband commented.

"I still think that man had a hand in it," she argued.

The woman was steadfast in her conviction and seemed ready to launch into a further argument when the proprietor's wife came and announced that supper was served. After the ladies were seated, Aurelia noted out of the corner of her eye the innkeeper preparing a tray of food, undoubtedly for Lord Chandler and his visitor.

Since other people had begun to descend, Aurelia rose from her place and wandered into the kitchen area, as if from curiosity.

Walking up to the proprietor, she asked, "Is that for Lord Chandler? I do not see him in the dining room."

He actually snorted. "No, this is for that scoundrel upstairs. Lord Chandler left instructions to feed him."

It was obvious that he did not enjoy having to serve Scurvy Joe, feeling, no doubt, that the task was beneath him.

"Left instructions? Did he go off somewhere?" Aurelia asked casually.

"Yes, my lady. He went into town. Something about having to talk to the constable. Excuse me, please," he said, carrying the tray out.

Aurelia followed him and resumed her seat just as his wife began to serve the first course. Talk at the table survived well enough without the ladies' participation, so they remained silent for the most part. Aurelia spoke to Gabrielle in a low voice so that no one else at the large table could hear what she had to say.

"Gabrielle! Chandler has gone off to speak to the constable about yesterday's affair."

"But why? Obviously Lord Dalton wasn't killed, so why the curiosity?" Gabrielle asked, sotto voce.

"I suppose he went to see if the two men whom we hit told Lord Dalton anything that could incriminate him in the affair. After all, there is no proof he did anything himself, and he would no doubt like to keep it that way."

"I would lay a wager that Lord Chandler had a hand in murdering that lawyer."

"Let us discuss this after dinner," Aurelia said under her breath, seeing that they were drawing attention to themselves.

Lady Standen and Lady Courtenay decided to retire directly after dinner and walked up the stairs to their room, where they intended to discuss matters further. Upon reaching the top of the flight, they heard the sound of a horse approaching the hostelry. Looking out the hall window, they saw it was Lord Chandler, returned from his trip to town.

They entered their room and quickly formulated a plan to eavesdrop on the conversation Lord Chandler and Scurvy Joe were certain to have.

While they waited for Lord Chandler to climb the stairs, Aurelia thought, how horrible it must have been for Lord Dalton to have him for a stepfather. She tried to imagine what kind of a life he must have had with a man who would as soon murder him as look at him. She shuddered at the thought and was grateful for her own loving parents. Perhaps his attitude was, in part, a result of living as he must have, she reasoned. One could hardly find it easy to love others when one was unloved as a child.

Just then her train of thought was interrupted by the sound of Lord Chandler's tread as he ascended the stairway. Aurelia motioned Gabrielle to listen as well. They heard him pass by their door and open the one to his own room. They waited a few minutes before venturing into the hall, being sure to make no sound. With their ears pressed to his door, they could clearly hear what was being said.

"So they're gone, are they?" a voice muttered. It was Scurvy Joe, as could be discerned by the strong cockney accent that accompanied this remark.

"Yes. The jailer let them go because my accursed stepson dropped the charges."

That had to be Lord Chandler, Aurelia thought as she pressed herself more firmly to the door.

"They didn't know nothin', anyway, me lord," Scurvy Joe uttered in between bites of his meal. "They musta left town by now. Too bad! Now Oi'll 'ave to get me some new men to do th' job."

"Do the job!" Chandler bellowed. Then, lowering his voice, he said, "You have tried to kill that little weasel twice now, and you still have not succeeded."

There was an almost insane fury in Lord Chandler's tone, and he was having a difficult time controlling himself.

"Well, now, me lord," Scurvy Joe responded slowly, "ye must know that yer stepson ain't an easy man to kill. Why, 'e could stop most men wit' just a look, that 'un could."

Chandler broke in harshly. "I'm not paying you to *try* to kill him. You had better deliver, or it's off to jail with you," he snarled.

"Oi think not, me lord," Scurvy Joe replied coldly. "Oi may not 'ave been able to kill Lord Dalton th' first few times, but then, few o' us got th' talent that ye 'ave fer slippin' winds."

Lord Chandler's voice was a hoarse whisper now as he asked, "What are you talking about?"

"Well, let's just say that a friend o' mine, a chemist and a good 'un, told me that a certain lawyer was poisoned wit' a rare drug that a certain lord bought from 'im. Oi've proof o' this, so don't be gettin' no ideas o' laughin' this off, me lord," he cautioned. "If Oi should die by foul means, a friend o' mine 'as instructions to deliver th' proof to th' law, and ye wouldn't want that, would ye, me lord?"

There was no answer to this, but Gabrielle could

imagine Chandler nodding his head, however reluctantly, in agreement.

"Now, then, Oi be needin' more blunt if Oi'm to pay fer more 'elp. Five hundred pounds would be 'bout right."

There was another pause. "I don't have that kind of money at hand, and you know it," Chandler said, barely audible.

"Pay me 'alf now and 'alf later, when ye comes into yer own. Oi trusts ye," the other laughed scornfully.

"I see I have no choice," Chandler replied tensely.

Aurelia motioned Gabrielle to retreat, for she could hear the chair in which Scurvy Joe was sitting scrape as he rose to leave. It was at this inopportune moment that the proprietor's pet cat dashed out from nowhere, and Gabrielle proceeded to step back inadvertently on the beast's tail.

Letting out a wail, the cat bounded away, and Lady Standen and Lady Courtenay were suddenly confronted by the unhandsome visage of Lord Chandler as the door to his room swung open.

"What are you doing here?" he snapped suspiciously.

Aurelia collected herself before Gabrielle did, and said, "We were simply going to our room when my friend accidentally kicked a cat."

With that she and Gabrielle turned their backs on Lord Chandler and walked to their room. Lord Chandler watched them go, a distrustful expression on his face.

Had they been listening outside the door? he wondered. No, you're becoming irrational, he told himself. All the same, they bear watching, he decided.

He turned and went back inside.

"Who be that?"

"No one. You had better go now and recruit some new men."

Taking one last swig of his ale, Scurvy Joe wiped his mouth on his sleeve and took his leave.

Aurelia and Gabrielle watched from their window as he rode away, and wondered what next to do.

Turning to her friend, Aurelia said, "I should go and say good night to Mama, but we definitely must talk when I return."

She left the room and Gabrielle began to undress, all the while pondering what they were going to do about Lord Dalton and Lord Chandler.

We just can't forget what we have heard, she thought as she pulled her evening gown over her head. Picking up her nightgown, she put it on slowly and continued to mull over the matter. Of course, Lord Dalton may already know that his stepfather is out to eliminate him. I know that Lord Chandler married Lord Dalton's mother for the money, so he must still be in need of that money.

Just then she heard footsteps coming toward the room. Aurelia slipped in quietly and also began to undress for bed.

"How does your mother fare?" Gabrielle asked, helping Aurelia with the hooks in the back of her gown.

"She's fine. I am sure she will be fit to travel by tomorrow. Now, what do you think we should do about Lord Chandler, Gabrielle?" Aurelia queried, slipping on her sleeping garment.

"We can't keep it to ourselves, of course. We have to warn Lord Dalton. He may not suspect that it is his stepfather who is out to murder him," Gabrielle said as she paced the room's length.

Aurelia shook her head. "We should get more information before we do anything on our own. After all, we may not know anything he doesn't already know. And if, after some questions have been answered, we find there is no real reason to interfere, we will not have to risk exposure. If he doesn't know, we can still tell him. He isn't aware it was women dressed as men who saved his life, so the chances are small we will be unmasked."

"That is quite true," Gabrielle admitted. "But do

you think he knows about the evidence Scurvy Joe has, incriminating Lord Chandler in the death of Mr. Caruthers?"

"I wish I knew," Aurelia sighed. "In any case, we shouldn't do anything until we have more facts."

Her face was thoughtful for a moment.

"I think that the lady we overheard this evening would be an excellent source of information. Perhaps we should attempt to cultivate her acquaintance on the morrow. Don't you think so, Gabrielle?"

"Yes, I quite agree. In any event, we must do *something*, though why we must I don't know. It really isn't our affair."

Aurelia smiled and climbed into her bed.

"All I can say is that as long as we have embroiled ourselves in Lord Dalton's affairs, it would be a shame not to see it through," she said, pulling the blankets up to her chin.

"What do you think of our Lord Dalton, anyway, Aurelia?" her friend asked, blowing out the lamp. She strained her ears for Aurelia's reply. Being a romantic at heart, Gabrielle thought it would be exciting if Aurelia developed a tendre for Lord Dalton.

Finally Aurelia answered. "I can't say I find him jovial or even pleasant in manner, but he is a most unusual individual."

Gabrielle pressed for more clarification. "How unusual, Aurelia?"

"Well, he is not fainthearted, for one thing. Did you see the utter contempt on his face when Scurvy Joe held him prisoner?" A small thrill of admiration could be heard in this keen observation.

"Better and better. Please elucidate further on his good points, as a review of them may make your opinion of him improve," Gabrielle said mischievously. "You admire his bravery. Go on."

"Well," Aurelia continued, undaunted by the amused tone in her friend's voice, "he is an excellent marksman; I admire that. He also displayed a passionate nature, of which I wholeheartedly approve. I never could abide anyone who was blasé about things."

"Most certainly he is not blasé," Gabrielle agreed. "What else?"

"And I must admit that he is extremely handsome, if a bit frightening," Aurelia conceded. "What do you think of him, Gabrielle? I know you prefer Lord Sheringham, but you must have an opinion, nonetheless."

Gabrielle flushed slightly at this but did not deny the statement.

"I would say that with that face he could break hearts, if only he were of that disposition. However, he doesn't look to be in the petticoat line to me. Looks like the solitary sort, to my mind."

"I'll tell you what I think," Aurelia said, turning on her side and fluffing her pillow. "I think he is probably very good to those people he cares for, and all the rest be damned. And I must now get some sleep, or I shall not be able to think at all tomorrow. We will need our wits about us if we are to help Lord Dalton and Lord Sheringham. Good night," she called out across the room.

At the moment when the girls were nodding off, London was ablaze with the lights of a thousand candles, lit in the homes of the aristocracy. Balls hosted by the cream of society were just starting and would continue well into the night, some into the following day. In the heart of the city, the lights of almost every house were aglow, the strains of a waltz drifting out of windows opened to alleviate the heat generated by so many people and so much activity.

One townhouse, however, was not having an entertainment that night. The largest and most impressive of the homes in that area, it stood out conspicuously, for it was almost completely dark, except for the lights that shone perpetually outside the main entrance. The lamps threw their glow onto the heavy mahogany door with its ornate knocker that awaited only the hand of the master of the dwelling.

It was at this house that a coach stopped. Two cloaked figures strode up the steps, and one extended his hand, gloved in black kid, and knocked on the door. No sound issued from within, and the gentleman lifted the heavy knocker and renewed his effort, sending a series of deep reverberations through the house. Scuttling noises could be heard, and suddenly the door was opened by an elderly butler, wearing a robe, who peered nearsightedly at the gentlemen standing before him. The lamplight set the men's features in sharp relief. Squinting, the servant recognized the shining blue-black hair and strongly etched features of the master of the house. Beside him stood a man whom he knew as his master's best friend.

As the two gentlemen entered, the butler was struck by the likeness of the black-haired young man to a portrait on the wall in the hall. The master had recently had it painted from an old picture of his father that he had unearthed.

Being well trained in his work, the manservant asked no questions, bowed deeply to his employer, and said, "Welcome back, Lord Dalton."

Aurelia and Gabrielle awoke, the light of day streaming through the cracks in the window shutters. As they dressed, they agreed to make an effort to engage the lady of the prior night's illuminating discussion in a conversation of their own. But first they visited Aurelia's mother.

"Mama, how do you feel?" Aurelia asked as she kissed her mother's cheek.

"I am feeling much better, but do tell the innkeeper to send my breakfast up. I will be ready to travel at ten o'clock," Lady Faye announced. With that she sent them down to their own breakfast.

They seated themselves in the dining room and watched the stairs to see if Lady Culpepper—whose name they had gleaned from a perusal of the establishment's register—would appear shortly. They very much wished for an opportunity to talk to her.

They did not have long to wait. Lady Culpepper's voice could be heard at the top of the steps.

"Do hurry, Tristan, my love. We must leave soon."

There was a mumbled reply to this as the lady entered the dining room.

Seeing the two girls, she nodded to them and seated herself in a nearby chair. She seemed to be a very pleasant woman up close, and appeared willing to engage in conversation with them, introducing herself with the ease of one accustomed to social niceties.

"I saw both of you at dinner last night," she chatted as she broke the top of her egg and spooned up some of its contents. "You didn't say very much. Did you arrive late yesterday?"

Aurelia smiled at the woman engagingly. "As a matter of fact, we did arrive late," she replied, introducing herself and Gabrielle. "We are traveling with my mother to London for the Season."

Lady Culpepper seemed very pleased to hear this.

"Oh, my, how nice for you. I remember when I came out. You will have so much fun going to balls and meeting all the eligible young men. I can always tell in advance which girls will really take right at the outset, and both of you will be successful."

She seemed to recall her own coming-out vividly and was rambling on about her London Season when Aurelia skillfully brought up the subject of the earlier activities at the inn.

"I heard from the proprietor that there was a little excitement here the evening before last."

Lady Culpepper was all too willing to discuss the matter, as her husband had not been very interested in it.

"Yes, and to think that I recognized the young man who killed that ruffian."

"Oh, really? Who was he?" Gabrielle encouraged.

"I believe he was Philip Dalton. I have known him since he was a little boy, and I knew his mother well, too. As a matter of fact," she addressed Gabrielle, "I saw that little set-to you had with that *gentleman* yesterday, my dear, and I nearly shouted bravo when you gave him that set-down. That atrocious man is Lord Dalton's stepfather, and a meaner individual I have yet to meet."

This was said with a great deal of sincere feeling.

"Why, that man is the worst of opportunists!" she declared.

"In what way, Lady Culpepper?" Aurelia inquired.

"Why, he pretended to be such a good, kind man. He tricked Lord Dalton's poor mother into believing he was in love with her, and she, poor lamb that she was, married the swine, even though I tried my best to dissuade her."

At this point she seemed overcome and drew a handkerchief from her sleeve, blowing into it and dabbing at her eyes.

"I take it he was not an ideal husband," Gabrielle said.

"Ideal!" Lady Culpepper exclaimed scornfully. "He was a swine, I tell you! He was a fortune hunter, pure and simple, and he made great inroads upon her estates."

"But the estates are now run by Lord Dalton are they not?" Gabrielle asked. "From your tone I assume that Lord Chandler no longer has access to the family fortune."

"Well, that's the interesting part. Alecia willed all her money to her son, and on reaching his majority at one and twenty, he claimed control. Lord Chandler, for all his title, is virtually impoverished, as Alecia left him nothing in her will."

This was announced with something nearing righteous satisfaction, and it was evident that Lady Culpepper believed this to be God's justice visited on the miserable person of Lord Chandler.

"The odd thing is," she continued with relish, "that should Philip pass on without an heir—and let me say that it is entirely possible, since he has never taken a fancy to any woman, to my knowledge—Lord Chandler would inherit the lot. Not the estates, of course, those are entailed, but the fortune that Alecia left behind would pass into his hands. It was part of Alecia's will. Poor girl, I suppose she still loved the wretch a little. Philip was not to have inherited unless he agreed to those terms. Of course, if he should marry, then the agreement is nullified; that is to be expected. Thank goodness Lord Chandler is hardly likely to outlast that boy, since Philip is, I believe, in the best of physical condition."

They spoke for a while longer, and soon Lady Faye joined her charges.

"Mama, let me introduce you to Lady Culpepper. Lady Culpepper, this is my mother, the Duchess of Harcourt."

The older women exchanged pleasantries and appeared to get along quite well. As they chatted, the innkeeper entered and informed her Grace that her coach was loaded and ready to depart.

Rising from the settee, Lady Faye bade adieu to her new acquaintance and asked the girls to do the same. As they rose they gave their promise to come to a ball that Lady Culpepper would soon be hosting.

After taking their leave, the three women were handed up the steps of their carriage. Looking out the small windows, they waved goodbye to the stableboy, who was half hidden behind a tree as he watched them go.

"Well, girls, we will be in London by this evening," Lady Faye announced with no little relief as the coach drove on at a goodly pace. "I'm sure you will find the city every bit as exciting as I did myself when I was first brought out." Her eyes glimmered with nostalgia.

"Oh, I am sure we shall, your Grace," Gabrielle agreed. In a low voice she added to Aurelia, "More exciting than you might guess, I'd wager."

꧁꧂ CHAPTER 4

THE SUN had just begun to set in the sky as the duchess
and her charges arrived at Berkeley Square. The coach
halted before a large house whose massive doors were
magically opened by several footmen who hurried to un-
load trunks and other packages. As Davis and Crane
supervised this process quickly and silently, the duchess
sailed into her city home like a galleon into port, passing through the double row of servants assembled for
her perusal without even a glance. She was quite sure
that her steward had engaged only those individuals
suitable to serve her. Aurelia was more inquisitive,
looking first from the groom to the footmen in their
familiar livery to the housemaid, laundry maid, and
under-cooks with their clean white linen. She noted
with curiosity a young lady's maid standing beside the
cook, who was approaching the duchess to welcome
her.

Suddenly confronted by this enormous woman, Lady
Faye halted in her progress.

"Welcome, your Grace, my ladies," the cook said as
she curtsied in her best manner.

This was an ill-advised move, as she could not rise
from this position without the assistance of two footmen who had rushed to her side. She appeared short of
breath as she regained her feet, but she managed to
wheeze, "All is ready for your Grace. Your rooms
have been aired and a fire lit in each."

Lady Faye did not require the woman's reassurances; she had observed the dark glow of well-polished mahogany when she entered, the lights of the candles reflecting off every surface. All was as it should be, and with a nod of satisfaction to the cook, the duchess motioned her to lead the way to the upper floor.

As they made their way up the stairs, Gabrielle saw that the lady's maid was following them, an uneasy expression on her pale oval face. When they reached the landing, Lady Faye glanced back and seemed to notice the girl for the first time. Raising her quizzing glass, she inspected the maid.

"Where do you come from, my dear?" she inquired suspiciously.

The cook twisted an apron string nervously and replied, "Your Grace, if you please, I hired this new maid to assist in the cleanin'."

Poking the girl, she whispered loudly, "Say what I told ya to say, child."

Blushing furiously, the girl managed a shy whisper. "*Bon jour, madame*. I am pleased to meet you."

"French?" The duchess looked surprised.

"Yes, ma'am," the cook replied quickly. "She was new here and needed the work, so I didn't see the harm, and she's a good worker, really she is, ma'am."

The cook had obviously become fond of the girl and seemed determined to plead her case as best she could.

Fortunately, her Grace had no aversion to foreigners and merely asked, "And what is your name? If you are to stay, we must call you something."

The girl looked at the ground. "Renée, madame," she answered.

"Well, Renée, you may stay, and you will be my daughter's personal maid for the time being. You will assist Lady Standen in her wardrobe as well. Can you manage that?"

A faint murmur and nod were taken for assent, so she accompanied Aurelia and Gabrielle to their rooms while the duchess retired for the night, her own maid being called to aid her.

Gabrielle and Aurelia found their chambers directly

next to each other, and there was a connecting door between them.

"How nice!" Gabrielle exclaimed.

"How convenient," Aurelia said feelingly. "This will make things much easier."

"I agree." Gabrielle began to wander about, inspecting various items.

Renée was in the process of heating the linens with a bed warmer when Gabrielle came over to her.

"Tell me, Renée, what brought you to England?"

The maid was hesitant to speak, but as both ladies seemed to be so kind, she told them.

"I came to England to work and try to raise enough money to free my fiancé from prison. If one has money, anything is possible, *n'est-ce pas*?"

The girl was close to tears as she spoke.

Aurelia was appalled. "In jail! What did he do?"

"He is a political prisoner, my lady. There is no specific charge against him. That is why, if I can raise enough money to have him released, they will, *à coup sûr*, let him go with no questions asked."

It was at this point that she broke down.

"But I fear I shall never be able to raise the amount needed," she sobbed.

The two women were distressed by her tears and told her to dry her eyes.

"There is no use crying," Aurelia said as she tried to comfort the girl. "I have a friend in the British Embassy who may be able to help him."

The girl's face lit up immediately.

"Oh, my lady, *merci*! If only you could, I would do anything for you," she swore fervently.

"Now, now, I haven't done it yet. I may not be able to get your fiancé out, but I shall try."

The girl kissed Lady Courtenay's hand in gratitude and quickly left the room before her emotions could once more overcome her.

Gabrielle looked at her friend, who shrugged and said, "Well, what could I do? I couldn't very well let the poor girl suffer and not lift a finger to help her, you know." Aurelia's tone was defensive.

"I am not criticizing you," Gabrielle explained. "I am simply trying to think of who it is you know in the British Embassy in France."

This launched a long discussion on a distant uncle of Lady Courtenay's, during which time they prepared for bed.

Just as they were ready to retire, Aurelia's mother entered.

"Girls, I meant to tell you before you went to sleep that we will be going shopping tomorrow afternoon for some clothing. I can see we are sorely out of fashion here, and I do want you both to be up to the mark. We will be making the rounds of all the different dress shops I have on my list. Get a good night's sleep," she admonished as she pecked her daughter on the cheek.

The prospect of a day's shopping expedition was quite welcome to Lady Standen's ears. She too had observed the fashionable gowns worn by several ladies as they had ridden in that evening, and she had felt a veritable dowd among them. Both she and Lady Courtenay wanted to cut a dash, so they went to sleep feeling very excited indeed.

The next day Aurelia, Gabrielle, and the duchess dressed with unusual care for their excursion. The duchess inspected them when they came down clothed in their best frocks.

"They are modest, but in excellent taste," Lady Faye noted as she led the way to the waiting carriage. "I knew you would not disgrace me."

As they entered the coach, Aurelia asked, "Did you have any specific articles of clothing in mind, Mama?"

"No, dear," her mother replied. "Just pick out a few gowns for teas and such."

Lady Faye's vagueness was characteristic, but did not distress her daughter, who was too engrossed in planning her new wardrobe. She was determined to make the best possible use of the carte blanche her mother had just presented her with, and the same was expected of Lady Standen.

Shop after fashionable shop was explored, and the ladies never failed to depart with a few parcels, leaving orders for more gowns to be delivered to the house later. They spent their money lavishly, and before they had emerged from the first establishment, it was flying to the ears of every clothier in town that Lady Courtenay and Lady Standen were to be treated with special care and service.

By the fifth dress shop Lady Faye's strength had begun to flag, and she proceeded home in a hired coach, ordering a footman to accompany the young women.

The two girls entered another shop with the name Madame Leconse on the door in gilt letters. Lady Standen had bidden the driver of their coach and the footman to refresh themselves at a local pub for an hour as she and her companion would be at Mme. Leconse's for some time. This they did gladly, for they could not imagine their services to be required.

Gabrielle had not been mistaken in believing this new shop would occupy a great deal of their time. As soon as they stepped in, she found herself looking at the most beautiful ball gown she had ever beheld. Made of white chiffon, it seemed to shimmer and glow of its own accord. She could see that strands of silver had been woven in the fine material and there, winking merrily among the puffy folds, were tiny diamonds.

"Aurelia, have you ever seen a more divine gown?" she breathed, but Lady Courtenay was not listening, for she had just spotted a blue walking dress with matching trim that would be perfect for Ascot.

With intricate embroidery accenting the cuffs and lapels, and with a hat topped by an arrangement of osprey feathers, the entire ensemble was exactly right, and Aurelia stepped back to view the creation from a distance.

"Is it not ideal?" she asked Gabrielle, continuing to retreat in order to get the full effect of the hat.

It was just at this moment that she bumped into

someone's back. Wheeling around, she uttered an embarrassed apology and found herself looking at a rather unattractive young man who appeared to be ogling her.

"My fault, I am sure," he said smoothly, with just the touch of an accent.

The man proceeded to eye her up and down, an action that Aurelia found most distasteful. Stepping away from him, she glanced about her for Gabrielle.

She saw her friend examining a dress in the corner of the shop and would have gone over to her, except that the gentleman, who was pointedly staring, was attempting to engage her in conversation.

"My name is Lord Torres. My friends call me Diego."

It was clear from the manner in which he had uttered these words that he desired Aurelia to address him by his Christian name, but she ignored the hint. Only the obvious fact that the gentleman was a foreigner prevented Aurelia from giving him the set-down he deserved. Instead, she said coldly, "I am pleased to meet you, Lord Torres," hoping he would leave matters at that.

The Spaniard was not going to cooperate, however, and asked, "And your name, miss?"

She gazed at him icily.

"I am Lady Courtenay," she replied in a toneless fashion.

Her eyes tried to hail Gabrielle, but she had her back turned to Aurelia at the moment. Just as Aurelia would have taken her leave of Lord Torres, somebody grabbed her by the shoulder and attempted to turn her around forcibly.

The owner of the hand announced loudly, "Who do you think you are? Get your own man!"

Aurelia struck the offending hand from her shoulder and spun around to see that the person who had uttered those words was a short young woman of only passable looks. She possessed a hard glint to her eyes that immediately pinpointed her as a woman of ill repute. Her small, kittenish features were contorted with rage at that moment, her anger directed at Lady Courtenay.

Aurelia's eyes seemed charged with destructive energy as she stared at the young woman, but, true to her upbringing, she decided to ignore her. With a final look of disdain at her bantam-sized foe, Aurelia turned on her heel to leave.

The woman, feeling insulted at this action, flew at Aurelia, fingers set in claws, trying to scratch Lady Courtenay's blue orbs from their rightful place. Aurelia simply lifted the thin girl off the floor and held her in the air as she kicked and screeched for all the world like a harpy.

Gabrielle had made her way to Aurelia's side as Lord Torres implored his "Light of Love" to be silent. Seeing that Aurelia had matters well in hand, Gabrielle merely suggested in a bored tone, "Why don't you gag her with a handkerchief?"

As the outraged young woman continued to plunge about, the proprietress of the shop came running out, along with her son, the tailor. They subdued the girl and had her carriage sent for. They had no wish to lose Lady Courtenay's patronage.

As they held the woman, she continued to rail at Aurelia, making accusations regardless of the lack of truth in them.

"You think you're so fine, don't you? Well, you won't steal my man from me!" she spat with fury.

Her coach clattered up to the front of the shop, and Lord Torres tried to negotiate the young woman into it, all the while attempting to apologize to the two ladies for her conduct.

Those who were familiar with Lord Torres would have been very much surprised by these professed apologies, since he had never been prone to any sort of politeness before. No, the gentleman had not reformed his ways. Truth be told, he had heard of the Courtenays, and of their immense wealth. As he himself was not of a wealthy family, he deemed it necessary to marry into money, and he now saw his opportunity being destroyed by his mistress right before his eyes.

Practically throwing her into the coach, Lord Torres picked up her purchase from another shop, a gaudy spangled dress of almost indecent design, and departed, promising to visit the two ladies at their home and to make the acquaintance of the duchess, of whom he had heard.

As the coach drove off with the disreputable woman still sticking her head out the window and cursing, Aurelia turned to her friend and said heatedly, "I certainly hope he doesn't come to the house. I would much prefer never to see his face again. Aside from the fact that he is afflicted with a terminal case of blemishes, he is also *most* impolite."

Gabrielle quite agreed with her friend, so they decided to instruct the butler to say they were not at home if Lord Torres should call.

This having been resolved, the ladies continued their shopping, Gabrielle purchasing the white gown of chiffon that had so enchanted her, and Aurelia purchasing the blue walking dress, which was to be delivered to the house after minor alterations. All told, the day's excursion had been very successful and pleasant, except for the incident at Madame Leconse's establishment.

By late afternoon both were exhausted, having visited enough clothiers to insure them of an adequate wardrobe for the duration of their stay in London. It was with a great deal of relief that Lady Standen observed that there remained only one last stop. They made the short walk to the store and entered its gold-gilt portals. Lady Courtenay was pleasantly surprised by the presence of Lady Culpepper, who, having discovered a deficiency in her wardrobe that demanded immediate attention, had elected to make her purchase at this selfsame shop.

Lady Culpepper was all smiles on seeing the two young women. Indeed, she had taken an instant liking to them and had several young men in mind to whom she wished to introduce them. Beckoning them with a hand gloved in pink kid, she soon engaged them in a discussion on the merits of the various trims and laces. As the three women chatted away, Lord Culpepper showed great forbearance when he was called upon to comment on matters totally alien to him, such as the distinctive differences between French and Italian crepe. They talked for fully thirty minutes as shopgirls presented dozens of dresses, capes, and hats for their inspection. Each item was appraised in turn, and at the end, all three women felt the time had been most constructively put to use. The proprietress of the store could not but agree, as she had succeeded in selling not less than six gowns for various occasions, three of which Lady Culpepper had purchased, and which Lord Culpepper eyed resignedly.

As the ladies waited for their garments to be wrapped, Lady Culpepper again extended an invitation for Aurelia and Gabrielle to visit her home.

"We are having a ball tomorrow," she informed them. "Do come. I am persuaded that it would be just the thing for you. It will give you an opportunity to become accustomed to large crowds," she added coaxingly.

Both girls consented to come with the greatest of pleasure, and it was with this exciting prospect that the ladies and Lord Culpepper took their leave of the dressmakers and stepped out onto the street pavement. As Aurelia and Gabrielle looked about, they realized that their coachman was glaringly absent, having no doubt lost track of time. Noting their dismay, Lord Culpepper offered to walk around the block to see if he could spot their transport. To this the young women were hesitant, since they did not wish to put him to such inconvenience, but Lady Culpepper waved their objections aside and bade her husband proceed. As Lord Culpepper strolled off, from the opposite direction Lady Culpepper saw Lord Dalton and Lord Sheringham approaching. Determined to make an introduction, she waved her hand to attract their attention.

"Look there!" she exclaimed. "Just the two gentlemen I most desired to see. I will introduce you to them."

Ignoring Gabrielle's faint protest, Lady Culpepper continued to wave, attributing the girls' reluctance to shy and retiring personalities. The ladies would have liked to retreat back into the dress shop, feeling unprepared for a confrontation. As it was, they were caught very neatly, and waited with some apprehension to be introduced.

Lord Sheringham glanced up to see the familiar figure of Lady Culpepper seeking his attention. As he waved back, he perceived the two women who stood next to her and was pleased to recognize them as the two beauties he had so admired back at the inn. Philip, who had been talking to his friend, peered out in the same direction upon seeing the pleased look on Brett's face. He was not overly surprised to view the sight that held his friend in thrall.

"I might have known that the only thing which could interrupt your never-ending speech would be the sight of a pretty girl," Philip said. "Now is the time to obtain an introduction, surely."

With amusement he watched Brett self-consciously adjust his hat and give his shirt cuffs a slight pull. Arriving at the spot where the ladies stood, the two gentlemen made their best bows.

As always, Lord Dalton's appearance was immaculate. His coat of black velvet was of the finest cut and showed his powerful build to definite advantage. Not for him the heavily padded shoulders, which so many gentlemen required in order to compensate for nature's unkindness. Philip was elegance itself, Lady Courtenay noted, her eyes appraising the cloth at his throat, which folded into a veritable cascade, and the tops of his Hessians, which gleamed in the fading light.

Aurelia had needed those few seconds to compose herself, and when, rising from his bow, Lord Dalton looked directly into her eyes, as was his wont with strangers, she did not flinch.

Lord Dalton was surprised by the lady's gaze, which did not waver and fall from his. He had never yet run across a woman capable of staring directly into what were commonly described as his "damned cold eyes," even by persons well disposed toward him, and he found himself in the unusual position of having to avert his own look.

He suddenly realized that Lady Culpepper had succeeded in her introductions and that all eyes were on him to make a gesture in response. Sensing that he had been taken unaware, Gabrielle quickly extended her hand for Lord Dalton to salute, which he did with rare form, duplicating the gesture for Lady Courtenay. Brett followed in his turn, and for a moment there was silence, everyone at a loss for words.

Lady Culpepper was about to make the first attempt at conversation when the group's attention was diverted by the return of Lord Culpepper, no carriage in evidence. A slight raising of his brow was the outward indication of his surprise at seeing Lord Dalton and Lord Sheringham as he greeted them.

Turning to Aurelia, he said apologetically, "There seems to be no trace of your coach, Lady Courtenay. We could, of course, take you up in our carriage."

Lady Culpepper added her voice to his suggestion, but the ladies were adamant against putting them out of their way.

"I am persuaded that our coachman will return in a little while," Aurelia insisted. "We can wait."

"But what will you do in the meantime?" Lady Culpepper asked. "Surely you can't stand here on the walk. It would be most improper."

A slight cough from Lord Sheringham caused all to turn to him.

"Very easily solved, madam," he said. "May I suggest a walk in the park? It will give the ladies a chance to enjoy the flowers in bloom."

This suggestion was made in the most earnest of tones and was well accepted by Aurelia and Gabrielle. Lord Culpepper, however, seemed about to disapprove of the idea, being somewhat of a stickler for convention. Though he was well acquainted with Lord Sheringham, and though he believed that Lord Dalton was respectable enough, he did not think it proper for the ladies to walk alone in the park with two young men. He would have given voice to his objection, but a glance from his wife quelled the words in his breast, and he and his lady took their leave of the four young people.

Aurelia and Gabrielle waved after the coach, then turned to their escorts. Brett seemed to be as one in a trance, content to stare, and appeared to have lost all mental faculties necessary to uphold a civil conversation. Seeing his friend at a standstill, Philip motioned the ladies to accompany them to the park, offering his arm for Aurelia to take. Brett took up his friend's lead and did likewise to Gabrielle.

Aurelia accepted the proffered arm, and as she did so, the slight contact had a surprising effect on Lord Dalton. It was something akin to being struck by lightning, but such a trite and fanciful thought was so unlike his usual self that Philip immediately cast off the idea. Still, he was feeling an unaccustomed sensation that he could not pinpoint, and he glanced out of the corner of his eye to see if Aurelia had also felt a reaction. She seemed not to have experienced a thing, continuing to stroll slowly along the path, admiring the flower beds.

Lord Dalton could think of very little to talk about, though he knew that Brett was depending on him to keep the conversation alive. The couples proceeded to walk about the park in silence. Brett struggled to think of something to say, since Philip had apparently misplaced his wits for the moment. Gabrielle started to make light conversation and soon put her escort at ease. Neither of them seemed to notice that Aurelia and Philip had not spoken a word since they had entered the park.

Though Aurelia usually was gregarious, she held her tongue now because she had sensed Lord Dalton drawing away from her, not so much physically as mentally.

Let him stew in his own juices, then, she thought indignantly as she walked stiffly beside him.

Lady Courtenay had the natural impression that Lord Dalton did not like her, since he had not spoken to her and was almost wooden in demeanor. If she could have read his mind, she would have been quite surprised. Indeed, Lord Dalton was himself amazed at his reactions. He seemed distant only because he could not readily analyze the attraction he was experiencing. The sensation was new to him; he had never felt anything remotely resembling his present state with any other woman of his acquaintance. Simply seeing this young woman from afar was one thing, but walking with her so closely was altogether a different matter. True, she was lovely to look at, perhaps lovelier than any other woman he had ever seen, but it was more than just her beauty, which, though considerable, could not solely figure in an explanation of his feelings. It could only be described as a natural affinity; it surely was not dictated by his common sense. It was this unusual sensation of unreasoning attraction that was hedging the normally glib Lord Dalton into silence. She probably thinks me an idiot, he reflected. He risked a glance at her face, but it was unreadable. He guessed that her placid expression was hiding her anger at his silence. He guessed correctly.

If he doesn't say something in another minute, I will simply leave him, Aurelia resolved, but even as she thought this she was experiencing a reluctance to depart from the young man. I must be going mad to put up with such behavior, she told herself.

Just as Philip would have said something, his attention was diverted by the approach of a lackey dressed in an all-too-familiar livery. The colors emblazoned on the man's clothing were those belonging to the bane of his existence, Lord Chandler. The lackey was apparently holding a bag filled with something. Suddenly the contents of the bag moved.

Aurelia had noticed Lord Dalton's attention being engaged, so she followed his gaze. She was horrified to see that a servant, with a sack that squirmed with life, was approaching the artificial lake in the secluded part of the park. She broke into a run toward the lackey, fury flashing a warning from her eyes.

Astonished at Aurelia's reaction, Lord Dalton followed in her wake. He watched with fascination as the young lady ran up to the cringing servant and seized the quivering bundle. As he neared, he could hear Aurelia's voice railing at the astonished and cowed man.

"How dare you even think of drowning this animal?" she demanded vehemently.

Lord Dalton faced the man, who was fiddling nervously with his cap, and asked, "Well, what do you have to say for yourself?"

The lackey was reluctant to answer, but as the expression on Lord Dalton's face boded ill if he refused, he capitulated.

"My master bade me to rid him of the animal. It bit him on the leg, you see, your lordship. It's vicious."

He was suddenly struck with fear as the face of Lord Dalton now took on an almost savage look.

"Your master is Lord Chandler, I believe."

This statement was made in a near pleasant tone of voice, but Philip's eyes were not smiling at all. The lackey gulped. Looking into Lord Dalton's eyes was like looking down the barrels of twin dueling pistols, and they seemed to bore a hole straight through him.

"Yes, sir," he acknowledged.

The bag in Aurelia's hand emitted a whine. She opened the sack and a sleek brown head popped out of the top. It was a tiny female dachshund, with which Aurelia was immediately taken.

"And you were going to drown this poor little dog? Well, you aren't going to now," she vowed as she pet the creature on the head.

The dog, sensing a champion in the lady, licked her face enthusiastically. It was quite a sight, the servant cringing before Lady Courtenay's verbal onslaught and the dog alternately licking her face and growling at the man. Chandler's servant turned to make an appeal to Lord Dalton, who was smiling slightly.

"Please, my lord," he pleaded, "I must do as I am bidden. Surely you know that."

In a calm but deadly voice, Lord Dalton answered, "I am confident that Lady Courtenay doesn't need any assistance in handling you, but just in case you have any notion of completing your task, let me tell you that it would not be prudent."

The threat was clear, and the slight smile that accented the statement nearly froze the lackey's heart with fear. Mumbling a vague reply, he beat a hasty retreat. Philip watched as his back disappeared from view.

"You were correct, Lord Dalton," Aurelia said after a moment. "I didn't need your help. However, thank you for your concern, all the same," she added with a warm smile.

She was cradling the dog, which appeared to be in high croak at the vanquishing of its foe. As she resumed her walk, Lord Dalton was impressed once again by this extraordinarily brave girl.

"That was more than a little foolhardy, confronting that man alone," he remarked keeping pace with her as she looked about for Gabrielle and Brett, who had seemingly vanished. "But I salute your bravery, my lady."

Aurelia shrugged off his comment.

"He wouldn't have been able to do anything in public, and with you bringing up the rear, I had little to fear. Besides, I am not afraid of a sniveling coward such as that," she huffed with a toss of her blonde head.

"I did not mean to imply that you should be afraid," Philip interjected. "I simply meant that most young ladies wouldn't have had your courage in such a situation. They are much more concerned with the possible repercussions of their actions. It just isn't done, you know," he added, sounding for all the world like a disapproving matron.

Aurelia was mollified by this move to break the ice, and began to unstiffen somewhat.

"You can be quite pleasant when you wish to be, Lord Dalton," she observed sweetly as they continued to walk. "I thought you held me in aversion from your earlier silence."

Lord Dalton looked down at the path, shamefaced at this reminder of his previous behavior.

"I shall endeavor to behave myself lest you become as displeased with me as you were with that lackey," he said jokingly, attempting to relieve his embarrassment.

Aurelia appreciated the jest and smiled again. Turning to look at Philip, she found herself gazing directly into his blue eyes. As their glances met, Philip again felt that peculiar shock, a thrill rippling along his every nerve. Once more, he was forced to avert his eyes. Aurelia, unaware of the effect she was having on Lord Dalton, experienced annoyance. Lord Dalton's distracted air only added to her displeasure.

Aurelia decided that she was not going to go through the silent treatment again, and proceeded to initiate the conversation this time.

"What do you think I should name this adorable little creature?" she asked pleasantly.

Looking up from his scrutiny of the path, Lord Dalton examined the animal.

"Perhaps something German?" he suggested tentatively.

Aurelia considered this.

"She is so small and impish, I think I will call her Elva, seeing as it means an 'elf.' "

"An excellent choice," he declared, reaching over to pet the dog. Elva responded to the caress, wagging her tail happily at the dark stranger.

"She seems to like you," Aurelia commented as they crossed over a stone bridge.

Just then they saw Lord Sheringham and Lady Standen waving to them from the opposite side.

"Well, at last," Gabrielle said when she reached Aurelia. "We've been looking for you two. Where did you vanish to? We thought we had lost you for good. What have you got there?" she asked, pointing to the dog.

Aurelia told her friend how she had come by the dog.

"It is darling," Gabrielle said, petting the animal.

Aurelia glanced about her and saw that it was starting to grow rather dark.

"I think we should return to our carriage. I'm sure our driver must have returned by now."

Lord Sheringham was unwilling to part company with such lovely women, but there was nothing for it, so the two men walked them back to their carriage.

In the gathering darkness Aurelia could hardly make out Lord Dalton's features, but she could feel him gazing at her. Gabrielle and Brett were walking somewhat ahead, and Aurelia could hear their laughter drifting back.

"Why do you stare so?" she asked him at last.

"I'm sorry. I didn't realize I was," Lord Dalton answered, averting his eyes. "I didn't mean to offend."

"I don't mind it," she said, proceeding on. "I just wondered why."

Philip made no answer, and in a few moments the two couples had reached the waiting vehicle. Aurelia looked out of the coach window at Lord Dalton and could see his eyes glittering.

"I hope we meet again," she said softly.

At first he did not reply, but as the coach began to move away Lord Dalton took her hand, which rested on the window, and kissed it.

"I truly hope that we shall, my lady. In fact, I am sure we will."

There was no time to make a reply, so Aurelia contented herself with watching the shadowy figure of Lord Dalton fade into the night.

Looking after the coach until it was gone, Philip turned silently on his heel and began to saunter toward White's, Brett following along in a stupor.

Glancing at his friend, Philip could see the absurd smile that dominated Lord Sheringham's face.

"La, Brett, do you realize what a damned foolish expression you are wearing at this moment?" he asked, breaking into a loud laugh.

Perplexed, Brett echoed, "Expression? What kind of expression are you referring to?"

Choking on his laughter, Philip replied, "You look downright queer in the attic, sort of vague and silly."

This statement set him off into another fit of guffaws, which was quickly shared by Lord Sheringham.

It was on this mirthful note that the lords arrived at their club, Philip relating to his friend along the way the incident that had occurred in the park. Brett had been all agog to know the details, which were supplied to him in short order.

They entered the club and were greeted at the entrance by the head butler, dressed in the manner prescribed by the establishment, black with gold braid.

As Lord Dalton handed his greatcoat to the footman, Brett couldn't resist remarking, "Why, the man is dressed almost as somberly as you are, Philip."

This comment, Philip thought, was beneath reply, so he merely ignored it, checking his cravat before entering the sitting room. As usual, the folds were intact, showing no inclination toward disarray.

Lord Sheringham, on the other hand, struggled to adjust his badly wrinkled neckcloth without success.

"Deuce take these things, anyway!" he cried as he accidentally pulled out yet another intricate fold in the snowy cascade.

Turning to his sorely tried companion, Philip straightened out the perverse article of clothing.

"There, good as new, but I know you won't leave it that way," Philip contended as he took one last appraising glance at himself.

Lord Sheringham would have replied to this, but at

that moment another guest was ushered into the hall-way. Nudging Philip, Brett nodded toward the new-comer.

"Now, who is that?" he wondered aloud. "I know I've seen him before, but I can't recall the name. Some sort of foreigner, an ambassador, I think."

Philip glanced over at the dark-haired gentleman with Latin features who was walking toward them. He would have been considered no more than mediocre-looking, even if his olive complexion had been present-able. As it was, he was a sorry sight.

"The man has the worst skin condition I have ever had the displeasure to see," Philip said casually. "The Spanish ambassador cannot be said to possess the most pleasing of features."

As he finished this sentence, the individual they had been discussing presented himself before them and made an adequate, if less than accomplished, bow.

"Lord Dalton, Lord Sheringham, we are not ac-quainted, but perhaps you have heard of me. I am Lord Torres, the Spanish ambassador to your lovely country."

Lord Torres's English was excellent, if a bit formal, and Brett, being the friendly type, immediately extend-ed his hand; but Lord Dalton, being a more fastidious person, and not prone to greeting those men with whom he was not formally acquainted, merely nodded his greeting.

Lord Torres was much offended by Philip's offhand manner, and seeing this, Brett quickly led the way into the gaming room.

"I am sure that there is quite a lot that English and Spanish gaming houses have in common," Brett com-mented, motioning Lord Torres to enter before him. Somewhat mollified by this courtesy, Lord Torres passed before Brett, oblivious to the exaggerated bow Philip made, mocking Brett's gesture. Brett was hard put to suppress his laughter at these antics, pressing his lips together tightly lest a titter escape.

"Perhaps a round of cards?" Brett suggested amiably.

Lord Torres agreed to this eagerly, as he was not often asked to play and was much addicted to games of chance.

As he seated himself at the card table, one of the club's footmen presented a letter on a silver tray to the surprised Spaniard. Lord Sheringham reached over and picked the letter up before Lord Torres realized it was indeed for him.

"Why, it's from a woman, by the looks of the writing," Lord Sheringham announced to Philip.

Raising the note to his nose, he sniffed for the telltale scent of perfume that would confirm his suspicions. It was indeed there, though it was a fragrance little admired by Brett.

Handing the missive to Lord Torres, Brett began to shuffle the cards, raising an inquisitive eyebrow at the man as he opened the note.

"Would it be indelicate to ask whom the letter is from?" Brett inquired. "I have an insatiable curiosity about such things, you see."

Looking slightly embarrassed, Lord Torres stuffed the letter into his pocket.

"It is from my mistress. Just a lovers' quarrel, you understand."

His tone implied that such men of the world as Lord Dalton and Lord Sheringham must surely understand such matters. Lord Dalton was many things, but one thing he had never been was a libertine. He little approved of those individuals who flaunted their mistresses and liaisons in public, and he knew instinctively that the brand of women Lord Torres would indulge in had to be of the crasser variety.

The look of scorn on Philip's face was ill-concealed, but Lord Torres's attention was engaged for the moment by Brett, who seemed intrigued at the idea of a Spaniard having an English mistress.

"Dashed queer things, women," Brett said jovially. "What did you quarrel about?"

Sensing that Lord Sheringham was truly interested, Torres decided to embellish his story a bit.

"I was flirting rather successfully with a young lady, and my mistress objected," he replied in a superior manner, obviously puffed out with his bragging.

Lord Dalton found it an irresistible temptation to inquire further into the matter, certain that any female attracted to Lord Torres must be in dire straits indeed.

"Just who was this fortunate young lady?" Philip asked.

Puffing out even more, Lord Torres smiled slyly.

"I was, in fact, speaking to *two* of the loveliest and wealthiest ladies in London, Lady Courtenay and her friend Lady Standen."

As he uttered their names, Ambassador Torres missed the reaction his words caused. Brett turned livid with anger, while Lord Dalton had murder written plainly on his face. Anyone who was even remotely sensitive to emotional changes would have realized that the atmosphere around the table had altered drastically.

Philip seemed to purr out the next sentence. "They were much taken with you, I gather. Who presented the ladies to you? Their mother, perhaps?" Lord Dalton's voice was calm but held an edge to it.

"Why, I believe they thought well enough of me," Torres replied uneasily, belatedly sensing the rise in tension. "I was not introduced to the ladies, since they were unattended, but I made myself known to them."

The Spaniard noted with alarm the high color of Lord Sheringham and cringed at the look in Philip's ice-blue eyes.

Brett had an overwhelming desire to land a facer to Lord Torres's sweating countenance, but managed to hold himself in check, though his fists clenched on the table clearly conveyed his desire.

"I think perhaps you would be wise to re-search your memory about the events you believe occurred," Lord Dalton suggested through teeth bared in a tight smile.

"I can hardly credit your claims of familiarity, as I am acquainted with Lady Courtenay and her friend."

This was said in a manner resembling more a demand than a suggestion.

Torres was aware of sweat trickling down his neck as he continued to gaze into Philip's eyes. The Spanish ambassador was not a brave man, and what little courage he did possess now deserted him. In a hesitant voice he said, "I may have been mistaken as to the ladies' feelings toward me, I must admit."

This statement did not seem to satisfy either young man, and Ambassador Torres decided on a tactical retreat in the face of such hostile opposition. Rising, he took his leave of them both, bowing stiffly.

Brett was happy to see the man go. Though he would have liked to teach Torres a lesson about lying, he could not but be glad that there would not be a row in the middle of the club. He had seen Philip's eyes narrow almost to slits and well knew that menacing look. It was deceptive in that no outer sign revealed his friend's anger, but the burst of violence that usually followed would surely have been detrimental to Lord Torres's health.

The entire scene had not gone unnoticed, but all who were in attendance were wise enough to continue with their gaming and not interfere. Nobody would desire to incur Lord Dalton's considerable wrath, and many were too fond of Brett to pry into something that was not their business.

The two young lords automatically continued to play cards with each other. Neither man spoke the thoughts that intruded on their concentration—the idea that perhaps there had been a grain of truth to Torres's words. Jealousy lurked in Lord Dalton's breast, but he refused to acknowledge such a feeling.

"Philip, you're not concentrating on your game at all," Brett commented.

Discarding two cards, Lord Dalton replied, "I am playing the same way I always play, and it has always been adequate to defeat you, Brett."

Lord Sheringham showed his hand.

"I win, Philip," he said with a sympathetic smile.

It was evidently going to be a long night for both of them.

As Lord Dalton added up the scores and proceeded to play another indifferent game of cards, Lord Torres sat in his coach, on his way to the Theater of Delights. It was in a poorer section of the city and consisted of a tiny stage surrounded by flimsy seats. This was where the baser tastes of those who were less discriminating could be satisfied. Every evening a huge number of women would entertain the audience by trodding over the well-worn planks in an uninspired imitation of classical ballet. These same females were always available to patrons who desired their company after the performance.

It was late, and Torres knew he had missed the last performance. He was not unduly distressed, however, since he knew his mistress would be waiting for him.

The hired coach ground to a halt in front of the small theater. There were still a few girls milling around outside, hoping to entice one of the stragglers from the audience into sampling their wares. As Lord Torres passed them, they threw out their hips in a lascivious manner more suggestive than mere words could have been. Looking them over briefly, he decided that they would not do.

Ambassador Torres was one of those unusual, and some would say perverted, individuals who preferred to bed with women who were, or at least looked, as close to the schoolroom as possible. It was this propensity that had attracted him to his present mistress.

Walking down the dimly lit corridor backstage, he did not even bother to knock on the door that bore the name Marie Manton.

Entering without preamble, he noted the figure that rested supine on the bed dominating the tiny dressing room.

The bed was covered by an old and soiled coverlet

of a faded shade of pink. When new, it had probably shone brightly of satin, but after innumerable years of use, with the bodies of innumerable numbers of men having lain upon it, it was now in ruins. The entire room had the tawdry look that inevitably occurs when a whore takes possession of it. The present occupant was definitely of that category, though she would have ripped the eyes from any man who dared use the word to her.

"So you've come at last, have you?" The voice uttering these words was caustic.

The speaker lay on the bed in a filmy dressing gown with little or nothing beneath it. Such apparel would have been provocative on another woman, but on Marie Manton it was incongruous with her physical appearance. The gown should have draped the voluptuous figure of a nymph; instead, it hung limply from Marie's thin and graceless shoulders.

She was short, under five feet in height, the smallest of the dancers at the theater. Though she possessed a delicate bone structure, she was painfully gaunt and gawky.

She looked to be a child of perhaps thirteen or fourteen, rather than her actual twenty-three years. The kittenish face that peered out from behind short black hair of lackluster quality could, on occasion, resemble that of a wild animal, especially when enraged.

While dancing on stage, the most charitable remark one could make about her ability, or lack of it, would be that it was only slightly better than the leaping of a frog.

To any normal man Marie would have been a laughable choice as a mistress. The figure that most men admired on other women was lacking in Marie. Her breasts were negligible and her slim hips those of a youthful boy. But it was for all these things, or rather for all the things that were absent, that Torres came to Marie's room every evening.

"I am not late, my dear," he replied, walking to the bed.

As he bent over her and attempted to kiss her, she rolled to one side, avoiding his caress.

"First you flirt with some slut in front of me, and now you come to me late," she hissed, rising from the bed and tying a robe around her thin frame.

She looked like a child, but her sentiments were those of a fully grown woman. Lord Torres knew that it was useless to argue with Marie in this mood, and he searched for something to divert her mind from her wrath.

"She would not be interested in me, anyway," he appealed. "She is being courted by a much more agreeable party than I."

The statement was meant to placate and distract Marie, and it succeeded on both counts.

"Who is he?" she asked curiously.

"Would you believe the *honorable* Lord Dalton has his cap set for her?" Diego replied in a mocking voice.

At the mention of Lord Dalton's name, Marie's ears immediately pricked up. She had seen Philip several times before, attempting to obtain his protection as a lover, but she had always failed.

In her mind's eye she could picture him, and had to admit to herself that his enormous wealth was not the only motivating factor in her desire for him. She could envision his leanly athletic and powerful body and had yearned on many an occasion to possess it. Also, she had always been attracted by the aura of danger that surrounded him. Simply conjuring up the image of his face sent thrills down her spine. Mesmerized by his cool eyes, she had longed to arouse the passion that she knew must exist beneath his gloomy exterior.

Looking at her lover Diego, the difference was striking.

"What makes you think that Lord Dalton wants that washed-out blonde girl?" she demanded, cutting haughtiness in her tone.

Torres proceeded to recount the events at his club in detail, watching his "lady love" for her reaction. She did not appear to have one from her outward demeanor, but her mind was working, nonetheless. She had a use for this information.

"I have a terrible headache, Diego. Would you mind if we didn't do anything tonight?" she pleaded as she propelled her lover toward the door.

Stupefied, Lord Torres did not resist, and made only a feeble protest as the door to her room was closed in his face. Staring for a moment at the wooden barrier, he shrugged and walked sullenly away.

"English women, I will never understand them."

Hailing a hansom cab, he settled himself in his seat and sulked all during the journey to his residence.

As soon as Marie had heard Diego's footsteps receding, she put on a dress and a warm cape. Slipping out of the theater by a side exit, she had watched as Lord Torres entered the coach and drove off.

Hailing a carriage for herself, Marie instructed the driver to transport her to an address in the fashionable part of town. Arriving at her destination, Miss Manton was admitted to a large mansion. She did not stop to examine the hall as she was led to a small room adjoining the library. She was sufficiently familiar with the place not to bother with inspecting the contents of the room. Walking over to a side table, she poured a drink from the decanter of brandy and took a large swig from the glass. As she felt the liquor burn down her throat she heard footsteps. Looking up, she saw a man in the doorway.

"Well, Marie, it is good to see you once again. I was just longing for someone with your particular talents."

The voice, deep and lecherous, was repelling even to someone as hardened as Marie.

Answering in a manner that was both languid and sensuous, she replied, "Perhaps you need a dance partner, Lord Chandler?"

A harsh crack of laughter followed her words as Lord Chandler walked to a wall lamp and lit it. The room brightened, and Marie could now see her host's face. It was even more dissipated than it had been a year ago, when she had first become acquainted with him. She had been his mistress off and on now for quite some time, and though he had other women, Marie did not mind; she also indulged in more than one *amour*. Now, smiling professionally into his face, she saluted him with her glass before tossing off the remaining liquid.

Turning to the side table, Marie poured another drink, speaking with her back to Chandler.

"I thought you might like to hear something I picked up tonight. Some information of interest."

Facing him once more, she could see by his expression that she had aroused his curiosity.

"What could you have that would interest me, other than your more obvious talents?" he asked as he poured a brandy for himself.

Smiling at him, she continued to sip her drink.

"I have some information about your arch foe, Lord Dalton," she mocked.

The mere mention of Philip's name had its customary effect; Chandler's features contorted to a mask of fury, but just as quickly, he seemed to regain control of his emotions.

His interest was evident as he looked intently into Marie's eyes.

"Do go on, my dear. You have captured my attention," he said quietly.

Marie proceeded to tell him all that Diego Torres had described to her. When she was done, she was pleased to find Lord Chandler silent for a change. Watching him, she saw his expression change from curiosity to frustration.

"Damn him!" he cried as he walked over to the large windows facing the gardens. "If he marries, the inheritance will go to her."

Realizing that Lord Chandler would have no further use for her, and fully intending to send him a bill for services rendered, Miss Manton left the house.

Chandler remained in the small study, brooding and swearing aloud. I must not allow this to happen, he told himself. I will have to deal with her as well.

Sitting down at the writing table. he began to pen a letter. As he would be attending Lady Culpepper's ball on the invitation of a friend, Lord Chandler chose that place as a rendezvous.

Sealing the missive, he rang for a servant, ordering the man to deliver it to a tavern outside London.

~~~~~ CHAPTER 5

AURELIA HAD WORRIED all night after formally meeting Lord Dalton. Now that she knew what he was like, how could she remain silent about the information she held? The urge to tell him of Lord Chandler's infamy was intense, but she was still unsure of the young man.

What if he thinks my behavior inappropriate for a woman of my station? she wondered.

Although she told herself that she did not care what Lord Dalton's feelings were, she knew that she cared very much what the rest of London would say about her escapade. The town could be most cruel to a young woman making her debut in society, and the thought of her name being bandied about on the tongues of the wags stiffened her resolve to wait.

Things are not yet desperate, she told herself firmly, though guilt hovered about the fringes of her mind. Besides, she rationalized, the only thing that could do him any good would be to find Scurvy Joe and the evidence he is supposed to possess.

Taking comfort in the fact that she had no idea where that nefarious individual was hiding, Aurelia settled down to a very dull morning, her frustrations well in hand.

While Aurelia gloomily pondered her position, Lord Dalton and Lord Sheringham awoke in the best of spirits. They had not remained long at their club after Torres had left, but had stayed long enough to receive an invitation to Lady Culpepper's ball from Lord Culpepper.

Tristan Culpepper had been surprised when his beloved wife had made the unusual request that he deliver the invitations personally to the gentlemen.

"But, dearest, why must I attend to it personally?" he had asked in perplexity. "A servant could just as easily deliver the invitation." But Lady Culpepper was not to be diverted from her request.

"Philip has refused so many times, and I do want him to be present at this assembly," she had insisted. "Lady Courtenay and Lady Standen will be there, and I am set on his presence."

Lady Culpepper had always been a matchmaker at heart and had long desired to be instrumental in bringing about Philip's marriage to a respectable girl. A firm believer in domestic bliss, she was sure that Philip's mother, Alecia, would have wanted her offspring to be taken care of.

Seeing the determined cast to his wife's face, Lord Culpepper sighed. He could not deny her such a small favor, so he found himself presenting the invitation to Lord Dalton, having steeled himself in advance for a chilly refusal. His astonishment at Lord Dalton's ready acceptance, and at the near gratitude he read in that gentleman's face had left Lord Culpepper befuddled. He had simply remarked that Lady Courtenay and Lady Standen would be attending the party when Lord Dalton and Lord Sheringham had both nearly snatched the embossed cards from his hand. It was all very curious to him, but as long as they were coming, and he had successfully dispatched his duty to his wife, he had been content to leave matters at that rather than question their unusual behavior.

Receiving that invitation had given Lord Sheringham a taste of heavenly bliss; he fairly floated back to Philip's townhouse. Before retiring that night, Brett had worried over what to wear in a most uncharacteristic fashion.

"I haven't seen you take such extreme pains with your wardrobe since we graduated, and at that time you were aspiring to dandyism," Philip had remarked dryly.

Ignoring the comment, Brett had continued to fret over his evening coats.

Though Philip had chided Brett about his overanxiousness, he privately proceeded to examine his own wardrobe, wishing to impress Lady Courtenay as much as his friend wished to do the same with Lady Standen. Though he generally confided in Brett, he was damned if he would let even his best friend know to what extent he had become captivated by Aurelia. Lord Dalton was not the type of man who admired other men's numerous affairs, and did not indulge in the petticoat line himself. For him to exhibit an interest in a woman was tantamount to a declaration of intent, so he had to be very sure before he would expose his feelings to anyone, least of all to the lady herself.

To pass the time until evening, the two men decided to witness what promised to be quite a spectacle. The evening before, at the club, there had been a near row. The delicate Lord Mince, a friend of Brett's, had been the recipient of an insult delivered by Lord Thrasham.

Even while driving to the boxing parlor, Philip was hard pressed not to laugh as he recalled Mince's blustering fury when Thrasham had pronounced that his lordship's rose-pink waistcoat was decidedly effeminate. This insult had led to a rash challenge, and the hour of reckoning was drawing near.

"Poor Ellie," Brett muttered as he watched the houses pass by the carriage window. "What could have possessed him to challenge Thrasham to go three rounds with him?"

"You would not have stomached the cut he was afforded, Brett," Philip admonished gently. "He may be unimposing in height, but he is a Mince for all of that. He has as much pride as any in his family, I dare say."

Brett groaned, thinking of the height differential between Mince and his opponent.

"Thrasham is at least six feet tall, and Ellie is not above five-six," he said. "Hardly a fair fight."

"We shall see," Philip remarked as the coach halted before Jackson's Boxing Parlor, an establishment catering to those afficionados of the manly arts.

Entering, Brett noted that a good many persons were congregated for the expected fiasco. There was none of the usual betting before a match, as nobody present doubted the outcome, and Lord Thrasham could be seen talking to Lord Royer in a corner of the room, confident as a cock on a dunghill. The sight made Brett's blood boil.

"I've a mind to call him to account myself," the young man fumed as he watched Thrasham laugh at some remark.

It was obvious that both Thrasham and Royer were celebrating the victory before the battle.

"One would have thought that Royer wouldn't encourage him to go after unworthy game," Philip remarked, following Brett's gaze.

"Wouldn't have mattered much," Brett commented. "Ellie can be such a shuttlehead about things."

At that moment the object of his concern entered the crowded room, his slight figure draped in a fighter's robe. He looked out of place as he walked toward the ring, which dominated the entire area.

"I'm going to him," Brett said to Philip, seeing that Mince would be in need of an attendant in his corner.

Left alone, Philip took notice of who was present. His eyes narrowed and his jaw set as he saw his foe enter. Lord Chandler was also a friend of Lord

Thrasham's though Lord Royer was known to shun Philip's stepfather.

"A bit of a commoner for all his blue blood," had been the caustic comment from this gentleman when asked about his lack of affection for Chandler. Still, as he neared, Lord Royer did not give up his place beside Thrasham. They appeared deep in discussion while Brett prepared Lord Mince for the fray. Philip walked slowly over to join the group, his face assuming a languid expression, his attitude decidedly nonchalant.

"Lord Thrasham, Royer," he greeted; then, turning toward Lord Chandler he added, "Sir." The tone was demeaning, and Royer smiled as color crept into his lordship's cheeks. The effect was lost on Thrasham, who did not have an overabundance of perspicacity.

"Well, Dalton, here to watch me pound that little sod into the canvas?" he asked jovially.

"Very certain, aren't you, my lord?" Philip answered. "It may be that the results will be contrary to your expectations."

Lord Royer took interest in this comment, which Thrasham and Lord Chandler seemed to dismiss entirely.

"You are aware of some facts to the contrary, Lord Dalton?" Royer inquired.

Royer was not one to underestimate anything that Lord Dalton might say. He had always had a grudging respect for Philip, though they did not move in the same circles or share the same interests, and he had recognized the satisfied gleam in Dalton's eyes, as if he possessed the knowledge to some secret.

"I am only saying that Mince may afford you more of a fight than you might anticipate, Thrasham," Philip replied.

"Nonsense," Lord Chandler put in, savoring the word. "There is no chance for Mince. If you knew more about boxing you would realize that, Lord Dalton." Chandler's tone dripped with heavy sarcasm.

"I was unaware that you were an expert in this sport, Lord Chandler," Royer remarked wryly.

"Aye, he is, and in others as well," Lord Thrasham bellowed, flinging a burly arm across Chandler's shoulders. "Not only is he an expert in the manly arts, he is one of the best damned hands with a foil that I have ever had the pleasure to lay eyes on."

This avowal was not denied by Lord Chandler in the least, and Lord Royer reflected that any self-deprecating gesture would have only screamed insincerity in any case.

Lord Dalton eyed his foe with a skepticism that rankled badly.

"Forgive me, but I cannot recall any mention from other members on your swordsmanship, Lord Chandler," Philip commented.

"Well, you needn't feel ill-informed, Lord Dalton," Royer interjected. "You can hardly be expected to know of Lord Chandler's fame, having been but a babe in arms at the time."

There were no words suitable to describe the look Chandler bestowed on Lord Royer at this remark. It was just as well that he did not try, since the fight was about to begin.

Thrasham was called away at that moment, and left reluctantly to prepare for the match. The three men watched as he disrobed in his corner of the ring. Lord Mince emulated his adversary, and there was not a man in the room who was unaware of the discrepancy in size and musculature between the two. Lord Thrasham's physique was enormous, with broad and heavily muscled shoulders. He was ham-fisted, his arms attesting to a mighty punch. Brett shuddered slightly and gave his friend a sympathetic glance.

Mince seemed unaware of the almost ludicrous sight he was presenting. Short in height, his slender form was dwarfed by Thrasham. Though he was puny-looking next to Thrasham's mighty presence, there was an odd stealthiness to his carriage, and the physique that was for the most part hidden by his normal clothing was not as underdeveloped as Brett had first suspected. As the two opponents shook hands, Lord Thrasham was surprised by the firmness of his adversary's grip, and by the clear and steady gaze his eyes presented. With Lord Dalton's words echoing in his ears, Thrasham returned to his corner to await the beginning of the round.

Meanwhile, Lord Chandler had compared the two men thoroughly, and was more convinced than ever of Lord Thrasham's superiority. Turning to his stepson, he wore an open smirk.

"If you think Lord Mince has a chance with Thrasham, my lord, perhaps you would be amenable to a small wager on the bout."

Chandler watched eagerly as Philip considered his suggestion. He had long wanted to part Lord Dalton from some of that blunt which he considered rightfully his, and he saw this event as a perfect opportunity.

Philip was well aware of Lord Chandler's eagerness and of Lord Royer's undivided attention.

"What odds, my lord?"

"Three to one against. After all, there is really little hope of your man winning," Lord Chandler answered, counting his profits in his mind.

"Done," Lord Dalton replied. "I wager a thousand guineas that Lord Mince will down Lord Thrasham before the second round."

"Very well. Will you hold the wager, Lord Royer?"

Royer agreed to this arrangement, and immediately the three men concentrated their attention on the ring.

The battle began as expected, with Thrasham lashing out brutally with his right. However, Mince was no longer standing where Lord Thrasham had seen him an instant before, and that confused individual became the recipient of several rapid blows from the left. Turning slowly, Lord Thrasham again struck out at his opponent, only to feel his fist whistling through vacant air. Three resounding blows were speedily delivered to the other side of Thrasham's head, and he found himself staggering under the assault.

Before long Thrasham was unable to lash out with his previous ferocity, and he was having difficulty in remaining on his feet. His foe constantly dodged and evaded his every attempt to make contact, and several times he embraced the ropes of the ring rather than Lord Mince.

Chandler watched with fascinated horror as he saw his friend fall slowly to the mat at the end of the first round, unable to rise. He had lost his wager, and Philip's silent acceptance of his winnings was maddening.

As quickly as Thrasham had hit the mat, the crowd of men who had witnessed the feat with dumb astonishment surged forward with their congratulations. Mince accepted them all with the cool calm he had displayed in the ring, and was accompanied by a sizable group to the club for drinks in order to celebrate his victory. Lord Dalton and Lord Sheringham, being part of that entourage, were in high spirits when they finally left the club sometime later to prepare for the ball.

It was total chaos at the Culpepper's mansion. There were last-minute details to take care of before the guests arrived, and Lady Culpepper thought her flower arrangements deplorable, but it was much too late to alter them. Tristan Culpepper arrived to witness his wife's usual preparty frenzy.

"My dear, *do* stop fussing about. Everything will be perfect as usual," he admonished, bestowing a peck on her cheek.

"I know," the lady sighed. "But you *know* how things are always popping up at the last moment. It's all just too much to bear, really."

Before her husband could answer, a footman announced that the first guests were beginning to arrive. Miraculously the furrows disappeared from Lady Culpepper's brow. Putting on her most gracious smile, she took her husband's proferred arm and walked to the hallway to welcome several old friends who had come early to assist Lady Culpepper in managing the entire affair. Soon after, more guests approached the residence in large numbers. Some brought along a friend or two, which was the usual custom of these affairs.

"I wonder where the duchess and her young charges are?" Lady Culpepper murmured. She had been keeping a watch out for their coach while she greeted the steadily accumulating number of people, but had not yet seen them. Lord Culpepper, peering out into the darkness, caught sight of the Courtenay carriage, Lady Faye's matronly head protruding from a window.

"Here are your matchmaking victims now, my dear," he said as the vehicle drew up to the entrance and two footmen helped the occupants down.

"My dear Duchess!" Lady Culpepper exclaimed, greeting the elder Courtenay with outstretched hands. "How good of you all to come to our modest little fete."

Gabrielle and Aurelia acknowledged the welcome warmly as they each gave a small curtsy to their hostess.

Lord Culpepper then proceeded to offer his arm to Lady Faye, and they led the way into the grand hallway.

As they entered, Aurelia and Gabrielle caught their breath in awe, for the entire house was lit with myriad candles. The effect was most spectacular. The strains of a waltz could be heard coming from the ballroom, and after giving their capes to the footmen, they stepped into the room.

Aurelia could sense all eyes turn toward them as they advanced. Everyone looked at the pair of divine young women, and there was a growing murmur of remarks such as "gorgeous" and "exquisite." This continued for some time, with couples actually stopping in mid-dance to stare at them.

Aurelia's eyes scanned the crowded room, hoping to find Lord Dalton, while Gabrielle was intent on locating Lord Sheringham. They were nowhere to be seen, but the ladies' glances had attracted several other individuals, who made haste to be the first introduced to the two beauteous women. By the end of the waltz both girls were fairly surrounded by men, and when a new dance began, they found themselves swept back onto the dance floor, still looking in vain for their absent gallants.

Lord Culpepper stood to one side of the ballroom, talking to the duchess, while his wife returned to the hallway to keep watch for latecomers. As she reached the door, she witnessed the arrival of the fashionable gentlemen whom she had been seeking all this time.

Lord Sheringham advanced with his hand extended in an apologetic manner.

"Please excuse us for being late. We had a slight delay on the way," he said as he bowed over her hand.

Lord Dalton walked more sedately toward his hostess and bowed elegantly.

"Let me beg pardon for our tardiness, madame."

She waved his words aside. "It's not necessary to apologize. What matters is that you have come. Let us join the other guests."

Philip offered his arm and escorted Lady Culpepper to the ballroom. Something similar to the murmuring that had accompanied Aurelia and Gabrielle's entrance could be heard when Lord Dalton's imposing and seldom seen figure appeared. It was true that Philip did not usually attend such functions and that this was a rare occasion, but it was more than just the novelty of seeing him that aroused such comment. Lord Dalton was standing under the archway leading to the ballroom, the candles of the hall chandelier softening what could normally be described as his wolfish yet handsome features. His eyes burned with a fire that appeared to consume his very soul as his piercing azure orbs seemed to rake across the room in search of someone.

His black velvet coat was cut to show to advantage a physique such as to elicit a reaction from one young lady: "What a man," she sighed.

This thought was in the minds of the majority of the women present, and Lady Courtenay was no exception to the general sentiment.

Suddenly Lord Dalton was arrested by the sight of

Aurelia dancing with her partner. His eyes rested on her as if he had finally found the form that could give him satisfaction. Power evident in his every move, and assurance in his bearing, he strode across the crowded ballroom floor and deposited his intimidating form before the dancers. Without so much as a veiled allusion to a request, Philip swept Aurelia from her unfortunate partner's grasp and waltzed her away.

She looked fearlessly at him, drinking in his very presence. He seemed to energize her to such an extent that she never tired while dancing with him, hardly feeling the floor beneath her.

She finally tore her eyes away from his and looked about the room, trying to gain some semblance of composure.

Philip took this opportunity to gaze adoringly at the face he had come to revel in. He wanted every feature, every contour, to become etched upon his memory so that he could at least possess a likeness in his mind, if not the actual person, for all time.

In truth, Lord Dalton, who had never doubted that the woman he would love would love him in return, was now jealous and unsure of his powers of attraction. After all, he had eyes in his head, and he could see that every man in the room was worshipping at the shrine of Aurelia's beauty. He continued to gaze at her face, at the hair so golden as to make the coin of the realm seem like copper, and at the delicately pale cheek that was now flushed to an exquisite pink from the exertion of the waltz. That cheek was more delicate than the wing of a dove, and softer than the petals of a rose. It took a tremendous effort on his part to refrain from caressing that lovely countenance.

Aurelia could feel his gaze on her face and looked once more into his eyes. The effect was such as to transport them away from an earthly existence and into another realm more suited to lovers who have found each other. They both broke the contact this time. Neither Aurelia nor Philip was ready to declare such a love outright without first knowing the other's feelings, so they withdrew into themselves and continued the dance on a more distant emotional plane.

Gazing about, Aurelia saw that Brett had found Gabrielle and that they were making no pretense at anything other than absolute delight in each other's company. Laughing and smiling, Brett guided his partner across the floor, eluding adeptly the approach of other men intent on claiming a dance.

Aurelia was amused by this observation and would have made a comment to Philip had she not abruptly realized that, unconsciously, Philip had been doing exactly the same thing. She could see several disgruntled suitors on the sidelines looking daggers at Lord Dalton's back.

They dare not do so to his face, she reflected, and laughed at the thought.

Philip marveled at her loveliness but maintained his outward composure. Only the most observant of individuals would have seen his hand tremble slightly as he led Aurelia from the dance floor when the waltz was ended.

Brett and Gabrielle joined them on the sidelines. Both women looked in need of the fresh evening air, and the quartet retreated to the balcony terrace that faced the garden and a marble fountain splashing gently. The rosebushes were in bloom, climbing the walls of the house alongside the ivy, scenting the air with their sweet perfume, and the moon flooded the garden with a strange intensity that resembled a rarefied variety of daylight.

Realizing that he was remiss in his duties, Lord Sheringham asked, "Would you like some punch, Lady Standen? Lady Courtenay?"

Gabrielle nodded at this, the long waltz having left her a trifle parched. Aurelia felt drunk with Lord Dalton's presence alone, but assented as well to receiving a glass of punch.

With a slight bow, the men took their leave of the ladies to obtain the required refreshments. It was then that her friend's emotional state became apparent to

Aurelia. Gabrielle looked completely blissful as she sighed loudly.

"Isn't he the most handsome, kind, and considerate man you have ever met?" she asked Aurelia, adoration evident in her voice.

Aurelia's reply was not laudatory, but it was sufficient. "He seems very nice, as well as to enjoy your company immensely."

Gabrielle did not appear to notice this less-than-enthusiastic comment, and was about to question her friend on the subject of Lord Dalton when their solitude was interrupted by footsteps approaching behind them. Turning in unison, expecting to see Philip and Brett with their refreshments, they sustained an unpleasant shock. There, striding purposefully toward them, was the rather ludicrous figure of Lord Torres, overdressed to the extreme in comparison with the other men at the ball.

Gabrielle emitted a faint groan at his approach, but there was nothing for it since Torres continued to advance. No avenue of escape was available, so the girls stood their ground, bracing themselves to face the pompous lord.

As Diego drew near, he had an opportunity to survey them more thoroughly than he had at the dressmaker's.

Lady Standen, even though she was not his first choice as a matrimonial prospect, might be a perfect second choice should his suit to Lady Courtenay fail to bear fruit.

She certainly is as striking in her own way, he thought, admiring her in a gown of silver gauze. Gabrielle seemed to be hardly of this earth as she glittered in the moonlight. Though Diego had a preference for younger girls, he was nonetheless aware that she was an extremely attractive woman.

Shifting his eyes to the figure beside her, he was blessed with the vision of the face and form of Lady Courtenay. Aurelia had chosen to don a dress of gold brocade, which contrasted perfectly with the gown of her friend. She had the air of grace and ease that was characteristic of the well-born, and her pale fine skin awakened a strong desire in Lord Torres to caress the object of his scrutiny.

He was so absorbed in his assessment of the ladies' various attributes that he failed to note the disdain with which they acknowledged his presence. Aurelia could barely suppress a shudder of distaste as he bowed before them, and Gabrielle even allowed her lip to curl momentarily. Both women were aware that Lord Torres's primary interest was money, and it appeared to be Aurelia upon whom he pinned his hopes of attaining this goal. As the Spaniard rose from his bow, he smiled at them ingratiatingly.

Obviously he wants to leave the door open should Aurelia reject his suit, Gabrielle mused knowingly as she surveyed his apparel with a fascinated eye.

"Lady Courtenay, Lady Standen," he said, putting on his most affable expression. "I am so pleased to see you both again. I have attempted to visit you at your home, but you have been out each time."

Putting on a false smile of her own, Gabrielle looked the man in the eye as she responded, "We have been so busy, you know, Lord Torres. We simply must have missed you by chance."

She batted her lashes as she continued to smile. Diego Torres was totally taken in by this explanation, which only an idiot would have believed had it not been delivered with such a sincere expression. Diego then suggested that Aurelia join him in the next quadrille.

Privately, Aurelia would rather have embraced a serpent than dance with him, but aloud, she merely declined on the grounds that "I must remain here to receive a glass of punch from Lord Dalton, who has gone to procure it from the banquet hall."

The mention of Lord Dalton's name incensed Torres, who had not yet forgotten the insult he had received at the club. Aurelia had not missed the look on his face when she mentioned Philip, and inquired, "Do you not like Lord Dalton? I find him unexceptionable myself."

This was said with a most innocent air, and the Spanish ambassador wisely decided to refrain from impugning Philip's honor until he knew more about his relationship with Lady Courtenay.

"I am a good friend of Lord Dalton's," he lied smoothly, his face all amiability.

Aurelia did not trust that toothy smile and knew not how to take this information. If Lord Torres was indeed a friend of Philip's, then all she could say was that Lord Dalton certainly was not particular about whom he chose as friends.

Still, many men had odd friends, so she merely said, "Oh," in the blandest of possible tones.

They seemed to be at a standstill for conversation, Lord Torres beginning to feel distinctly uncomfortable. Gabrielle stepped reluctantly into the breach.

"I personally think Lord Dalton an impressive figure," she said, watching for a reaction. There was none, much to the lady's disappointment.

"Do you find him so, Lady Courtenay?" Diego inquired cagily. He had a strong desire to discover the extent of Lady Courtenay's affection for Lord Dalton.

Aurelia hesitated a moment before answering. "Well, yes, I do. It's undeniable, is it not?"

Though she tried to keep her voice light and unconcerned as she spoke these words, her face betrayed her true veneration for Philip.

Diego nodded absently to himself. He would brook no interference with his own wooing of Lady Courtenay, a pursuit he was sure would be successful as well as profitable.

His usually dull wits pondered over the best method to break off this affection. He could think of nothing, so he let the matter rest for the time being.

Small talk was the prime activity now engaged in by the ladies in an attempt to bore Lord Torres into absenting himself from their presence.

Diego watched Aurelia's reaction to all that was discussed, but the blasé look on her face remained intact for the most part.

What did she think of the races? he asked; her answer was obscure.

What did she think of Parliament? She did not think of Parliament at all, she averred.

It went on like this for some time, during which Aurelia wondered what could have befallen Philip and Brett that they should be so tardy in their task.

These gentlemen were at that very moment cornered across the ballroom by a veritable dragon of a matron who was bent on extracting a promise from them that they would indeed attend her card party next Wednesday. Philip and Brett attempted to extricate themselves from their predicament when they realized that the lady's two unattractive but enthusiastic daughters had consumed the punch intended for Aurelia and Gabrielle. The lords, upon managing to escape, had to return to the dining area for more punch, Lord Dalton cursing the matron under his breath for the delay.

In the meantime, Gabrielle was on the verge of yawning in Lord Torres's face, and Aurelia wore a look conveying to him very well what a dashed dull dog she thought he was. Desperately trying to think of something interesting to say, Diego hit on a subject that seemed to rouse both ladies from their lethargy. "Did you hear about Lady Lovill's escapade?" he asked conspiratorially.

Neither girl had, so he proceeded to describe the event that had so recently made Lady Lovill's name common gossip.

It seemed that this young woman was well known around London as an excellent whip, and had raced several female companions on her estates for fun. She had won consistently and become more daring with each successive victory. Finally she had challenged the notorious Lord Harrington to a race, with a lock of her hair as the forfeit if she lost. Well, the lady had won the race, and Lord Harrington had purchased a new gelding for her stables as his payment. It was the talk of the town, and as the woman in question was married, it was simply opprobrious for her to have raced with the most infamous rake, short of Lord Royer, in the country. Many of the wags and gossips were convinced that the lock of hair was not to be the only thing forfeited had the lady lost.

Diego noted that Lady Courtenay did not seem terribly scandalized by this behavior, and inquired into her lack of condemnation.

"I think it was perfectly innocent. She has a right to behave as she wishes, and there is no reason she shouldn't race with Lord Harrington, though *I* am a bit more particular," Aurelia insisted with a toss of her head.

She wore such an expression of defiance that Ambassador Torres realized she felt deeply on the matter of women's rights and privileges. This revelation spawned an idea in his mind, a way to alienate Lord Dalton from her affection. As if starting on another subject, he casually mentioned that Philip had labeled the lady's conduct reprehensible.

Hardly believing her ears, Aurelia exclaimed, "You are sure? I did not think he would hold judgment over another person so easily."

Lord Torres smiled in such a manner as to make Gabrielle shudder, and continued to lie in his teeth. "Quite sure, Lady Courtenay. His exact words were, 'Any woman who would engage in such scandalous behavior is not deserving of respect.'"

Aurelia's face was suffused with incredulity, but the first signs of uncertainty were creeping into her expression. The fear rose within her that Philip could disapprove of her own actions.

Diego had no way of realizing that the subject was more than just a matter of rights to Aurelia, but he could see that his words had given her pause for reflection.

Gabrielle did not know what to make of all this herself. She did not trust Lord Torres; nor did she readily believe that Philip would say any such thing. However, if it were true, he most certainly would not approve of a woman who had dressed in men's clothes, ridden around the countryside armed with pistols, and placed his lordship in the uncomfortable position of being beholden to her for the saving of his life, not to mention the humiliation of having been deceived.

As she reflected on her misgivings, Gabrielle slowly scanned the ballroom through the terrace doors. Her eyes were halted in their progress by familiar figures attempting to negotiate the circumference of the room while holding full glasses of punch.

"There they are," she said with relief.

Torres looked up, appearing rather like a fox caught poaching in the henhouse. He decided that a confrontation with Lord Dalton was not in order at this time. Apologizing, he quickly took his leave of the ladies, kissing their hands, which were reluctantly offered up to his grasp.

Aurelia was unprepared to see Lord Dalton after the false revelation that had been so evilly provided for her. She did not entirely believe it, but the suspicion persisted in her mind that it could be the truth.

She resolved, however, to appear as if nothing had happened. Turning to her friend, Aurelia warned, "Don't let on that Lord Torres has been talking to us."

Gabrielle complied with the request, thinking that Aurelia must have her reasons.

So it was that Philip returned to his lovely companion, who appeared to be well rested and perfectly composed. He did not have any indication that there was anything amiss, and when he suggested a walk, Aurelia seemed pleased with the idea. Leaving the empty glasses on the terrace, they proceeded to the garden below. Tall shrubbery shrouded some of the benches that bespeckled the premises, providing a comfortable retreat for those individuals seeking privacy. In the center, Lord Culpepper had ordered constructed a maze of hedges. Aurelia was enchanted.

"Let us go in," she urged delightedly.

Gabrielle was game, so they convinced their escorts

to try to find them in the maze while they would attempt to hide from them. As neither gentleman believed there would be any difficulty in locating them, they agreed indulgently. The truth be told Aurelia intended to test Lord Dalton's temper. Even if he had never held the sentiments that Lord Torres had attributed to him, she had been piqued at the mere idea that he could harbor such views.

As the ladies entered the maze, Aurelia whispered in Gabrielle's ear, "Let's lead them a merry chase. We will go out of the maze and then let them thrash about looking for us."

Gabrielle was by no means adverse to a little prank, so they left their gentlemen to search in vain. They exited quickly and hid in a dark arbor behind a large bush to await the outcome of their trick. They could hear the sounds of Brett's and Philip's feet as they trod in circles searching for them. When faint curses emanated from the hedges, the girls could barely suppress their laughter. Just as Aurelia would have spoken, the girls heard the faint sound of talking coming from behind the spot where they were hidden.

"What can that be?" Aurelia wondered.

Lady Standen shrugged her shoulders in bewilderment. Her curiosity aroused, Aurelia found a hole in the bush through which she could see the structure of a small gazebo. It appeared to be occupied at the moment. Motioning Gabrielle to look as well, she could just make out the silhouettes of two men at the narrow entrance to the gazebo. Suddenly there was a flare of light, then the soft glow of lamplight. They could now see the occupants of the structure as clearly as if they were standing before them. The girls stared with astonishment as they realized that the illuminated figures were the notorious highwayman Scurvy Joe and the murderous Lord Chandler.

Aurelia heard her friend's soft gasp of surprise, but she said nothing, trying to distinguish what was being said. The voices were low, but the hedge was so close to the enclosure that almost every word of the discussion could be heard.

Lord Chandler was dressed in an unimpressive coat of puce, but his clothing was finer by far than that of his wretched companion in crime, whose ragged coat was encrusted with filth from his ride.

He looked very uncomfortable in Scurvy Joe's presence. Due, no doubt, to the fact that the bandit had just recently extorted from him a large sum of money.

"Ye sent fer me?" Scurvey Joe asked, looking directly into the older man's eyes.

Bending forward slightly, Lord Chandler answered in an urgent voice, "Yes. I'd previously planned no specific time for my stepson's demise. However, circumstances have changed. I want him dead within the next two weeks."

Lord Chandler seemed firm on this, and Gabrielle could plainly see the speculative expression on the outlaw's face.

"Why now, all o' a sudden, yer lordship?"

Chandler's patience was being sorely tried by this ruffian, but he managed to retain his calm and proceeded to explain. "My devil of a stepson has his cap set for a wife, and we both know that the last thing I need is for him to marry. Wives are damned inquisitive things, always poking about."

Scurvy Joe digested this information.

"Well, why not just put th' girl to bed wit' a shovel?" he suggested. It was all the same to him, man or woman. "It'd be considerable easier to me mind," he reasoned.

This twisted logic resulted in Chandler's nearly losing his patience. In a slightly louder voice than he had hitherto used, he said, "I have thought of that, but we can't go killing everyone he knows. It won't do. Too many questions would be asked. No, she is not to be harmed unless there is no other alternative. You must take care of Philip soon. It wouldn't do for the lady he's dangling after to inquire too much about his death.

Best to kill him before her attachment to him becomes fixed."

This made sense to Scurvy Joe's limited intellect, and he could find no fault with Lord Chandler's assumptions.

"Well, then, Oi'll 'ave to 'urry up and get rid o' yer lordship's little stepson," he snickered.

As Scurvy Joe seemed ready to leave, Chandler added, "Mind you, it must look like an accident!"

The highwayman looked down at the restraining hand that had been placed on his arm to detain him, a deadly glint in his eyes. Chandler removed the offending member, which action seemed to satisfy the ruffian. As he reached the door of the gazebo, Scurvy Joe turned one last time.

"If someone is wit' Lord Dalton when Oi tries to kill 'im off, what then?"

Chandler did not hesitate in his reply. "Kill anyone who gets in the way. Make it look like an accident."

Scurvy Joe made to leave, but Chandler called out after him in a tight but controlled voice, "About that evidence you have."

"What o' it?"

"Perhaps I could buy it from you for, say, double the sum you originally asked."

Lord Chandler's voice was just a trifle too eager, and this merely caused a smirk of satisfaction to appear on Scurvy Joe's face.

"Oi think not, me lord," he taunted. With that he turned and left.

There was naked rage on Chandler's face, and Aurelia thought she had never seen such a look of savage hatred before. It was almost primitive in its intensity, and it made him look like some demoniac spirit of destruction. He spun dizzily out of the structure's concealing security and disappeared into the darkness.

Gabrielle had found the entire scene unnerving. She could not utter a word, however, as she again heard a sound, footsteps nearing the recently vacated building. The women strained their eyes as another light was lit in the gazebo. To her astonishment, Aurelia saw that Scurvy Joe had not yet departed. He had apparently waited until Chandler had left, then returned to meet someone else. They watched as a second figure came into view, another highwayman by the looks of him, and obviously in league with Scurvy Joe.

He was a thin, emaciated individual with ratlike features that befitted his high and squeaky voice.

"Oi watched just like ye said to, Joe."

"Yer sure 'e's gone, then, Rufus?"

"Aye, aye, 'e's gone," the cohort replied, his nose twitching convulsively.

Aurelia could almost imagine the man sprouting whiskers and a tail.

"Well, ye 'eard, we's goin' to kill Lord Dalton soon," Scurvy Joe said with a sadistic sneer. "It'll be jolly good fun to pay 'im back fer th' men 'e cost me."

The confederate laughed along with the master, like a cur who has learned its place from having been kicked constantly.

"Did ye see 'is lordship cringe when Oi says, 'Oi think not, me lord?'" The leader snickered derisively. "Ye still 'ave them papers safe, don't ye?" he asked threateningly.

Rufus was profuse in his assurances.

"Aye, aye. They be safe as a flea in a rug in me room, or me name ain't Rufus Kane. The Golden Inn has loose floorboards."

"Well, take care ye don't lose them," Scurvy Joe growled. "Where be th' 'orses?" he demanded after a moment.

Kane scurried off, and eventually brought back a pair of animals. Mounting up, Scurvy Joe reminded his underling, "Wait at th' inn until Oi calls fer ye. Oi'm goin' ta need ye on this little job."

They left at a gallop in opposite directions and were soon out of sight.

Aurelia turned to her friend. "This has gone too far," she said, the worry obvious in her voice.

"I agree; we must tell them," Gabrielle responded.

It was the only reasonable thing to do, yet the two women were uneasy. They were not positive that Lord Dalton would object to their masquerade and subsequent behavior, but lesser things had been cause enough to cool a romance's flame.

But Aurelia and Gabrielle knew they had to apprise the young lords about Chandler's plot in spite of what that might do to their respective relationships. The only question was how to go about it.

It was then that they became aware of uttering coming from the maze.

"Oh dear! We forgot all about them!" Gabrielle exclaimed.

It was true. Rather than admit defeat, Philip and Brett had continued to search in vain for the girls for the past twenty minutes. Lord Dalton's bursts of profanity had become increasingly frequent, and gradually more irritation could be heard in Lord Sheringham's milder exclamations.

Aurelia was most amused as yet another stream of curses drifted on the still night air. She should have guessed that Philip would not be one to give up on an effort, no matter what the task.

"Perhaps we should go back in and let them find us," Gabrielle suggested. Aurelia agreed. It was only fair since they had looked for such a prolonged period.

"It will give them a feeling of accomplishment," Aurelia giggled, trying to force the miserable thoughts from her mind.

For appearance' sake, Aurelia put on a false smile and entered the maze, Gabrielle in her wake. Lady Standen was worried herself but also put on a façade of enjoyment to deceive the two lords, whose voices could be heard more clearly as the girls neared the spot where they were searching. Gabrielle again felt a chill at the thought that she might be deprived of the one man to whom she had ever been attracted. She knew she could never bear it if Brett were killed, which was quite likely since he went everywhere with Philip.

The women reached the middle of the maze which

showed no signs of having been traversed by either Philip or Brett. Was it possible that they had not found the center during all this time? Apparently this was precisely the case. All the other paths had been trampled by the men's boots in their search, but here the grass remained undisturbed.

"Perhaps they will never find us," Gabrielle commented in despair.

Aurelia was inclined to agree.

"This calls for positive action," she declared.

Lord Dalton was becoming decidedly exasperated, Brett surmised from the way in which his friend kicked pebbles aside and from the increasingly profane exclamations issuing from his lips. They had been searching for a good half hour by Brett's estimation. Philip's profanity was directed at his inability to discover the center of the maze. At the suggestion that they call out to the ladies, Lord Dalton's visage took on a stubborn mien. He intended to continue looking for as long as it took to find them. Just as Brett would have called out himself, risking even Philip's ire, with which he was well acquainted, he heard the clear, untrammeled sound of female laughter rising into the air from a direction just in front of them. The tautness that had dominated Lord Dalton's features disappeared, and with it Lord Sheringham's fatigue.

As they broke through the last hedge, Gabrielle quickly whispered to Aurelia, "Pretend to be surprised."

It was with apparent astonishment that the lovely ladies greeted their escorts. Philip's face showed undisguised satisfaction at finally having reached his goal, never suspecting that Lady Courtenay had purposefully laughed aloud to attract his attention.

Lord Sheringham allowed himself to puff up slightly as he took in Gabrielle's admiring gaze.

"It wasn't so difficult. Philip and I knew where you were all along," he fabricated. "We were just funning."

Philip cast a look of surprise at his handsome friend, wiping the expression from his face almost immediately. Aurelia noticed it but made no comment about the obvious falsehood.

As they made their way out of the maze, Philip found himself gazing at Aurelia in unabashed devotion. He was now admitting to himself that he was in love with this extraordinary woman, and he was no longer attempting to hide the fact from anyone. His eyes seemed almost to caress her countenance, and their defensively cold and aloof look was gone, never to return in Aurelia's presence.

Though the look now was gentle, it possessed an intensity that spoke volumes. Aurelia seemed to be numbed by his presence, and for a moment she could see nothing but his blue eyes as she returned his gaze measure for measure.

The moment was broken by noises from the ballroom. Gabrielle and Brett stepped through the door onto the ballroom floor, too enthralled with each other's company to notice if Aurelia and Philip were following. Aurelia would have joined them, but Philip had stopped just outside the louvered doorway. She turned to him, a puzzled expression on her fair face.

"May I have the pleasure of calling on you and your mother tomorrow?" Philip asked suddenly.

The manner in which he said this made her head spin with a breathless rapture. By his tone she was sure his purpose in the visit would be to ask permission to pay court.

In as calm a voice as she could manage, she answered, "You may, my lord."

He bent closer to her pink mouth, which tempted him to an impetuousness in which he would not otherwise have indulged.

Just as their lips would have met, Lady Culpepper came outside and interrupted their moment of bliss. Seeing that she had intruded, she made as if to leave. Unfortunately, it was too late. Philip recovered himself sufficiently enough to bow to that august personage. She hastily acknowledged the greeting and walked hurriedly away.

The moment was lost, however. Under control once more, Lord Dalton bent low to kiss Lady Courtenay's hand. This was a more proper action for him to indulge in, but to his impassioned heart it was similar to giving a drop of water to a man dying of thirst; it was a gesture, but far from satisfying. If anything, this civilized salute was fuel for his burning ardor.

Knowing that his control would be sorely strained if he continued to remain alone in her company, Philip at last led the object of his adoration back into the teeming ballroom.

Aurelia was also disappointed at the turn of events. Lady Culpepper's interruption could not have come at a less opportune time, but she resigned herself to her fate for the moment.

As they made their way past the dancing couples, spectators along the walls were much struck by the expression on the lovers' faces. Aurelia was radiant, and Philip bestowed a look of sheer idolization upon his precious lady.

Many matrons tried to put this new development off by saying that Lord Dalton was only toying with the girl, but they knew better. It wasn't in his makeup to deceive a young and apparently innocent girl in such a manner.

The duchess was aware of her daughter's happiness and was well pleased with the match. She was not at all surprised when Lord Dalton asked if he might call on her the next day. She gave her assent, being quite sure she knew his intent, just as her daughter had been. And when Lord Dalton asked to accompany her daughter home, she made no objection, except to insist upon a footman accompanying them. The duchess remained behind to renew old acquaintances.

The couple left the ball with Gabrielle and Brett. There was not much opportunity to exchange more than trifling comments during the ride home, but both women knew that the silence which would occasionally come over their escorts was indicative of deeper feelings. The ride was over all too soon, and as the carriage halted before the house, Brett saw that there was at last a chance to be alone with Gabrielle for a few seconds before parting. He quickly helped Lady Standen down from the coach and stood with her in the shadow of the doorway of the duchess's residence.

This left the carriage to Philip and Aurelia. The footman, torn as to which couple to observe, chose Brett and Gabrielle, since they seemed all the more anxious for privacy.

Lady Courtenay was experiencing the most sublime feelings imaginable as she looked at Philip, the light from the doorway making it possible to see his features clearly. As he gazed back into those intrepid, blue-gray eyes he found her to be a mixture of confounding but alluring paradoxes: lovely yet bold, delicate but with a will unmatched by any other.

Aurelia sat poised with expectancy; surely such a superb and commanding man could not be too timid to make his feelings known. Lord Dalton did indeed feel an immense desire to let his passions burst forth. As before while on the terrace, he knew an overwhelming longing to kiss those lips that beckoned him. Though his ardor was aroused, he still resisted the insistent urge, and quickly opened the carriage door. Aurelia was upset by this, thinking that there was not any true emotion on Lord Dalton's part.

Her suspicions were unfounded. She perceived how he trembled at her touch as he helped her from the coach, and she saw the distracted look in his eyes. The arms that so yearned to embrace and protect her encircled her waist as Philip lowered her to his side. Aurelia's closeness, and the maddening passion he felt for her, were too much to bear any longer. Drawing her to him, he held her pressed against his heart. She could feel the wild pounding within his breast that matched her own heart's turbulent beating. Leaning back for one breathless moment, Aurelia looked adoringly up into the face of the man she had come to love so well in such a short span of time.

Slowly and with deliberate intent, Philip bent his

mouth to Aurelia's, drawing her still nearer in his embrace. She could feel his frame shake with emotions barely suppressed, and his eyes spoke more eloquently than any voiced declaration. With an unexpected gentleness, their lips met, and Aurelia experienced such a moment of utter bliss that it seemed to elevate her to some other existence. Though the kiss had ended, Aurelia could still sense the lingering pressure of Philip's lips on hers. Lord Dalton could not bear to relinquish his possession of her, nor was Aurelia inclined to withdraw from that sweet embrace.

Sadly, their brief period of mutual happiness was short-lived. The footman, seeing that Lady Courtenay had thrown restraint to the wind, rushed over to them, a horrified expression on his face. A single glance from Philip, however, brought him to an immediate standstill.

Looking at Aurelia, Lord Dalton said, "Don't think that I am impetuous or insincere; I am not a man who takes these matters lightly. Perhaps you will think me foolish to say this, but although I have not known you long, I feel that we were meant to be together. I hope you share my feelings in some small measure, if not in total."

He watched fervently for a reponse that would set his agitated mind at ease. He waited for her answer with an emotion approaching fear, should her reply prove negative.

It was at this point that the footman could be heard coughing himself into a fit to remind them of his presence. Seeing that she must go, Aurelia said quickly, "I do share your feelings, Philip—more than you can know."

With that statement she was gone.

Although Aurelia was no longer in sight, Lord Dalton continued to stare at the spot upon which she had so recently stood. Her words had been like a balm to his troubled heart, and he gave his imagination free rein. For a moment he could almost see her still, so close that he wanted to reach out and touch her.

Philip would no doubt have been happy to remain rooted to the pavement until dawn, but Brett was not inclined toward such bizarre behavior. Walking up to his friend, he had to shake Philip's arm to rouse him from his preoccupation.

"Come, now, Philip, it's time we were off." Then, noticing the blissful expression on Lord Dalton's face, Brett cajoled, "You are obviously happy about something. Care to tell me what great good fortune has befallen you?"

Philip waited a moment before answering. "Brett, for the first time in my life I find myself—" He cut off his speech with a gesture of impatience. "I was about to say 'in love,' but that does not even minutely express my feelings for Aurelia."

This statement was so incredible coming from someone like Philip that Brett was half inclined to believe his friend was shamming. Before he could voice this suspicion, Philip abruptly decided to move on. With an exuberant leap he bounded up the step of the coach and deposited his slender form into the seat. Turning to look out the window at Brett, he saw that his friend appeared even more incredulous than ever.

"You said it was time to go, Brett. Come along, then; don't dally. One would take you for a lounge lizard," Philip said patiently, as if to a child.

Brett took his place beside Philip without another word, unable to think of anything to say, and the coachman headed homeward.

Meanwhile, at the Courtenay residence, Aurelia was in transports as she and Gabrielle sat in the library.

"Gabrielle, Philip is in love with me," Aurelia said at length.

This did not surprise her friend in the least. Gabrielle had suspected as much from the looks the couple had been exchanging all evening, and she was overjoyed with the news.

"That is wonderful, Aurelia! Brett has said much the same thing to me, but not, I gather, as definitely or as forcefully as Lord Dalton must have, judging from your ecstasy."

They hugged each other affectionately, overcome by their mutual joy, and talked gaily about the future. Walking into the hallway, they were met by Renée. Beside her stood a gawky young man of about nineteen years of age, and at his feet a very drowsy Elva wagged a tired tail in greeting to her mistress. Bending to pick her up, Aurelia observed the man, as did Gabrielle. He was obviously new to the country, for he wore the rough clothing of a French peasant. This was, they deduced, Renée's love, whom Lady Courtenay had brought out of imprisonment and had sent to England.

Looking him over thoroughly, Aurelia decided he must concern himself with a bath almost immediately, in as hot a tub of water as could be provided. Gabrielle appeared especially fascinated by the tiny insects crawling around in the newcomer's hair. Tearing her eyes from the sight, she shuddered slightly.

All during this silent inspection Renée's beau was becoming more and more indignant.

Finally Aurelia spoke. "Please introduce us to your fiancé, Renée," she said gently.

Realizing that her swain was becoming increasingly restive, Renée complied quickly.

"This, my lady, is Antoine Scarron. He is a bricklayer, or at least he was one in France."

Her pride in his abilities was evident by her tone and had the desired effect of putting the Frenchman more at ease. He seemed to unbend a bit, and the scowl he had been wearing disappeared.

"You are welcome in my home, Mr. Scarron," Aurelia said, her voice possessing no trace of condescension. The greeting was warm and friendly, and Antoine appeared almost at a loss. He had not expected the aristocracy of England to be any different than that of France, and he was visibly touched and confused by turns.

Making his best bow to the two ladies, he responded, "I am at your service, my lady."

Gabrielle was still fascinated by the quantity of lice on his head, but managed to express her hopes that Mr. Scarron would discover a new and prosperous life in Britain. "For I do not think France has dealt with you in a proper manner," she declared.

"France! I am ever faithful to France, but I detest and abhor the present government," he spat. Calming down, he turned to an astonished Aurelia and said, "If there is anything I can do to repay you, be sure that I shall do so without question. I say this *au grand sérieux*."

Aurelia accepted this statement with a gravity matching his, and Renée led him away for a good wash, taking Elva along for her evening meal.

As soon as he was out of earshot, Gabrielle said, "I do hope she will bathe him thoroughly."

Lady Courtenay laughed at this. "I'm sure she will. Did you notice the little creatures milling about in his hair?" she asked as she and Gabrielle climbed the stairs to their rooms.

Gabrielle made a face indicative of her feelings on the subject.

"How could I not have noticed?" she responded. "His pate seemed to have a life of its own. You are fortunate if Elva does not become infested as well!"

Aurelia was much amused by these comments and was about to reply in the same humorous vein when her thoughts turned to Philip. Her expression changed drastically, a look of horror seeming to grip her face.

"We have forgotten about Lord Chandler!" she gasped. The very name of that depraved individual sent shivers of apprehension down her spine. "We must warn Philip!"

"And how are we to warn him, pray?" Gabrielle wondered distractedly. "I cannot think of how unless we disclose all to him."

"I should go and tell him myself, but I cannot face him just yet," Aurelia said, her mind a confused whirl of guilt and worry. "What if we wrote an anonymous letter to him, warning him of his danger?" she suggested anxiously.

"Would he trust such a message? After all, Chandler could just as well have sent it, for all he would know. He would suspect a trap."

The problem elicited all of Aurelia's mental faculties as she struggled to think of an answer to her dilemma.

Suddenly she hit on an idea.

"My signet ring!" she cried. "We can seal the letter with that. Surely he would trust the information then."

Gabrielle considered this suggestion.

"If he had an impression of the crest, he would eventually find out who we are," she pointed out.

"I know," Aurelia replied in a strained voice, "but we have to take the chance. If he discovers my identity, I would almost welcome it."

Gabrielle could see that Aurelia's conscience warred with her inability to face Philip with the truth, and she finally nodded.

"I suppose you are right. I will get ink and parchment from the desk."

Gabrielle hurried into the adjoining room, and Aurelia seated herself before her escritoire to compose the missive. She could feel her heart beating and strove to calm herself. Philip's life depended on her at that moment, and if he did not believe the message she was about to send, Lord Chandler might succeed with his diabolical scheme.

Gabrielle returned, a trifle breathless, with paper and quill. Aurelia began to write with the greatest of care, describing all the events in great detail: where Scurvy Joe's cohort was to be found, the plans for Philip's ultimate demise, and the incriminating evidence that this certain underling possessed. On completion, Aurelia reread the neatly printed note and handed it to Gabrielle, who looked it over and nodded in mute agreement.

Fetching hot wax from her own writing desk, Gabrielle held it at the ready while Aurelia walked over to the jeweled casket on her vanity. From among the glitter of gems accumulated over the years, Aurelia extracted her signet ring. Clasping it to her breast for a moment, as if in prayer, she returned to the escritoire.

Gabrielle ceremoniously applied the sealing wax to the note, and Aurelia carefully pressed the ring into the center of the fast-cooling mixture. She waited a moment, then removed it. There in the wax was a perfect impression of the Courtenay crest.

"Now we must have it delivered," Gabrielle stated with a briskness she did not feel.

Aurelia seemed as one in a daze; the effect of writing and her fear for Philip's safety had sapped her strength.

"The Frenchman, Antoine, can deliver it," Gabrielle decided. "We can trust him, I think, and he is not known in town."

"Let us do it, then, and have done," Aurelia said wearily.

She had tried her best; the rest was up to fate.

Gabrielle rang for the maid, and a few moments later they could hear her footsteps coming toward the room. Renée entered and glanced about her expectantly. Lady Courtenay still sat in the chair by the writing table. She looked pale and distressed.

"Renée," Gabrielle said, "I have a task for Mr. Scarron to perform. Is he dressed?"

The maid was surprised, but was not brave enough to inquire what the errand was.

"He is ready, my lady. I shall send him up directly," she replied, leaving the room.

The two women waited, Aurelia becoming more forlorn and desolate as time dragged on. She stared fixedly at the letter in her hand, and Gabrielle did not think it wise to intrude on her friend's private sorrows. Finally there was a knock on the door, and Mr. Scarron entered the room, curiosity stamped on his visage.

Bathed and fed, he looked much more respectable. His coarse clothing had been discarded for a rather conservative gray ensemble provided by Davis.

Bowing before both ladies, he asked, "What is my mission?"

Gabrielle regarded the young man sternly in order to convey the gravity of the entire matter.

"You are to deliver this note to Lord Dalton's townhouse. You must go alone, and try not to let anyone see you. It is imperative that this remain a secret."

She then gave Mr. Scarron the traveling directions he would need.

The idea of an adventure appealed to Antoine. He clicked his heels and bowed.

"*Bien entendu,* I will do all that is required, my lady. Trust me." With that he marched purposefully from the room.

CHAPTER 6

LORD DALTON'S ostler had finished rubbing down the horses for the night. He had lavished his usual care on the animals, for he knew that his master would spare no expense to keep his mounts in the best of condition. As he left the stables and made his way back to the house, he saw what he took to be the shadow of a man across the lawn. He blinked, rubbed his eyes, and looked again.

"Must be me bloomin' imagination," he mumbled to himself.

He could see nothing amiss, so he put the illusion down to too little sleep and too much ale. What he did not know was that the shadow belonged to one Antoine Scarron, who was at the moment hiding behind a shrub in the garden. Silently, the Frenchman waited for the ostler to move on. He had tried to leave the letter in his possession at the front of the house, but there had been too much light from the street for him to remain unnoticed by any possible passerby. Now he must attempt to leave it in some more secreted area. He watched the servant make his way slowly toward the rear entrance and disappear into the recesses of the house. Rising from his cramped position, Antoine padded quietly toward the goal he had chosen, the open doors of what appeared to be his lordship's study. The doors had been left slightly ajar, as it was a rather warm night, and when he heard sounds from within, he checked himself at the entranceway.

A lamp was lit, and through an opening in the drapes Antoine received his first glimpse of how the men of English aristocracy appeared. His eyes appraised the forms and visages of Lord Dalton and Lord Sheringham, who had not yet retired for the night. As he observed the gentlemen he decided that at least the British looked less arrogant than the French nobility. Having served for a time in the home of one such notable in France, where he had learned to speak English, Antoine saw that there were indeed differences between the nationalities. It was fortunate that Antoine had not viewed Philip Dalton in one of his more defiant moods. As it was, the events of the evening had left a rather blissful appearance on his attractive features.

"Will you join me in a glass of sherry, Brett?" Philip inquired, turning his back to the curtained doorway.

Lord Sheringham's faint reply was lost to Antoine as he saw his chance to slip the note through the portal. As he did so he inadvertently made a noise. He quickly fled the area in fright, since it was imperative that he not be seen.

Lord Dalton had jerked round at the slight sound and motioned Brett to be silent. His piercing glance shot across the room, and he spotted the letter lying on the parquet floor. Walking carefully over to the doors, he pulled back the drapes with a quick thrust.

"Well, whoever delivered this is gone now," Philip said as he bent to collect the packet. "Now, who would—" He stopped in midsentence as he examined the seal on the letter.

"Brett, come here!"

"What is it?" Brett asked as he took the paper from Philip's hand.

"That, my friend, is the same seal that was engraved on a ring that one of our rescuers was wearing. I recognize it now," Philip explained patiently.

Retrieving the missive from Brett's unresisting grasp, Philip managed to open it without breaking the seal. As he read the contents, he pocketed the small bit of wax. Brett watched his friend examine the letter with characteristic care, and then read it himself after Philip handed it to him. Finishing his perusal, he was left speechless.

"What is their interest in my affairs, I wonder?" Philip mused.

"Well, I dare say that they could be in league with Chandler, you know," Brett recovered enough to suggest. "It could all be a trap, for I am positive you are going to that inn to have a little talk with Scurvy Joe's henchman."

"True, Brett. That is exactly what I plan to do, but I think you are wrong about those two being in league with Chandler. After all, they did save our lives. No, I don't think they are setting a trap," Philip decided.

"Then we are going to the inn," Brett said in a resigned voice.

"Poor Brett, yes, we will be going, but not just yet."

This was surprising to Brett, for it would be more in character for Philip to leave immediately. Looking inquiringly at his friend, he found that Philip was not attending to him. Instead, he seemed to have a distracted air about him, as if he were reliving in his mind a moment of bliss. It was then that Brett realized there was something far more important on Philip's mind than the matter of his own survival. He could not contain his astonishment at the thought of this.

"Philip, you are actually afraid to leave London because of Aurelia, aren't you?"

Philip's face was as impassive as stone as he regarded his friend, but his eyes, as always, showed his discomposure.

"I am to see her tomorrow. I can't possibly leave now, not when there are so many things I have to settle with her."

"She will be here when we return, Philip," Brett reminded him.

"Yes, but I am not the only suitor for her hand," Philip retorted sharply.

Lord Dalton was immediately ashamed of his sharpness.

"Forgive me, Brett," he apologized. "I simply can't depart now. I will go at the end of the week. There is time enough for all of this," he added cheerfully.

Brett's fears were not allayed, but he knew he could not dissuade Philip; besides, if it had been he, he would not have left Gabrielle at that moment, either.

"Well, I suppose there is no real danger at this time," he conceded.

"Of course not."

"And we will go at the end of the week."

"Of course."

"Well, let's go to bed, then," Brett recommended with a yawn. "Tomorrow will be an important day for you, and you will need all your strength," he added laughingly.

Lord Dalton and Lord Sheringham retired for the night, each in his own way concerned with the future—Philip, mainly for his future happiness with Aurelia; Brett, with the imminent danger to Philip's life. Neither man enjoyed a restful sleep.

The following morning Lord Dalton's valet, Packer, found that his master was in a particularly irritable mood. Nothing he set out for his employer seemed to please him. This was unusual, since Lord Dalton normally did not care very much what he wore as long as it was black.

"It simply won't do, Packer," Philip snapped.

Packer sighed and replaced the fifth suit of clothing he had brought forth for Philip's approval.

"My lord, if you could perhaps tell me what you have in mind, I might be able to find something to your specifications," Packer proffered in a strained voice.

Lord Dalton then realized he was being unreasonable.

"Oh, never mind, Packer. I will wear the last suit. It will do very well, I'm quite certain," Philip assured him.

"Very good, my lord," came the reply as the valet rummaged within the confines of the clothes press for the suit Philip had so recently rejected.

After laying the ensemble out on the bed, Packer retreated silently from the room. He had been in the earl's service long enough to know that his master would not welcome his help, expert as it was, that morning.

Truth be told, Philip was more than just a trifle nervous, though he would have been loath to admit it.

He was taking special pains with his appearance because he did not wish anything to be out of place when he made his call on the duchess. His brief meeting with that lady had assured him that only the most proper of gentlemen would win her approval, and he was determined that no mistake on his part would be the cause of his losing favor with the mother of the woman he intended to wed.

He was in the process of tying a very difficult but entirely appropriate cravat when there came a rapping on his door, and the voice of Brett smote his ears, inquiring if he was awake.

"Oh, yes," Philip replied as he put the final touches on his masterpiece.

Turning, he opened the door. "Well?" he asked, waiting for an opinion.

"Well!" Brett exclaimed, circling his friend so that

he could take in the full impact of the clothes. "You are certainly out to impress the lady, Philip."

Lord Dalton smiled tightly.

"Well, if not to impress, then at least not to offend her," he admitted.

Seeing his friend's discomfort, Brett put on his brightest smile.

"Come, now, you look every inch the proper aristocrat. The woman can't but adore you in all your splendor," he said jokingly.

Though Philip did not seem to agree with this prophecy, he need not have worried so, for the person in question was fully appreciative of his attire when he arrived at her residence sometime later.

"Lord Dalton," Lady Faye said as Davis showed his lordship into the sitting room.

"Your Grace," Lord Dalton returned. "I am honored that you could receive me, madame." He saluted the proffered hand, tightly encased in a glove of pale green kid.

The elder Courtenay seemed pleased at this very correct greeting and bade his lordship be seated. This Philip did, and for the next half an hour Lady Faye engaged him in light conversation while tea was being served.

The duchess was accustomed to having tea in the morning as well as in the afternoon, since she found that the practice tended to fortify one for the events of the day. Though Philip had already partaken of breakfast, he willingly accepted the cup of tea and the slice of sponge cake that her Grace pressed upon him. The man who had often been described as fearless on the hunting grounds and ruthless at cards could not summon the nerve to refuse the undesired cup of tea for fear of giving offense. Of course, Lord Dalton must be excused for this sudden and uncharacteristic lack of courage, which emanated from the fact that he had had little to do with the mothers of any young women, or indeed with the young women themselves, and he was unsure how to proceed to the matter that was foremost in his consciousness. Had it been Aurelia's father to whom Philip would direct his proposal, he would have had no hesitation at all. However, something told him that he must advance with more conventional care in the case of Lady Faye than he would have lavished otherwise.

Though Davis strained his eager ear against the wooden barrier, he could not hear what was being said within the duchess's inner sanctum. So intent was he on listening that he did not see Lady Courtenay descending the stairway with Elva under her arm. She stopped in midflight and looked down on the thinning pate of Lady Standen's butler. The dog's nose twitched a bit in curiosity as she watched along with her mistress.

The loud "ahem" she made caused the butler to rise from his unseemly position with haste.

"Davis, who is in there?" Aurelia asked with her customary nonchalance.

"Lord Dalton has come to call on her Grace, my lady," he answered stiffly.

Aurelia flushed slightly at hearing Philip's name. Seeing that the butler was observing her, awaiting further orders, she said imperiously, "You may leave now."

With a sniff Davis bowed and retreated belowstairs.

Aurelia approached the sitting-room door and rapped sharply on its thick mahogany surface. There came a faint sound from within, which Aurelia took for assent to her entrance; placing Elva on the polished floor, she pulled open the door and walked gracefully inside, the small dog following close behind. She saw her mother and Lord Dalton seated on the sofa having tea, and Aurelia thought, not for the first time, that he was the handsomest man she had ever beheld. Lord Dalton quickly rose from his seat as Aurelia came toward them.

"Good morning, Mama," Aurelia said, kissing her mother on the cheek.

Greeting Philip, she extended her hand, on which he

implanted a chaste kiss. Elva pranced playfully about their feet all the while, but the couple appeared oblivious.

Lady Faye would have had to be blind not to see the glow of happiness surrounding the pair. Not only was there happiness, but also an intensity that convinced her that this adoration was no freakish fit of fancy.

Lord Dalton was at a loss for words upon seeing the love of his life, and the best he could manage was a murmured, "Good morning." Aurelia was equally reserved before her mother and also could discover little to say.

There was an awkward silence as both struggled for words; then a brilliant stroke came to Philip.

"Madame," he said, turning to Lady Faye, "may I ask your permission to take your daughter to the races today? I have a horse running this morning that I am persuaded will win."

The duchess was hesitant to agree to this, so Aurelia added her voice to that of Lord Dalton's, hoping to sway her. "I would enjoy that immensely, Mama," she pleaded, "and we could be accompanied by a footman."

Her Grace gave in to her daughter's persuasive tone.

"You would not mind a footman coming with you, Lord Dalton?" Lady Faye asked.

Philip's reply was prompt.

"Not in the least, madame, if it will assure me of Lady Courtenay's company."

"Very well, then," the duchess declared, rising from her seat. "You must go and change, Aurelia, at once. I will have the footman wait outside."

Aurelia left the room, after promising Philip that she would only be gone briefly.

She handed Elva over to the fastidious Crane just beyond the polished doors.

"You must take care of my baby until I return, Crane," she admonished, sweeping quickly up the staircase to her chamber.

"Yes, Lady Courtenay," Crane replied. Butler and

dog eyed each other somewhat balefully as he retreated to the kitchen with his charge.

When Aurelia had left, Philip again found himself at a loss. The duchess did not need to be asked the question that hung on his lips to know what it was. Before Philip could say a word, she spoke.

"You have my permission to pay court to my daughter, Lord Dalton."

Philip was astonished, then he smiled.

"Thank you, your Grace. I shall try to be worthy of her," he declared elatedly as he bent to salute her hand.

Without further conversation, the duchess left Lord Dalton to await Aurelia's return in privacy. Quite suddenly she realized that she might cry, and was determined to take herself off to some quiet corner of the house and give vent to tears. She had only just then become aware that her little Aurelia would soon leave and be a married woman.

So it was that Lord Dalton greeted Aurelia alone, which gave him the opportunity to press a kiss tenderly into the palm of her hand before escorting her to the waiting carriage. He did not relinquish his hold on her hand until they were forced to separate for the benefit of the servants, who had just appeared.

"Must not shock them," Aurelia whispered mischievously as they passed Davis, who had evidently seen the kiss, and who now wore a look of solemn disapproval.

Philip had the utmost difficulty in maintaining an impassive face as they walked by the butler; Aurelia, on his arm was looking much like the proverbial cat in the cream. The moment the door closed behind them, they broke into peals of laughter.

"Did you see his face?" Aurelia asked between gasps for air.

"Yes, I did," Philip replied breathlessly. "What a look he gave you!"

His laughter subsiding, he gazed into Aurelia's eyes, which sparkled with mirth, and wanted to take her in his arms for all the world to see. Though the temptation was great, he resisted, for he felt an obligation to the duchess as well as to his lady to act in such a way as to be above reproach.

"You look so serious all of a sudden, Philip," Aurelia said, smiling enchantingly. "Is something wrong?"

"No, my darling. I was just thinking how very much I love you," he answered feelingly.

Before she could reply, Philip handed her up into the carriage.

"To the races," the earl shouted to his coachman, and with a flick of the whip they were off, no one able to see what went on behind the drawn shades.

The crowd at the racing green was confronted with an unheard-of sight that bright morning: the notoriously unromantic Lord Dalton, totally besotted by love, was escorting Lady Aurelia Courtenay across the smooth grass of the track.

"Good God, Louisa!" exclaimed Lady Chatalot upon viewing them. "Can it really be Lord Dalton with that young lady?"

Her companion could only nod in silent assent. The women watched Philip convey Aurelia to a spot by the railing to watch the upcoming race, her footman following at a discreet distance behind.

Aurelia was well aware of the stir that they were causing, and she heard snatches of conversation when they passed some of Lord Dalton's acquaintances. These gentlemen were obviously surprised by this turn of events, but they could certainly understand why Lord Dalton had at last succumbed to the Goddess of Love. Aurelia had never looked better as she walked along in her becoming new dress of light blue accented by a darker blue braid. A glow of happiness radiated from her being, and she seemed to light up the sky, rather than the other way around.

"Philip," Aurelia said as she watched the thoroughbreds lining up at the gate, "do you really think your horse will win today?"

Lord Dalton studied the printed list that one of the lackeys had handed him when he descended from the carriage.

"There are quite a few good horses running," he replied thoughtfully, "but I think the best must be the animal owned by Carburry, and my horse has beaten Carburry's several times in the past."

He pointed out the prized animal to Aurelia, and as she followed his hand, she happened to notice a familiar and most dreadful figure on the other side of the racing green. It was the sinister Lord Chandler, and he had apparently caught sight of his stepson and her. Aurelia could not suppress a shudder after glimpsing his depraved face, and Philip, seeing her look of utter aversion, gazed across the track to determine what had elicited such a reaction.

"Why, what is the matter?" he inquired, scanning the area. His eyes passed over Lord Chandler, for he had just disappeared into the crowd. "Has something displeased you?"

Aurelia shook her head in mute reply. She dared not tell him that she knew Lord Chandler at all. She was sure that Philip would wonder about her reaction to having seen his stepfather, and she did not want to give away her secret just yet.

"I just saw a girl of whom I am not fond."

Philip found this response a bit odd, since he thought the look she had shown was much more intense than one caused by mild irritation or dislike, but he decided to make no comment for the time being. Just as he would have spoken again, Lord Dalton halted in midbreath and stared off into the crowd. Aurelia followed his gaze, and to her horror she saw Lord Chandler wending his way through the mass of people toward them. Wearing an expression that could only be described as devious, he halted before Philip, making an elaborate bow. Chandler instantly recognized Aurelia as one of the ladies he had suspected of listening outside his door at the inn, and he was appalled.

On any other occasion Lord Dalton would have been inclined to be rid of Lord Chandler's company, but now he saw a chance to put his stepfather out. He knew very well that Chandler was living on the expectancy of obtaining his money, and the opportunity to bait him was irresistible.

Returning Lord Chandler's bow, Philip failed to notice Aurelia's face flush and then turn deathly pale at being confronted by this dreadful individual. Then suddenly she was filled with determination.

There is no reason to be afraid, she thought. I shall make *him* uncomfortable, in fact.

As Chandler's eyes shifted from his stepson to Aurelia, he immediately noted her changed temperament. She was no longer pale or hesitant, and he was disturbed to see a certain baleful glint in the young lady's eyes that was distressingly close to Lord Dalton's own glance. Feeling somewhat nonplused, Lord Chandler considered a quick retreat but decided against it. He had deliberately accosted the young couple to ascertain just how serious this affair was becoming, and he intended to go through with it. A wife was definitely more trouble than Chandler could afford, and if the attachment proved deep, he would have to make arrangements to break them up.

Besides, he thought, I can certainly match these two in a battle of wits.

Putting on his most felicitous smile, he asked, "Well, Philip, are you not going to introduce me to this lovely young lady?"

Chandler's voice grated on Lord Dalton's nerves, and he was loath to introduce Aurelia to such an ugly customer, but there was nothing for it.

"Lady Aurelia Courtenay, may I introduce you to Lord Chandler, my late mother's second choice as husband," Philip said smoothly.

Aurelia's eyes twinkled as she watched Chandler's color rise, then recede. The control it took to suppress an outburst of anger on his part was great; he stood there and fumed in silence.

"I am sure that any blood relative of Lord Dalton's must be worth knowing. As for the rest, we need not bother with them." Aurelia gave Chandler a deceptively sweet smile.

Philip looked at Aurelia approvingly. He was well pleased by her reaction, though he did not realize the extent of her knowledge as to the lord's bad conduct. He simply assumed that she was picking up on his lead, and he anticipated with pleasure a good bout of raking his stepfather over the coals. Chandler, on the other hand, was resolved to keep the conversation as civil as possible, at least until he had the information he sought. Aurelia's joining in Lord Dalton's insults was only partial proof that she was inclined to favor his detested stepson.

He tried an obvious ploy to discover how long Philip had known Lady Courtenay. "You are just recently arrived, Lady Courtenay. Pray, when did you meet her, Philip?" he asked, turning to Lord Dalton.

Philip could plainly see that Chandler was attempting to gain insight into his attachment for Aurelia and to learn if he had a definite tendresse for her. Just as he would have replied, Aurelia answered in his stead.

"We have known each other for some time," she said, deliberately vague.

"And we intend to see each other much more in the future," Philip added. He smiled devotedly into Aurelia's blue-gray eyes and placed a possessive hand upon hers.

This was quite enough to convince Chandler that immediate steps would have to be taken to disrupt this happy romance. He had a plan brewing in the back of his mind, but in order to execute it, he must manage to see Philip and Aurelia Courtenay again together, preferably at a public event or a ball.

It was toward this end that Lord Chandler inquired, "Ah, Lady Courtenay, surely you will be attending Lady Bellvue's ball this Thursday evening?"

"Why, yes, I will be," she responded suspiciously.

"Good, then I shall have an opportunity to see you again," Chandler declared. "Now, if you will excuse me," he said as he bowed again, "I must leave."

Extending her hand reluctantly for his unwanted salute, Aurelia gave one last parting shot. "Perhaps we will see you at Lady Bellvue's ball, Lord Chandler, but then, one never knows what sort of people one will meet in such a mixed assemblage," she asserted wickedly.

The earl did not bother to conceal his amusement at Aurelia's veiled allusion that Lord Chandler was no more than a mistake on Lady Bellvue's guest list and that he could be labeled with the riffraff whom one occasionally found at even the best of affairs.

Chandler managed to hide his incensement at this final aspersion on his character, but Aurelia could tell by the abrupt manner in which he subsequently took his leave that he had been greatly discomforted by her remarks.

She could not help but feel satisfaction from having aided Philip even in a small way. She knew now that in all matters she would always take his part.

From where they stood they could not hear Lord Chandler mumbling a vow of vengeance against them. Aside from his desire to retaliate, Chandler also had a much more practical reason for wanting to break up the couple. He knew that Scurvy Joe had failed before in his attempts on Philip's life, and as an extra precaution, it would be wise to sever the relationship as fast as possible.

As Aurelia turned around to say a word to her beau, she found that he was staring at her in obvious admiration.

"There are few women I know who would have had the nerve to speak to my stepfather in the manner in which you just did. But why did you cut him so? After all, you have no quarrel with him."

Aurelia thought for a moment.

"Well, you evidently don't think well of him," she

replied. "So if you don't approve of him, there must be something wrong with him. Besides," she added, "he doesn't seem very pleasant to me."

Philip looked surprised. "What gave you that impression? Not but what you're right about him, but he didn't offer any prior indication of his character."

Aurelia fell back on a common feminine myth. "Oh, just my intuition, I suppose," she answered vaguely.

This was hardly an adequate response, but Lord Dalton knew better than to pursue the subject.

Lady Courtenay regarded Philip for a long moment, trying to decide if he had accepted her answer. As she looked into his eyes she was struck by their intensity, which was apparent even when their gaze was not in direct contact with hers.

Suddenly he smiled down at her, altering his entire demeanor. He didn't care why Aurelia had taken his part—it was enough that she had—and Philip was feeling better at that moment than he had ever felt before. One could hardly deny that the earl appeared at last to have everything in life that a man could need or want. He was in love with a beautiful girl who he had every reason to believe shared his feelings, he was very wealthy, and he had just twisted a figurative knife into his worst enemy's wound. He looked carefree, and everyone watching the lovers could instantly see the change that Aurelia had wrought in Philip in such a short time.

While Lord Dalton and Lady Courtenay continued to follow the racing, Chandler wended his way back to his coach. Several couples made it their express business to avoid contact with him, since he was not favored by the majority of the ton, but he was oblivious to these snubs. Indeed, his mind was on matters of much higher importance to him. Specifically, Lord Chandler was aiming all his mental faculties at the problem of the blooming romance. Arriving at his coach, he ascended the steps and sat down to contemplate the scheme brewing in his mind.

Rolling up the window shade, he shouted to the driver, "To the Theater of Delights!"

The coachman roused himself from a drunken stupor—his lordship often employed the worst possible menials as servants—and started the horses in the direction of the theater.

As the carriage drew up before that establishment, Lord Chandler realized that an afternoon performance was in progress, for a number of rowdy individuals were lined up before the box office to pay their tuppence and receive an eyeful. As he descended from his coach he could hear a bawdy song issuing from within the dance hall, and he knew that the object of his trip would be on stage at any moment.

He entered the darkened theater after handing his money to the half-witted youth at the window. The seats were well filled for an afternoon show, and Chandler decided to stand rather than to risk his cloak to the possibility of grease or ale on a seat.

Several ruffians glanced up at this unusual-looking man. He was obviously not a regular denizen of the Theater of Delights, and he had a strange air about him, but their attention was soon diverted by the gyrations of a particularly well-built young woman on stage. Chandler raised a quizzing glass to inspect the new talent, whose figure was voluptuous, but found her lacking the peculiar traits in which he reveled. Specifically, she was too mature for his tastes and too overly endowed. He was more desirous of innocent-looking girls, since his inclinations were of the more depraved variety.

He watched the entertainer as she finally made her exit from the stage in a flurry of petticoats and visible flesh. The audience was obviously appreciative of her charms and made it known by repeated baying noises and wolf whistles. Lord Chandler contented himself with a faint clapping of his gloved hands.

Suddenly the stage went black, with only a single spotlight in the center. Into this oasis of illumination leaped the slim, if awkward, figure of Marie Manton, clothed in barely more than a few well-placed leaves and vines. The music played by the orchestra was an unbridled native rhythm, and Marie performed a series of wild movements around the stage. The local hooligans were so much impressed by her scanty clothing and her want of propriety that they did not notice that her dancing was stilted and odd, or that her figure was not of the type that would ordinarily fire their lust.

Chandler was used to viewing the dubious charms of Miss Manton, and with even less on than at present, so he was not particularly inflamed by her performance. As a matter of fact, he could watch her dance with objectivity and could offer up several criticisms of her style, or rather, her lack of it. He knew, however, that this was not Marie's major talent and that her appeal to the horde herded like cattle into the stuffy confines of the theater depended on her negligible apparel and little else.

As the beat of the music rose to its crescendo, Marie continued to writhe across the stage, shedding several vines and leaves as she went. In her mind Miss Manton was imagining herself at the most prestigious of ballet theaters, but, truth be told, her ability was such that she would have been fortunate even to clean the floorboards of an establishment of that quality.

With a last flurry of her vines, Marie Manton dissolved into the darkness. There was a smattering of applause at the finale, since the majority of the audience, which had at first been interested in her performance, had soon tired of watching.

As one rowdy individual put it, "Cor, she looks like me little brother Charlie."

This comment went unheeded by Lord Chandler, who had already started to make his way backstage to speak with Marie on the matter of a business proposition. He pushed his way past several paint-covered women. As he did so, one of them, a disheveled-looking nymph with tinny blonde hair, shrank back at the sight of him. She had seen many strange men in her day, but none with such a strong aura of villainous intent. She shuddered slightly and then pranced out onto the lighted stage.

Chandler reached Marie's room and knocked on the grubby door with the silver head of his walking stick.

A voice from within said, "Come in, my love."

Obviously Miss Manton was expecting someone else, but Lord Chandler had no compunction about interrupting her plans for his own gain. He entered without comment and stood on the threshold looking at Marie, who was seated before her vanity. This piece of furniture had been aptly named in the case of Miss Manton. She was brushing her scraggly hair and admiring her own visage when Lord Chandler rudely appeared. Seeing that the form reflected in her mirror was not that of the gentleman she had invited to her room, Marie whirled around in her seat, her eyes flaming and her face screwed into an expression of fury. She resembled for all the world an alley cat ready to spit.

"What do you want here?" she screeched in her shrill and grating voice.

Chandler flinched, just for a moment, then his features assumed a passive, almost agreeable look.

"Why, Marie, what type of greeting is that for one with whom you have shared hearth and home, not to mention financial rewards?" he asked pleasantly.

She immediately picked up the closest object at hand and flung it at his head. The porcelain figurine, which had originated in the flea markets of Piccadilly Circus, burst into shards scant inches from Chandler's pate.

"Marie, what have I done to incur such a show of disaffection?" He continued to speak while dodging yet another piece of porcelain.

"Done?" she shouted as her hand darted out for a bottle of champagne that had been delivered earlier in the day. "You haven't paid me for that information I gave you, that's what you've done!" She tossed the bottle at Chandler's retreating figure.

Catching the bottle deftly with one hand, Chandler attempted to calm Miss Manton's ruffled sensibilities by opening the magnum and pouring the bubbling liquor into the accompanying glasses.

"Now, Marie, I will pay you by and by, I assure you. In the meantime, I have a proposition to make to you that would more than triple the amount of money I owe you. Are you interested?" he asked in a sly voice as he handed her a glass.

He had aroused Marie's sense of curiosity, so she decided to listen to his offer. Reaching for the proffered glass, she said, "Well, what is it you want me to do?"

Chandler smiled slightly. He could always depend on Marie's naturally avaricious nature to get the better of her.

"It is like this, my dear," he replied smoothly. "You know, of course, of my stepson, Lord Dalton."

Marie nodded as she visualized the earl's handsome face. The image made her tingle with unexpressed desire.

Seeing that he had Marie's full attention, Chandler continued: "Well, there is a young lady in whom he has taken an interest, one Aurelia Courtenay."

Marie looked at him, trying to make out his message.

"What of it?" she said at last. "I told you as much already, and it was bound to happen, a strong good-looking man like that. What did you expect?"

"You're right, of course, my dear," Chandler replied, "but I do not want him to get married for many reasons. That is why I have sought you out."

Marie drained her champagne glass and laughed. "What do you want me to do about it?"

Chandler smiled evilly. "I want you to break up this little romance, Marie. You must use your charms to the utmost—tempt Philip from her side. If that fails, then give my Lady Courtenay a disgust of him by implying that he has had doings with you in the past. Unless I miss my guess, a past liaison with you would prove intolerable to Lady Courtenay, thus ending the romance for all time."

He was obviously assured on this point.

"What makes you think she would give him up even then?" Marie demanded scornfully.

"Because," he retorted, "Lady Courtenay is a woman of quality. Something you wouldn't understand, Marie."

She was sorely tempted to sacrifice yet another object of porcelain in her room, but thought better of it.

"I'm every bit as good as anyone!" she shrieked, then gradually calmed herself. "Well, how do I meet this Lady Courtenay?"

"I will arrange the meeting myself. I am invited to a ball that the couple will be attending, and you shall accompany me. You will bide your time, and when you see an opportune moment, you will strike."

This plan appealed to Marie because she had never before had the chance to attend a legitimate ball given by "quality" people.

"That is an excellent idea, my dear Lord Chandler," she said sweetly. "I shall enjoy this assignment very much."

"Good! I shall send my carriage for you around nine."

Chandler then took his leave of Miss Manton so that she might contemplate her strategy.

Strategy was not the only thing occupying Marie's waking hours. Her mind was filled with the possibility of acquiring Lord Dalton as a lover at long last. She had the firm belief that once Philip saw her clothed in all her glory, he would change the tune he had so often sung before—that of disinterest.

Yes, she said to herself, he will be mine yet.

With a lascivious laugh, Marie swept open her closet to survey her finery for the battle ahead.

Little could she know that Lord Dalton was not likely to be swayed by her charms, which were not of the least interest to him. He had often commented that he would far leifer watch Miss Mantón dance than have her as a mistress; and seeing that her dancing did little to recommend her, this was an unabashed insult.

Miss Manton did not have long to wait, since the ball was only a few days away. This ball was to be the grandest yet presented that Season, and a good percentage of the ton would be in attendance.

Alfred, Lady Bellvue's butler, surveyed the gathering coaches with pleasure and an increasing sense of pride. Earls, dukes, and other assorted nobility were congregating before the mansion. Lady Bellvue was renowned for her lavish affairs and her impeccable sense of taste. She carried out to the very letter the dictates of propriety and of good form, and her balls were always attended by only the very top of the social crust.

Being the best of all possible butlers, Alfred took great care to maintain the proper posture, which he deemed necessary for one employed by Lady Bellvue. As he directed the footmen to relocate several carriages, he spied an approaching vehicle with more than a hint of trepidation. Even by the flickering light of the front-hall lamps, Alfred could make out the crest on the door of the coach belonging to one Lord Chandler, an individual whom Lady Bellvue had often referred to as "that black-hearted scoundrel."

Alfred was at a loss as to how best to negotiate the situation with which he was about to be faced. Knowing his mistress's feelings on the subject of Lord Chandler, Alfred was sure she would not want him present at her party, yet his rank was of the first nobility and not at all in doubt.

He was still at a loss when the carriage door opened and Lord Chandler and a young woman descended the steps. Alfred parted his lips to speak just as Marie swept past him into the hallway. Before he could protest this intrusion, Chandler followed his companion in.

Turning to the gaping servant, Miss Manton, resplendent in the finest gown she owned, demanded, "Well? What are you waiting for, man? Take my cape at once!"

Alfred's face, normally impassive, grimaced at the obviously common accent that the "lady" demonstrated. Gulping not once but twice, Alfred meekly removed the cape from her shoulders. He did not wish to cause a scene and did not know what else to do.

A footman appeared and relieved Lord Chandler of his cloak, openly goggling at the spectacularly clad Miss Manton.

The gown she had chosen to wear that evening had been constructed by a French seamstress who was famous for her gaudy creations and whose clientele was limited to the special social class referred to as courtesans. The neckline of Marie's dress plunged almost beyond the point of decency, and the close-fitting waist and bodice left nothing to the imagination. The garment had been designed to draw attention to the wearer, and this it did, being a striking shade of pink.

Unfortunately for Miss Manton, the eyes that gazed on this creation as she entered the ballroom on the arm of Lord Chandler were not accustomed to seeing women clad in gowns generously encrusted with flame-red sequins. The effect her entrance produced was immediate and most definitely arresting. Lady Bellvue nearly fainted in her shoes as she saw what had caused the abrupt silence that had just fallen over her guests.

Among those now digressing into a state of shock was Lord Sheringham, who had looked up at the precise moment when Miss Manton entered. His silence was especially noted by Gabrielle, who had just been conversing with his lordship. She too was amazed at Miss Manton's presence, since her previous behavior at the clothier's was enough to convince her of Marie's ineligibility.

The silence lasted only a moment, but for Lady Bellvue it seemed an eternity. She slowly made her way toward the unwelcome couple, framing in her mind what she would say. As she reached them, she suddenly noticed that Lord Chandler held in his hand an invitation that appeared to be one that she had issued.

Where on earth did that man get an invitation? she wondered in consternation. I certainly never sent him one.

Now there was no possible way in which she could object to his presence. She could not know that Lord Chandler had gone to a greal deal of expense to have an invitation forged for that evening's entertainment.

Chandler, noting her approach, had already presented his bow to her scrutiny.

"Lady Bellvue, so good of you to have me to your ball. May I introduce my friend, Miss Marie Manton."

All of this was said with the utmost civility and propriety.

Lady Bellvue was so taken aback that all she could do was extend her hand for Lord Chandler to salute.

As she wondered what to do next, Chandler scanned the crowded ballroom for his stepson. He had previously noted that both Lord Sheringham and Lady Standen were present, so he reasoned that Philip and Aurelia must be near as well. He was correct on this point, for just at that moment Lady Courtenay and Lord Dalton entered the ballroom from what appeared to be the terrace. Seeing that they were oblivious to his presence, Chandler started to maneuver Marie toward the couple.

Aurelia was intent on gazing at the face of Lord Dalton, who was in turn reciprocating the action. Since this was mutually satisfying to both parties, it was with great reluctance that Philip allowed his attention to be drawn from Aurelia by the loud clearing of someone's throat.

He sustained more than just a mild shock when his inquiring look met the eyes of his stepfather. Aurelia had already shifted her own gaze to Chandler's companion. There was no outward sign of Lady Courtenay's thoughts, but the earl was not as subtle in his feelings.

A frown suffused his face as he was formally introduced to Miss Manton by Lord Chandler. He eyed her with distaste, but Marie took his long scrutiny as an indication of interest.

Striking a ludicrously seductive pose, she said, "Lord Dalton and I are acquainted with each other, Lord

Chandler. I'm sure you remember me," she added in a languid tone to Philip.

Lord Dalton remembered her quite vividly, as a matter of fact. He recalled the numerous times she had flung herself at him and the numerous rebuffs he had given her in return.

"Well, I'm sure you must remember Miss Manton's dancing at least, Philip," Chandler put in with mock joviality.

Philip looked pensive for a moment, and Marie waited expectantly for what she thought would be the compliment he was forming.

"Oh, yes. I remember your dancing very well, Miss Manton," Philip drawled. "And I must say that, judging from your performance, I assume you are talented in quite a few different areas."

Talking this as a bona fide compliment, Marie replied in her most alluring tone, "Yes, I have quite a few outstanding talents, Lord Dalton. I would love to demonstrate them to you sometime."

She looked at him through her long, artificial lashes, waiting for some sign that he understood her innuendo.

He gave no indication of understanding. Instead, he declared, "It is well that you have other attributes to fall back on as a source of income, since it is unlikely that you could earn a living from your present occupation."

It was with the greatest of willpower that Aurelia resisted the overwhelming desire to giggle at Philip's affront to this pretentious young woman, but her face betrayed her amusement.

Seeing that Lady Courtenay was on the verge of laughing at the insult just inflicted on her, Marie instinctively stretched out her hand to slap Aurelia's face.

She remembered Aurelia as the woman Diego had been flirting with at the dressmaker's shop, and since she had been thwarted in her efforts to assault Aurelia the first time, she was determined to succeed on this occasion.

Before she could complete the move, however,

Aurelia's hand darted out and caught Marie's in mid-flight. Holding it tightly in her grip, she forced the hand down and made a pretense of examining Miss Manton's garish rings to avoid a scene.

"How nice of you to honor us by wearing *all* of your jewelry," Aurelia remarked caustically.

Marie regained enough control of herself to say, "Yes, I certainly did want to honor you all. Though you should thank Lord Dalton, since he helped me acquire these jewels—indirectly, of course."

With that last word Marie flounced off, Lord Chandler hurrying after her.

Philip was livid and took a step in pursuit of Miss Manton. He was determined to make her retract that statement, by force if need be. Just as he would have caught up with her, he felt a restraining hand on his arm. It was Aurelia's.

"Let her go, Philip. You don't think that I would believe such a story, do you?" she asked with a smile that charmed him overwhelmingly.

"I swear to you I have never had anything to do with that 'lady,' and I use the term loosely," he said heatedly.

"I trust you, and I do not need any assurance of your fidelity other than your own word."

Lord Dalton beamed at her. She had made him feel so wonderful that it was beyond his ability to express it in words.

"Well, then, my lady, dance with one who is your willing slave," he suggested only half jokingly as he made an exaggerated bow.

Aurelia curtsied delightedly in return, and Philip whirled her onto the ballroom floor.

Although he made an effort to hide it, Lord Dalton was by no means satisfied with leaving Miss Manton and his stepfather in peace. He knew that Chandler had put Marie up to this ploy to place him in disfavor with Aurelia, and he resolved to have his revenge in due course.

It will be a pleasure to see him convicted of murder, he reflected.

The evidence that Chandler's henchman held would be all that Philip would need. He thought again of the despicable tactic Marie had tried on him. Glancing across the room, he could see her spinning about in her flamboyant dress.

How can one do anything *but* see her? he wondered disgustedly.

He compared Marie's tasteless attire with Aurelia's beautifully cut and elegantly decorated gown, and Marie came out looking cheap and boorish. He watched Lord Chandler propel her across the dance floor and thought her particularly graceless for a dancer. She reminded him of a gawky, gangly colt that was just learning to walk, but she had none of the colt's charm. In summation, she embodied everything Lord Dalton found most contemptuous.

He was only thankful that he was dancing with his beautiful, beloved Aurelia instead of with that annoying and obtuse young woman.

While Aurelia and Philip glided across the floor to the flowing strains of a waltz, Brett and Gabrielle watched them from their vantage point at the far end of the ballroom.

Aside from the moment's disturbance when Chandler and his tawdry companion had first entered the room, Gabrielle was having a most enjoyable time. She and Brett had not yet bothered to dance at all that evening. They had been content to sit and talk to each other, a propensity that Lady Faye approved of wholeheartedly, since visions of double weddings danced through her head.

If she could have heard the couple's conversation, however, she might have had her doubts about Gabrielle's abilities to interest a man. They had been discussing horses for the last half an hour. This was a subject that most individuals would hardly consider conducive to amour, but it was one that interested Lord Sheringham very much. While it was not romantic, it did prove that a life with Gabrielle would be one of shared interests.

Brett had just completed an exciting story about a past race in which he had participated. Gabrielle had been vastly entertained by his rendition of the events and was eager to have a glimpse of Lord Sheringham's horses.

"Brett," she said excitedly, "I do so want to see your animals. May I come out to your stables and look at them tomorrow?"

Brett would have thought this a splendid idea at any other time, but he and Philip were about to undertake a trip on the morrow. Thinking quickly, he formulated his reply carefully, for he did not wish to arouse Gabrielle's curiosity overmuch.

"I'm afraid that won't be possible, Gabrielle," he told the lovely girl. "You see, Philip and I are going away tomorrow."

Seeing the disappointment on her face, Brett felt a particular beast. It was true that Gabrielle was disappointed, but at the mention of his leaving, her senses had become alert to the possibility that this journey might be the one that she and Aurelia had been anticipating.

Determined to obtain more information, Gabrielle replied in the sweetest of voices, "Oh? A trip? Where are you going off to?"

Brett, relieved that she was taking things so well, decided that it could harm nothing to tell her at least their destination, if not what reason had spurred their departure.

"We are off to Hertfordshire, to a place called The Golden Inn."

"For what purpose, pray tell?"

Brett was rather taken aback at this inquiry and was loath to answer it.

Gabrielle goaded him on a bit.

"Could it be that you are off to see another woman, perhaps?" she asked in a slightly accusatory tone.

Her words did indeed produce the desired effect. In

an effort to smooth what appeared to be Gabrielle's ruffled sensibilities, Brett explained hurriedly, "This trip is for Philip, not for me."

"Philip? What of Philip? Does he go on *personal* business?" she inquired, her brow arched, implying that perhaps it was Lord Dalton who was about to be faithless to Aurelia.

Realizing he was falling deeper into trouble, Brett decided to tell Gabrielle as much as he dared.

After all, she will not inform anyone else, I am sure, he thought.

So he told Gabrielle, as vaguely as possible, that a plot had been hatched to take Philip's life and that the two of them were going to the inn to take care of the matter.

"But you must not mention this to Aurelia," he emphasized. "Philip does not want her unduly alarmed. Now promise me."

He looked at her expectantly, so Gabrielle swore not to divulge his secret. This promise reassured Lord Sheringham's troubled conscience, but if he could have spied Gabrielle's left hand, which was hidden from view behind her voluminous skirts, he would have found cause to feel less secure. Gabrielle's own conscience was eased somewhat by the crossing of those dainty fingers that Brett had so often admired. She fully intended to inform Aurelia of the entire conversation, because, she reasoned, it *was* for the young lords' own good.

CHAPTER 7

So IT WAS that on the following morning, as Lord Sheringham and Lord Dalton started off for their destination, they were followed unobtrusively by two mysteriously cloaked figures on horseback. When they stopped several times during the day to water their mounts, so too did the two figures, making themselves as inconspicuous as possible. Neither Brett nor Philip took notice of the strange pair, for the road on which they traversed was much used during that particular time of year.

As this curious caravan progressed toward their mutual destination, events that would affect the outcome of their trip were even at that moment occurring at The Golden Inn.

The proprietor of this establishment, a man with two gold front teeth, hence the name of the inn, observed a single horseman approaching his modest abode. As the rider drew near, the innkeeper was disappointed to discover that the man was only a common-looking individual with at least a few days' growth on his chin. He sighed resignedly to himself, knowing that his good wife would never be persuaded to change this person's sheets once he had left, and the task would be his instead.

Putting on a professional smile, he asked, "Well, now sir, is it to be a room for you?"

The dusty rider dismounted from his long-suffering horse, sending a cloud of dirt flying in all directions.

Looking at the proprietor in a churlish manner, he replied, "Nay, no room. Oi've come to see a friend o' mine, a Rufus Kane."

A knowledgeable look sped across the innkeeper's face as he recalled a scruffy-looking being who almost forcibly resembled a rodent.

"Oh, yes, Mr. Kane. He is here. Who may I say is calling?"

The stranger scowled. "Tell 'im Scurvy Joe is 'ere to see 'im, and be quick about it."

The proprietor immediately recognized the infamous name, so it was with the utmost haste that he hurried off to fetch Mr. Kane.

Scurvy Joe walked into the dining room to await the arrival of his subordinate. Seeing nobody within shouting distance, the bandit helped himself to a freshly roasted chicken, which he inelegantly ate directly off the spit, having removed the entire apparatus from the fireplace. As he was making vast inroads into his newly acquired meal, he heard voices approaching. Wiping his mouth on his sleeve in haste, he pulled out his pistols and aimed them directly at the doorway. Just as he would have fired, he recognized the figures of the innkeeper and Rufus. He replaced the pistols at the waist of his breeches and seated himself.

"It's 'bout time," he growled, picking up the chicken once more. "Leave us!" he commanded the innkeeper.

The proprietor, glad to be set free, scuttled from the room.

Rufus greeted Scurvy Joe cautiously, for even though he had been associated with him only recently, he realized that Scurvy Joe was not entirely in his right mind and must be handled carefully.

"What brings ye 'ere so early, Joe?" he asked as he watched grease dribble down the front of Scurvy Joe's already filth-laden shirt. "Ye warn't supposed to come till tomorrow."

Scurvy Joe simply snorted at this.

"Oi can change me mind, can't Oi?" he snarled.

"Of course ye can," Rufus agreed quickly, his fea-

tures twitching nervously, his eyes seeming to start
from his head. "What are we goin' to do about Lord
Dalton, then?" he continued as he settled himself opposite his leader.

Scurvy Joe looked at his partner through half-closed
eyes.

"Well, now, the first thing we's goin' to do is go and
get them papers Oi put in yer safekeepin'," he said
slowly to the cringing man. "Ye do still 'ave 'em,
don't ye?"

"Aye, aye, to be sure. They be up in me room."

"Let's go up and see 'em first, and then we'll talk
business."

Scurvy Joe rose from the table, throwing the remainder of the fowl's carcass into the fire. Motioning Kane
to lead the way to his quarters, he followed a few steps
behind.

As they started up the stairs, they were suddenly
halted by the sound of approaching horses. Looking
out onto the courtyard through a nearby window,
Scurvy Joe could make out the figures of two horse-
men.

"We may be takin' care o' our business sooner than
Oi thought," he observed in a menacing tone.

Scurvy Joe and his cohort watched from the window
as Philip and Brett dismounted from their horses and
surveyed the area.

The ratlike man was beginning to sweat profusely,
knowing of Scurvy Joe's usual brashness.

"Joe," he whispered urgently, "ye can't just kill 'em
'ere and now."

Scurvy Joe didn't take note of his partner's plea.
Kane tried again.

"Th' rest o' th' guests will be sure to 'ear us and 'unt
us down if we do it 'ere."

Scurvy Joe could see the sense in this statement, but
was loath to let the opportunity slip through his fingers.
Then a thought occurred to him.

"Why would them be 'ere, Oi wonders?" he asked.
Shooting a glance at Rufus, he looked particularly

vicious. "Ye wouldn't be plannin' on sellin' me out to them two, now, would ye?" he added slowly.

"No, Joe!" Rufus sputtered through chattering teeth. "Oi 'aven't left this inn since Oi got 'ere. Oi couldn't 'ave sent word to 'em."

The highwayman seemed to believe him.

"Just fer safekeepin', why don't ye 'and over them papers and we'll call it even," he said in a deceptively pleasant voice.

Kane, understandably relieved by this change of temperament, was only too anxious to comply with the suggestion, so he hastily led the way to his room.

Meanwhile, Philip and Brett, having searched unsuccessfully for the proprietor of the establishment (who was at that moment hiding under a woodpile from fear of Scurvy Joe's unpredictable temper), walked into the inn unannounced. None of the other travelers were in evidence, either, since most of them were indulging in a nap before dinner.

Philip, ever perfect in attire even after a long and exhausting journey, seemed as fresh as if he had just stepped from his townhouse in London. Brett, on the other hand, did not appear to be in such fine fettle; his cravat was slightly askew, and his coat of fine broadcloth, usually immaculate, was a sorry array of wrinkles and creases, spotted by slight dabs of mud that his horse had kicked up.

"Lord, Philip," Brett sighed tiredly, "I feel as though I've been riding on cockleburs all day."

Lord Dalton looked down with sympathy at his friend, who had deposited his weary coil into a plushly cushioned seat.

"You should have stayed in London, Brett," he said. "I could have handled this myself."

Brett smiled up at Philip in his usual easygoing manner.

"Now, now, you know you need me to take care of you," he said whimsically, ". . . until you get married, that is. Then it will be every man for himself."

Brett had to duck quickly as Philip tossed one of the overstuffed pillows at his head.

Upstairs, Scurvy Joe was surveying the papers that Kane had produced from the recesses beneath a loose floorboard.

"There they be, Joe," Rufus said nervously. "Just like Oi told ye. Oi warn't goin' to sell them papers."

Kane's taskmaster was somewhat placated by the fact that he now had the papers in his possession. Then a malevolent look crept into his eyes once again.

"Oi 'ave an idea," said the tyrant. "Oi wants ye to meet wit' 'em two down there."

"What fer, Joe? Oi told ye Oi was never goin' to sell them papers."

Scurvy Joe looked at the little man contemptuously.

"Oi know, ye idiot!" he snarled. "Oi wants ye to lure Lord Dalton into th' woods by th' river so Oi can get me job done."

Rufus Kane had never been known for his quickness of wit, and he still did not grasp the intricacies of the task.

" 'Ow will Oi get 'em there?" he queried.

"Offer 'im th' evidence," Scurvy Joe said curtly. " 'E'll take th' bait, if Oi'm any judge, and that's when we take care o' that troublemaker and earn a tidy sum to boot."

The satisfaction was evident on Scurvy Joe's face as he looked out the window. "They must be inside by now," he continued. "Oi wants ye to go down and tell 'em to meet ye by th' river when it be dark, so there'll be no problems surprisin' 'em."

His cohort, having finally grasped the gist of the errand, was visibly appalled.

"Bot' o' them?" he squeaked. "We don't need to finish bot' o' them!"

He had grave doubts that it would be possible to get the better of these men. They're young, he thought, and the one in black looked to be an ugly customer in a fight.

"We should just leave it at th' one, Joe," he added, gulping convulsively.

Scurvy Joe considered this for a moment.

"If ye can manage it, so much th' better. Just go down and arrange it, and make sure th' right one comes."

Kane did as he was ordered and descended to the drawing room with a great deal of apprehension. He was trembling as he looked upon the forbidding visage of Lord Dalton. The features that had endeared Philip to Aurelia certainly did not produce the same effect on the ratlike man, who saw the deep blue eyes as threatening and the dark brow as scowling and ominous. Nonetheless, his fear of Scurvy Joe urged him on, and he approached cautiously.

Taking him for the proprietor, Brett roused himself from his chair and said, "Ah! Do you have a Mr. Kane staying here at your establishment?"

Presenting Lord Sheringham with his most ingratiating of smiles, Rufus replied, "Oi be th' man ye seek."

Brett was somewhat taken aback at his mistake, but Philip, with his usual aplomb, addressed Kane in something akin to an accusatory tone. "We have a proposition to make to you about certain papers that we know you have in your possession."

Seeing that Lord Dalton was the man to deal with, Kane aimed his conversation directly at him, ignoring Brett for the most part.

Brett would leifer not talk to the man, anyway, since his fastidious sensibilities were repelled by Kane's physical appearance. He paid attention to what was said, in any case, and heard Philip agree to a meeting by the river at dusk.

"Come alone," the ferret-faced individual warned with unusual bravado, "and come on time. Oi won't wait a minute past th' set time."

To this Philip agreed, and the man left.

"Philip," Brett said when Kane was out of earshot, "I don't think it's wise to meet him alone."

The earl did not appear to be unduly concerned with the possibility of danger.

"Brett, I've waited too long for my revenge, and I would agree to meet the man in hell to get the evidence I need." Then, seeing the worried expression on his friend's face, he added gently, "I know. I will be careful, I promise. But you must not follow me. I don't want him to be scared off."

Brett promised, and Philip was satisfied.

"I meet him in a few hours. That gives me plenty of time to do a little errand beforehand," Lord Dalton said.

Brett looked bewildered. "What errand is that?"

Philip walked over to a wall mirror to adjust his already perfect neckcloth.

"Remember I told you I would find out who those men were who helped us on the road?"

Brett nodded.

"Well, I took the seal from that letter I received and had my man Jenkins look up the crest in the *Royal Book of Heraldry*. He's supposed to meet me in town, at the inn we passed coming here, and tell me what name accompanies the seal."

Brett was impressed.

"I can see you've been working diligently at a solution. What do you intend to do when you find out to whom it belongs?"

Philip shrugged. "I'm not sure. Thank them in person, perhaps offer them a reward if they'll take one."

Brett shook his head at this. "They looked to me to be young men of means, Philip. I doubt there is anything you can give them."

Lord Dalton walked toward the door and turned at the threshold.

"Then I suppose I must simply be content to know to whom I am beholden for my very life."

He gave a short laugh, but there was no humor in it.

"Don't wait for my return. I'll go directly to the river."

So saying, he passed out into the arms of the approaching twilight.

Brett watched him go, thinking all the while that Philip was ever an odd fish, and then settled himself down for a little nap on the lounge in the sitting room, as there was nowhere else to go.

He found sleep hard in coming, the reason due to his excessive feelings of foreboding; but he had sworn not to follow Philip, and he would keep his promise.

Lord Dalton proceeded slowly. As he rode, riders approached him, cloaked in heavy capes and wearing hats pulled far down, obscuring their features. He did not give them a second glance, but, unbeknownst to him, they turned in unison to look at his retreating figure. Only after he had passed them and was completely hidden from view by the gathering darkness did the two tear their eyes away and continue on their journey in total silence.

It was only a short while to where Philip would be meeting his lawyer, and he soon arrived. Dismounting, the earl was met at the entrance by the proprietor. Ushering him in, the innkeeper took his cloak and hat.

"My lord," the little man asked as he led the way to the parlor, "will you be wanting a room for the night?"

Philip, finding the large room devoid of other persons, shook his head and replied, "I am meeting a Mr. Jenkins here."

The man had not yet arrived, so Lord Dalton ordered a light meal and sat down to await his coming.

Philip was halfway through his repast when Mr. Jenkins entered the room. Motioning him to be seated, Philip offered him a glass of wine, which was refused.

"Jenkins, have you the information I require?"

A very dependable man, Mr. Jenkins produced the wax impression Philip Dalton had entrusted to his care, along with several pages of what appeared to be a family tree.

"Lord Dalton," Mr. Jenkins began as he laid his papers on the table, "I have investigated the crest you gave me, and it is without a doubt a variation on that of the Courtenay family."

The advocate proceeded to elaborate on the background of the Courtenays, but Philip was no longer listening. To say that he was dumbstruck would have been the mildest description of the condition in which he now found himself.

When Philip finally recovered his voice, he interrupted his lawyer, who had been delineating one of the Courtenay forebearers.

"Mr. Jenkins, are you *quite* sure that the crest belongs to that particular family?"

His advocate immediately took on an expression of wounded pride.

"I assure you, Lord Dalton, my research has been most thorough. It is, of course, a variation on the original crest in that it must have been made for a female descendant, but the change is minimal. The Courtenay crest is most recognizable even without alteration."

Seeing that Lord Dalton was apparently appeased by this reassertion of the facts, Mr. Jenkins continued to outline the ancestors of Philip's beloved.

How could I have been so blind? the nobleman chastised himself. How could I have overlooked the similarities between my young benefactor and the lady I adore? Nonetheless, it was true, and Lord Dalton oscillated between stages of feeling ranging from embarrassment to being stupefied. Fortunately, none of his emotions approached anger. On the contrary; after the initial shock of knowing who his rescuers were, Philip was finding it most difficult to present a straight face to his lawyer.

Mr. Jenkins was unaccustomed to seeing the reserved earl mirthful even to the minutest degree, and was momentarily nonplused.

"Lord Dalton, I seem to have said something amusing. Pray, what was it?"

Philip composed himself a bit and replied, "Nothing, nothing at all. I am quite satisfied with your report, Jenkins. That will be all."

Philip's advocate had not yet finished reciting even half the material he had gleaned, but collected the papers resignedly. Placing them in Lord Dalton's hands, he removed himself with a bow in his employer's general direction.

Now, how do I handle this? Philip wondered as he raised a glass of wine to his lips. I can understand that Aurelia would not trust a stranger with her secret, but after she met me she should have confided in me.

Lord Dalton pondered over several possible reasons why Aurelia might not tell him of her masquerade, but could not come to any logical conclusion. It never occurred to him that she might not have wanted to divulge this information for fear of displeasing him.

He started from his thoughts and began to worry about the hour. He looked at his timepiece. He had taken longer to conclude his business than he had planned. He would have to hurry.

Tossing a few coins on the table, Philip summoned the proprietor and bade the man fetch his coat and hat, and prepare his horse. This was done straightaway, and Philip Dalton was soon galloping along the road in the darkness toward the river and his rendezvous with Rufus Kane.

The sky was pitch-black, as a covering of rain clouds had hidden the moon, and Philip was having the utmost difficulty in avoiding the many ruts and potholes that had been made by a recent rainstorm.

As he approached a turn in the road, he slowed his horse a trifle, guiding it toward the outer rim of the curve, which, in theory, being less traveled than the middle of the road, should have been safer. This was a miscalculation, since many other persons had followed the same reasoning.

All of a sudden Lord Dalton's mount stumbled laterally and fell heavily on its rider. While the animal labored to its feet, Philip lay senseless on the ground, oblivious to the minutes passing quickly by.

Back at the Golden Inn, Lord Sheringham was finishing his solitary evening with a glass of the proprietor's finest claret.

The innkeeper had not yet returned from his hiding place, but his wife had appeared earlier to silently serve the guests their dinner.

The others had by this time retired for the night, which should have afforded the woman some relief, yet as time dragged on, she seemed to become more and more upset.

Finally, Brett had to ask, "My good woman, what is amiss? Perhaps I can be of assistance."

The worried woman fairly snatched at his offer, seeing no other aid available.

"Oh, my lord," she moaned, wringing her hands in dismay, "my husband has not returned since that man sent him away."

"What man is that?"

"That awful one who came to see Mr. Kane this afternoon. I was watching from the kitchen door," she explained.

Suspicion ran rampant through Brett's mind, and after pressing her for a description of the man, he was positive it was none other than Scurvy Joe.

"Oh, sir! Please help me find my poor husband. He may be dead for all I know."

The proprietor's wife was near tears, but at that very moment the object of her anguish appeared in the doorway, bedraggled and grubby from his stay under the woodpile.

Finding that the innkeeper's story matched that of his wife, Brett knew something had to be done. He was certain that a trap was being set to catch Philip off guard and kill him; that would explain why Kane had wanted Lord Dalton to come alone. Looking at his gold pocket watch, Brett deduced that his friend must be very near the river by now, and most likely, approaching his destruction.

Taking up his greatcoat, Lord Sheringham walked over to his saddle and extracted a pistol from the depths of his saddlebag. He loaded the weapon, tucked it into his waistband, and set off on foot toward the river, wary of every sound and shadow along the way.

Under the circumstances, he felt little guilt over breaking his word to Philip, for if he were correct in his assumptions, his friend would most certainly need his help.

Even though Brett proceeded carefully, he remained unaware that silent individuals dogged his tracks, and had been doing so ever since his departure from London. They merged into the darkness with such complete harmony that they were no more visible to Lord Sheringham than the air he breathed.

He reached the designated spot and could hear the river, swollen with the recent rains, rushing past. He could not see anyone in the thick blackness, try as he might.

Just as he would have called out Philip's name, the clouds that had for so long obscured the moonlight parted, shedding a faint light on Lord Sheringham's form. So brief and weak were the rays, however, that he was silhouetted only for a moment. But it was long enough for Scurvy Joe and his partner to ascertain Lord Sheringham's position, but not long enough for them to see that the man standing by the riverbank was not their intended victim.

Stealthily the men eased their way toward the unsuspecting Brett, and they were nearly upon him before he became aware of their presence. Almost as one, the two leaped on the young lord, Kane attempting to pinion his arms while Scurvy Joe raised a dagger, ready to plunge it into Brett's heart. There was a short struggle, but Brett could not possibly handle both these villains at once.

Suddenly the clouds ceased to block the moon, and just as Scurvy Joe would have sealed Brett's fate, a shot rang out. Joe jerked convulsively, his body propelled backward as he fell heavily into the rushing river.

Kane, seeing that his leader had met with his doom

at last, attempted to flee. But Brett was more than a match for him and held fast to the thin little man.

The bullet had been fired from a pistol that still smoked in the hand of its owner, one of the cloaked strangers. Both forms turned, intending to leave, but were halted in their tracks by a most surprising sight. Lord Philip Dalton was approaching them with purposeful strides, gun drawn, primed, and at the ready.

"Drop your weapons," he commanded.

The strangers, seeing no reasonable alternative, did as they were bidden. The earl glanced over at Brett, to see that he was unharmed, holding Kane captive, and walking toward the group.

Philip now gave his full attention to the two individuals before him. Examining them as carefully as the limited light allowed, he found that their features were obscured for the most part by their hats and the turned-up collars of their cloaks.

"Who are you?" Lord Dalton demanded, still staring intently. He thought the pair vaguely familiar somehow.

A muffled reply issued from the one who had killed Scurvy Joe.

"We were simply passing by when we saw this gentleman struggling with two assailants . . ."

Muffled though it was, Lord Sheringham immediately recognized the voice. With a look of utter astonishment and disbelief, he asked hesitantly, "Gabrielle, is that you?"

In answer to this question, the other stranger stepped forward and stood in a patch of bright moonlight. After removing the concealing hat, this person was revealed to be a pale and somewhat unearthlylooking Lady Aurelia Courtenay.

Though apprehension showed plainly on her face, Aurelia regarded Philip unfalteringly, ready for the words that would determine if they were to share a common future.

She was distantly aware of a gasp of astonishment

that had issued from Lord Sheringham, and realized that Gabrielle must have removed her disguise as well.

Lady Courtenay continued to wait for some sign from Lord Dalton. Finally he whispered, "Aurelia, dearest to my heart, why did you not tell me?"

He moved toward her, arms outstretched, and tightly embraced the slight figure drenched in moonlight.

"You are not shocked? You do not even seem surprised!" she exclaimed. Looking up into his face, her hands resting on the soft material of his coat, she tried to discern his expression. He appeared to be smiling at her.

"Well, my lord, here I have been so reluctant to tell you of my scandalous lark, and far from being shocked at my impropriety, you seem to be amused. Have you known all along?" she asked suspiciously.

Shaking his head, Philip replied, "No, my darling. I have only just found out your true identity earlier this evening. You had me fooled all this time. But why didn't you tell me before? You could have trusted me, you know."

This was said in a light manner, but the slightest note of disappointment and hurt could be detected.

"I thought you disapproved of females who engaged in unconventional behavior. Your friend Lord Torres assured me it was so."

Philip only wished that Lord Torres were present so that he could land him a facer.

"Your behavior may have been unconventional, but I hardly think it warrants censure on my part. I personally have done much worse in my time."

Aurelia raised her eyebrows at this but said nothing.

Lord Sheringham and Lady Standen then joined the pair. Much the same words had also passed between them, but an embrace on their part had been prevented by the presence of Kane.

With that bit of business concluded, all eyes became fixed on the captive.

Giving Rufus one of his characteristically penetrating glares, Philip demanded tersely, "Where are those papers?"

Kane seemed to shrink down into his coat.

"Well, me lord," he replied fearfully, "Oi 'ad to give 'em back to Joe. 'E 'ad 'em when 'e fell in th' river."

For a moment anger blazed in Lord Dalton's eyes, but the intensity soon dulled and was replaced by an expression of frustration and exasperation. The man was too frightened to be lying, of this Philip was sure.

"We appear to be at a standstill, then," Brett said at last.

Lord Dalton nodded reluctantly.

"There is nothing for it, I suppose. We'll just have to hand in this wretch to the authorities."

The group began to walk back toward the inn in silence. Gabrielle was very much distressed by the turn of events, since it had been her shot that had sent Scurvy Joe and the evidence into the river's current. She had only intended to wound him.

Seeing that Gabrielle was vastly upset by the death she had accidentally caused, Brett ventured, "You know that scoundrel never did a good deed in his life, and you have unwittingly performed a service to society and have saved Philip's life. There was nothing for it. You could never be held accountable."

These were just the words Gabrielle needed to ease the pain that gripped her heart. She realized, however, that there would always be a memory of the incident that could not be dispelled.

"I wish there were some way we could still prove Lord Chandler guilty of his crimes," she sighed.

Aurelia threw a glance of support at her friend, which further comforted her. She had been thinking much the same thing herself; surely there had to be some means of entrapping this man who had eluded justice for so long.

Unexpectedly, new and intriguing possibilities began to unfold in Lady Courtenay's mind. Turning to their prisoner, Aurelia asked, "Did you by chance happen to read those papers?"

The ratlike man looked rather uneasy.

"Aye, Oi did. But just fer a minute!" he admitted.

"What good is that?" Brett wondered. "We can't prove anything without physical evidence, and I hardly think a court of law would accept the testimony of *this* individual.

Philip nodded. "Yes, of course. I begin to see the implications now."

"What implications?" Gabrielle inquired.

"I am referring to the contents of those letters," he replied. "We can use that information to trap my stepfather into a confession of guilt or into making an unwise move against me."

Looking again at Mr. Kane, he said, "Well, the decision is up to you. If you cooperate with us, you will be better off for it. The constable may be persuaded to let you go if no charges are issued against you. Make up your mind."

All eyes turned to stare at Kane. He glanced from face to face, weighing his chances carefully.

"Oi'll 'elp ye," he conceded, "but ye 'ave to promise to 'elp me."

"Agreed," Aurelia confirmed.

The five of them continued their walk while the culprit divulged the information he had obtained from the papers. Philip absorbed the details, and by the time the group arrived at the hostelry, he had begun to formulate a plan of attack.

As they entered the courtyard, the doors to the inn opened and a voice called, "Who is there?"

A man peered out, lamp in hand, and from behind him the proprietor extended his head.

Recognizing Rufus Kane and Lord Sheringham, he said, "That's them, constable."

The innkeeper had apparently summoned the town's law officer when Lord Sheringham had failed to return.

"Constable," Lord Dalton began, stepping forward with their captive, "this man has done no real harm. The one you want, Scurvy Joe, is dead. He attacked my friend and was shot during the scuffle. He fell into the river and was carried away by the current. I suggest this man be allowed to go free, since there will be no charges issued against him by any of us."

The constable considered this proposal for some moments. There seemed to be no point indeed in holding the offender, and since the constable much preferred peace and quiet, he was inclined to agree with the young gentleman's assessment of the situation.

"Very well, my lord," he said. To Rufus Kane he added, "Don't let me see ye again, or I may not be as charitable a second time."

Kane was only too grateful for the opportunity of escape—especially from Lord Dalton—and he beat a hasty retreat.

The innkeeper ushered the four young people into the sitting room, leaving them immediately thereafter to attend to the preparation of their rooms.

After they had seated themselves, Brett looked puzzledly over at Gabrielle. "My love, how is it you were able to get away from Aurelia's mother to make this trip? I saw no trunks; surely you did not travel all the way from London in the clothes you are standing in."

Philip added his voice to that of his friend's:

"Yes, how did you manage all of this? Surely you will be missed."

The girls smiled at these questions.

"Mama thinks we are visiting a friend for a few days, Philip, and our trunks and baggage are being held for us at an inn a short distance from here. My maid, Renée, and one of my footmen, Antoine, are awaiting our return. They can be trusted and will bear out any story Gabrielle and I wish to tell. So, you see, there is no reason to be worried."

Once again Lord Dalton was struck with admiration at the ingenuity displayed by this young lady. He would have liked to discuss the events that had passed between them at length—the rescue they had masterminded previously, the discovery of Chandler's assas-

sination plot, and a thousand other things—but there
was no opportunity just then, for the innkeeper had
come to show them to their rooms.

Brett and Philip escorted their intendeds up the
stairs, the proprietor never realizing that two of the
young men were in reality women.

The next morning the ladies descended to the sitting room in their male attire, looking for all the world
like a couple of gentlemen fresh from Eton. The Lords
Dalton and Sheringham were already in the room and
rose when the girls entered. There was no one else
there, as none of the other guests had yet awakened.

Taking Aurelia's hand, Philip bestowed a tender kiss
upon it. Rising from the greeting, he said, "I have sent
one of the stableboys to hire you a closed carriage.
You can ride concealed until you reach the place
where your servants are staying. It would not be wise
for you to continue to travel as you have been doing,
so I will have no arguments."

Lady Courtenay had no intention of disagreeing with
Lord Dalton, since she considered his plan the wisest
course.

Breakfast proved to be substantial, consisting of
eggs, bacon, and sautéed kidney. Whilst they ate, they
discussed what strategy would best be suited for the am-
bushing of Lord Chandler. Several plans were suggested and discarded as too impractical.

Lord Dalton was silent for the most part, a look of
intense concentration on his face.

Noticing his preoccupation, Brett remarked, "Well,
Philip, it appears as if you may have an idea already."

He gazed expectantly at his friend, for he knew from
past experience that Philip Dalton must have formulated at least a skeleton of a plan by now.

Putting down his cup of tea, Philip proceeded to explain his scheme to the rest of them.

"It's simple, really. What do we know? We know the
name of the apothecary to whom Chandler went for
the poison. We know there was a receipt for the drug,

which was lost with Scurvy Joe, and we know there were several letters written by my stepfather to the apothecary, alluding to blackmail. We can only assume that Chandler had the apothecary killed, since the man was blackmailing him. What I propose to do is to make Chandler nervous. A nervous man will make mistakes that he would not otherwise allow himself. I want him to become desperate, and consequently to take desperate chances. To accomplish this, Brett and I will hint that we possess evidence that we really do not have, in order to push him to some overt move against me that can be witnessed and proved."

Aurelia pondered this plan. As Philip said, it was simple, but it was also frought with danger.

"Philip, there is no guarantee that he will believe you. Besides, what if he moves against you in secret? He could have you killed, as he has wanted to for some time. There are plenty more Scurvy Joes in the world."

The earl was not a man who could be easily dissuaded from a chosen path, but Aurelia was the one person to whom he could deny nothing.

"Pray don't say you disapprove, for if you cannot like it, I will not go through with it." He was seriously discomforted by her evident distress.

It would take only a word from Aurelia to alter Philip's strategy, but loving him as she did and knowing of his need to bring Lord Chandler to justice, she could not bring herself to hinder him.

"I would not stop you from doing what you felt you ought, but do have a care for your safety," she implored.

"I shall endeavor to do so for both our sakes," he replied, smiling. Then, turning to the others, he said, "We must provide Chandler with a perfect opportunity to strike at me, so that he won't be tempted to murder me in advance—one where there will be plenty of people to see what transpires.

"We want him to make the move in public, but in a manner that will afford him some chance of escaping unnoticed, else he would never attempt it. It has to be enticing enough for him to risk discovery," Brett thought aloud.

"But where?" Gabrielle asked. "He will never try anything against Philip openly. I say he will make his move when you least expect it."

"Not if we ensure that the opportunity is rich enough," the earl asserted.

"I have it!" Brett exclaimed. "What could be better than a masked ball? That assures anonymity, but there will also be plenty of people present. We could have it on your twenty-fifth birthday, which I know is in six days' time. We'll be ready for Chandler, and if we push him to the point of desperation by saying that we will reveal the proof on that night, he will almost certainly have to do something."

"Yes, yes, that sounds just right," Philip agreed enthusiastically. "I can stage the masquerade with servants on guard at all the exits."

Seeing that the worry was back on Aurelia's face, he took her hand across the table.

"I promise I will give him no occasion to reach me before the appointed time. It will be then or never for him. There is no way in the world he will be able to reach me beforehand. I will surround myself with people day and night." Laughing, he added, "I'll even go so far as to insult my solitary nature and invite several of Brett's friends to remain in my home until the night of the ball. Surely you must believe me safe among so many," he wheedled.

Lady Courtenay could not resist his playful tone, and smiled.

"I suppose you will be safe enough. I am silly to worry so. Don't give me another thought."

"That I could never do," Philip replied seriously.

Aurelia said no more and tried to hide her apprehension. She knew that if he had to concentrate on her anxiety as well as his own, he would be hard pressed to protect himself from Lord Chandler.

The hired carriage halted in front of the inn, and Lord Dalton and Lord Sheringham escorted the two women to it. They had agreed that they would return to London by separate routes in order to bring as little attention to themselves as possible.

There were no parting embraces since arriving guests with prying eyes had to be considered, so with a handshake that could hardly be deemed satisfactory, the ladies bade goodbye to their beaus.

Aurelia's face remained at the carriage window until she could no longer see Lord Dalton; then she lowered the blinds, which were not raised for the rest of the trip.

The duchess had just finished her evening meal and was about to ring for Crane when he entered the dining room of his own accord.

"Madame," he said as he stood stiffly by the side of her chair, "the young ladies have returned from their trip."

Delighted with the news, her Grace rose hurriedly.

"Where are they, Crane?"

"In the salon, resting, madam."

"They are home early," she remarked to no one in particular as she hurried along the hallway toward the salon. When she reached the foyer, she saw a footman and the girls' maid bringing in the packages and trunks. She was met there by Gabrielle, who was on her way upstairs.

"Gabrielle, my dear, did you have a pleasant time at Corinda's?"

Lady Standen was caught unaware by this question and hesitated a moment before remembering her lines.

"Oh, yes, madame," she replied. "I had a lovely time. I'm just sorry you were too ill to come with us."

Hearing voices in the foyer, Aurelia entered the hall to greet her mother.

"Mama!" she exclaimed, hugging her affectionately. "It is ever so good to be home."

"Did you have a nice time?" Lady Faye asked.

"Yes, it was very nice out at Corinda's estate. She

had a marvelous hunting party, and she is planning to
come out for the Season next year."

"Well, dear, if she does, we must throw a party in
her honor, since she was so considerate as to invite you
for a visit," her Grace decided.

Aurelia was more than just a little relieved that the
invitation could not be made until next year, for
Corinda would have no idea what she had done to
deserve such a kindness.

As it was, Aurelia was exerting the utmost energy in
preserving a jovial and calm exterior. Within, she was
tense with worry. Even though Philip would be surrounded by people until the end of the game, there was
no telling how things would progress, and Aurelia was
more afraid for him than she had ever been before. She
almost regretted not having insisted that he not go
through with his plan, but there was nothing for it
now.

Lady Faye saw none of the emotions that were
plaguing her daughter. Why should she indeed, when
Aurelia played her part to such perfection? Gabrielle,
however, knew what must be going through her
friend's mind, and made the excuse of exhaustion to
obtain a chance to speak with Aurelia alone.

"Oh, of course. How silly of me! You can tell me all
about the trip later," the duchess fluttered. "Renée,
prepare the rooms for Lady Courtenay and Lady Standen."

After kissing her mother on the cheek, Aurelia ascended the stairs with Gabrielle. Upon reaching their
chambers, they saw the French maid turning down the
covers of Lady Courtenay's bed.

"Renée," Aurelia cautioned, "remember, not a word
to the other servants or to anyone at all."

"Of course not, my lady," she replied, and curtsied.

When she had left, Gabrielle laid her hand on her
friend's shoulder and reassured her. "He will be all
right, Aurelia. It would take a better man than Lord
Chandler to outwit your Philip."

Aurelia smiled slightly and nodded, but Gabrielle

knew that the consternation would still be there no matter what she said. She could hardly blame Aurelia for worrying about Lord Dalton; even though Lady Standen tried to sound confident, she too feared the outcome of their scheme.

CHAPTER 8

TRISTAN CULPEPPER was in the middle of a boring conversation with Lord Innane. It was always thus whenever he chanced to patronize White's. Lord Innane was almost a permanent fixture at that establishment, and he never failed to seek out Lord Culpepper to relate the common gossip of the day into his unwilling ear. Only civility of the highest order kept Lord Culpepper from abandoning Innane, that and the knowledge that Lady Culpepper would not appreciate the slighting of her closest friend's spouse.

"It's disgraceful," Lord Innane's nasal voice grated out. "The way that Royer takes up and discards mistresses is most inconsiderate, not to mention wasteful."

Lord Culpepper simply nodded. It was unnecessary to reply verbally to the man, who was perfectly capable of sustaining a conversation alone and without aid.

Culpepper prayed silently for some form of diversion to draw the irksome gossipmonger from his side, and was surprised when his prayers were answered almost immediately.

"Look there, Tristan," Innane said, pointing toward

the doorway. "It appears that Lord Dalton and Lord Sheringham have returned from their trip."

"So it would appear, Innane," Tristan Culpepper replied. "You have something to discuss with Brett Sheringham, if I am not mistaken."

Lord Innane nodded. "Ah, yes, yes. The matter of my four friends . . ."

Rising from his seat next to Lord Culpepper, Innane approached the two gentlemen, who had just discarded their greatcoats into the ready hands of the footmen.

"Lord Sheringham! The very man I wished to see," Lord Innane said as he drew Brett aside.

Philip was oblivious to the gossiper; his eyes searched the room for the presence of another. His sweeping glance was arrested by the sight of his prey, playing at the card table, unaware of Lord Dalton's arrival. Touching Brett on the arm, Philip advanced toward the players. Brett followed, and was in turn trailed after by Innane, who had not yet ceased nasalizing.

Philip halted alongside one of the players and looked down at the cards the man held.

"Winning?" he asked.

Chandler stiffened at the sound of his stepson's voice and clutched his cards more tightly.

"Lord Dalton!" a rotund gentleman chortled. "As you can see by his long face, Lord Chandler has been losing."

"But about to make a turnaround, eh, my lord?" another player added.

"Is there any room for Philip and me to join?" Brett queried.

Greetings filled the air at the knowledge of Lord Sheringham's presence, attesting to his general popularity, and a place was cleared for both young men.

Lord Chandler had not yet spoken, but he did not wish to appear put out by Philip.

"I don't believe I have had the opportunity to play with you before. It will be novel at least," he said at last to his stepson, who was now seated across the table from him.

The tone was even, the voice firm—nothing to indicate unease on Chandler's part—so why is Dalton staring so intently at him, I wonder? mused Lord Culpepper as he watched from his vantage point by the fire.

He knew well of the hatred that existed between the men. He could not understand, then, why Philip was all of a sudden playing cards and keeping company with his stepfather. Realizing that his wife would never forgive him if he did not give an accurate recounting of the events that were about to take place, Tristan Culpepper rose from his chair and wandered over to the card table. Besides the Lords Dalton, Sheringham, and Chandler, there sat Lord James, a rather corpulent but friendly individual, Lord Royer and Diego Torres, who appeared to be unaccountably put out.

Upon seeing Lord Culpepper, Brett greeted him fondly. "Tristan, how are you?"

Philip looked up from his cards and nodded to the old gentleman.

"Brett, Philip. I'm fine, just fine. Where have you both been these past three days, anyway? Lord Innane was inquiring after you, Brett, but not even your man knew where you were off to. A mystery, my boy?"

"A mystery indeed, Tristan," Brett replied. "Philip and I had the most incredible of adventures, did we not?"

He turned toward his friend for confirmation of his words, all heads following suit.

Philip never ceased his scrutiny of Chandler as he answered, "An adventure of sorts, gentlemen. You have no doubt heard of the rumors surrounding my mother's attorney's death? Well, I have recently acquired documents that will verify these rumors and pinpoint the person responsible for the deed."

Culpepper and the rest turned to stare at Lord Chandler, who had been at the vortex of the accusations during the hearings regarding the death of Mr. Caruthers.

Retaining mastery over his emotions regardless of Philip's words, Lord Chandler said, "That will be extremely interesting. I'm sure we would all like to know whom those papers name, Lord Dalton. Where did you acquire this evidence, if I may ask?"

Brett answered instead, drawing the crowd's attention to himself.

"That is precisely the adventure I was speaking of. Philip and I had a run-in with a certain person with whose name you may all be familiar—Scurvy Joe."

A general murmur of recognition could be heard.

"What does he have to do with it, Brett?" Lord Royer inquired, glancing at Chandler for a moment. "Never tell us that the man responsible for Caruthers' death had dealings with the likes of Scurvy Joe, a common rogue and highwayman."

Lord Chandler fidgeted uncomfortably at Royer's words but remained silent, feigning interest in his cards.

"Your powers of deduction unman me, Royer," Philip said with a straight face. "Indeed yes, the man implicated in those documents did have dealings with the *late* Scurvy Joe."

"The man is dead?" Lord James asked.

"Of course. How else could I have come to possess the documents of which I have spoken?" Lord Dalton replied levelly.

"Those documents, do you have them with you?" queried Tristan Culpepper. "I for one would like to know who the man is."

The others at the table added their voices to this sentiment.

"Yes. I too would like to hear who it is," Diego put in loudly. "Why do you not reveal that man's name now, if you really have proof, Lord Dalton?"

Philip looked over at the Spaniard, scorn in his eyes.

"You doubt my word, Ambassador Torres?" he prompted slowly.

Lord Torres had spoken more from low spirits than from a true sense of dislike. He had just that day received notice that he was to return to Spain, inasmuch as his presence in England was no longer considered fruitful. The recall had left him in a bad mood, but confronted by the accusatory glare from Lord Sheringham combined with the cold blue portals to hell that Lord Dalton possessed for eyes, Diego Torres did not have the courage to continue with his attack.

"I merely meant that we are all anxious to hear who the man is, Lord Dalton, nothing more."

Philip accepted this explanation and turned his attention once more to his stepfather.

"Are you not curious as to the nature of those papers, Lord Chandler?" he asked pointedly.

"Not at all," came the answer. "I have no taste for sensationalism. If you truly have proof, you would have submitted it to the authorities by now. No, Lord Dalton, I will not fall into the trap."

"Trap?" Philip repeated with an air of innocence. "Why should I try to trap anyone?"

"I simply meant I was not going to be fooled like the rest of these gentlemen. You have no proof of anything at all," Chandler asserted somewhat defensively.

Uncertainty could be discerned in his voice, and Philip pressed his advantage.

"Perhaps you would doubt less if you knew the nature of the documents: correspondence between an unscrupulous apothecary and the man whom the papers accuse, written letters from that man in answer to blackmail threats, a bill of goods for several ounces of a fast-working, almost undetectable poison—all leading to the individual we discuss."

"And the name, Dalton, what is the name?" demanded Lord Royer. "The suspense is killing!"

"All in good time, Royer," Philip said, his gaze slipping from Chandler to encompass the entire group. "I will reveal the name of this man on my birthday, which is in a couple of days. I am having a small celebration to which all you gentlemen are invited. At midnight I will reveal the man's name."

Philip looked again at his stepfather, and with a provoking smile he added, "You are invited, of course, Lord Chandler. It is to be a masquerade, a masked ball."

"How novel," Lord Culpepper commented. "Why masked?"

"A whim, Lord Culpepper," Lord Dalton answered. "Merely a whim. You will all come?"

Everyone accepted the invitation with much relish. Even without the added enticement of a revelation, the unprecedented invitation to Lord Dalton's residence would have been enough of an inducement for their attendance.

"Oh, yes," Brett added in a voice loud enough for all to hear, "Innane, about your four friends. Since they are new to London and their lodgings are not yet furnished, I am sure Philip would not mind putting them up at his townhouse."

Philip's eyes darted to his friend, a startled look on his face. Then, recalling his promise to Aurelia, he said, "Yes, Innane. I will be happy to put up your friends until their lodgings are prepared; they are most welcome in my home."

Lord Dalton's words totally astonished everyone within earshot, for he was not well known either for his amiability or for his hospitality.

"He must have mellowed," was one comment as Philip and Brett left the table to wander about the room.

"Shall we continue, Chandler?" Royer asked languidly, searching for a reaction.

Lord Chandler appeared to be calm, but Royer could see the knuckles of his hands turning white as he clutched the playing cards.

"By all means. Let us proceed," he replied, his voice steady, almost bored in tone.

Within his soul Lord Chandler was far from self-assured. There would be no mercy from Philip, of that he was quite certain. There would be no opportunity to catch his stepson off guard, not with five men accompanying him everywhere he went—an army of bodyguards. He had no resources with which to bribe Philip, and he harbored no illusions that that would be a successful move in any case. He had to think of a new way to attack.

Lord Royer had watched Chandler lose the last few hands, and was sure that he was attempting to bluff on the one he now held.

Unexpectedly Lord Chandler smiled; it was a twisted grin, and Lord Royer felt such evil exude from this man that for a moment he was repelled. The smile vanished as quickly as it had appeared, and Chandler placed his cards on the table.

"You win," Royer said incredulously. "I thought surely you were bluffing."

"I never bluff," Lord Chandler replied, "and I feel my luck is about to change."

The following morning was altogether dreary, since the sun did not deign to show itself, hiding behind a screen of dull gray clouds.

It did not seem dismal to Lady Aurelia Courtenay, however, for she was in the pleasurable process of describing to her mantua maker the perfect ensemble, consisting of pastel blue satin embroidered with gold and silver threads, for Lord Dalton's ball.

"It will be most difficult to complete the costume, my lady," the seamstress said, measuring Lady Courtenay from every conceivable position.

"I'm sure that I can depend on you to finish it by tomorrow night, Monette," Aurelia said confidently.

"For such a customer as yourself, I think we shall be able to, my lady," the woman agreed. "We have so much to do with all the orders for costumes, you understand, that it will be necessary to hire extra help, but my lady will no doubt consider the creation well worth the price once you behold it complete."

"I'm positive it will be beautiful, Monette," Aurelia

returned as she sorted through the samples of material and lace the seamstress had brought for her scrutiny.

She was about to comment on a particularly attractive bit of braid when a knock sounded on the door.

"Enter," Aurelia said.

Crane came in, silver salver in hand, and presented the note on its surface to Lady Courtenay.

"This arrived by special messenger a moment ago, my lady," he said, waiting for further orders.

Taking the letter, Aurelia dismissed him with a wave of her hand.

"Who could this be from?" she wondered out loud, turning the note over to view the seal. She did not recognize the crest. Shrugging slightly, she opened it and read the contents.

Soon afterward a smile of delight appeared, because the signature at the bottom read "Philip."

"Good news, my lady?" Monette inquired.

"Yes, good news indeed! Have you completed your measuring? For if you have, I have another appointment with someone whom I must not keep waiting."

The seamstress was used to the caprices of the rich and instantly gathered her materials together.

"I am done, my lady. The gown shall be ready, as you requested, by the night of the ball."

Bowing, she left the room. She was determined not to lose Lady Courtenay as a patroness. It was not every day that one acquired a customer who was unconcerned by extra costs and expenses.

Aurelia opened her expansive closets in search of a change of clothing. She eyed the many gowns she owned for something suitable for a walk in the park. She chose a dark brown dress of taffeta with a matching jacket and dashing bonnet.

He wishes to be alone with me, she thought joyfully, little questioning the irregularity of the request.

She rang the bellpull for Renée to assist her with her toilette.

The maid answered her mistress's summons immediately.

"Renée, please help me with this dress. I am to meet Lord Dalton in an hour, and that is hardly enough time in which to become presentable," Aurelia said, brushing her golden hair vigorously.

Taking the brush from her hand, Renée proceeded to arrange the thick, shining locks into uniform curls.

"Will you be requiring my presence, my lady?" she questioned, knowing that Lady Faye would wish her daughter chaperoned. It would not do to have Lady Aurelia compromised, and besides, the French girl did not feel comfortable about Lord Dalton, whose features she found most disturbing.

"No, that won't be necessary, Renée," Aurelia replied.

The maid shook her head disapprovingly but kept her silence on the matter of propriety, or lack of it.

After a moment she asked, "Will Lord Dalton be arriving soon?"

"No, I'm to meet him by the stone benches in the park," Lady Courtenay replied, stepping into the gown Renée held out for her.

Renée found this statement particularly odd, since she had thought that Lord Dalton would adhere to all the social niceties.

Observing the maid's look of uncertainty reflected in the mirror, Aurelia teased, "He will not eat me alive, you know. He only wants to be alone with me. See," she continued, handing the note to Renée, "it says right here that he wishes to have a moment alone with me. That means no chaperone, no footman, no one at all."

"*Tiens!* At least allow Antoine to drive you to the rendezvous in the carriage, my lady," Renée pleaded.

Lady Courtenay, touched by her maid's concern, decided it might be a good idea at that for the footman to drive her to the park.

"All right, but he must leave the moment Lord Dalton arrives."

Gazing at herself in the full-length mirror, Aurelia determined that her garb was complete except for jewelry. She opened her jewel chest and looked over the shimmering gems it contained. Her eyes rested on the gold signet ring she had been forced to abandon wearing. Smiling, she took up the ring and restored it to its rightful place on her third finger. Throwing a light tan cloak over her shoulders to keep out the early-morning chill, she was ready at last.

Fifteen minutes later, Antoine Scarron, resplendent in his new livery, handed Lady Courtenay up into her carriage.

Renée watched with apprehension from the front entrance of the house. She would have felt much more reassured if she could have consulted Lady Standen or the duchess, but seeing that both were out shopping, she could only hope that Lady Courtenay knew what she was doing.

Just as Renée would have closed the door, she was startled by a streak of brown scurrying outside. It was Aurelia's dog, Elva. The animal barked at the coach, begging to be taken along.

"Antoine, hand her up to me," Aurelia requested. "There is no reason why she cannot have a little romp with Lord Dalton and me." Amusement showing on her face, Aurelia added to the maid, "Here, then, is a proper chaperone."

So saying, she motioned Antoine to proceed.

Scarron felt particularly proud of his new clothes, and he drove the horses as well as he knew how, attempting to present a picture of expertise to befit his sartorial splendor.

As he approached the park he took note that there were few carriages traversing its smooth lanes. The early hour was the probable explanation, since most members of the gentry preferred to make the rounds in the afternoon.

Pulling the vehicle onto a side path, just as Lady Courtenay had described to him, Antoine negotiated it down the winding road toward the stone benches secluded among several large trees and bushes. He saw what he took to be Lord Dalton's coach waiting by the side of the benches.

After bringing the horses to a halt, he assisted his mistress in descending from the carriage.

Aurelia hurried toward the rendezvous site, anxious to be with her love. All of a sudden someone caped in black appeared from behind a tree, his back to her. Mistaking the man for Philip, she broke into a run, her little dog hurrying to keep up with her. Then the form turned around. Aurelia stopped in confusion: the man was masked. Thinking it a joke or a hoax, she smiled at him, taking a step forward. Abruptly the smile was wiped from her face. Elva's snarling and barking warned her too late of the danger in which she now found herself as three other figures surrounded her, all masked and cloaked as well.

She attempted to scream, but her cry was stifled by a heavily gloved hand. Struggling fiercely, she struck out at her assailants and succeeded in landing a few solid blows, but her adversaries were too many for her to battle with.

She was aware that her footman was attacking her captors, but he was soon laid unconscious by a severe rap on the head.

Three of the ambushers dragged her across the grass toward the carriage, whereupon she made a last attempt to break free in front of the coach door. Wrenching her shoulder loose from the grasp of one of her foes, she again struck at them, but the man she had originally mistaken for Philip was out of reach behind her and attempting to push her through the doorway. Suddenly he swore and shook his leg violently.

Elva, who had been forgotten for the most part, was steadfastly nipping at the disguised man's legs, managing to draw blood in the process. Growling and barking, the little dog lunged at him again and again, until with another oath he kicked her savagely, sending her flying into a bush.

With a furious shove the man finally forced Aurelia

into the dark interior of the coach, where yet another cloaked figure attempted to bind her feet and hands.

Lady Courtenay, freed of her recent assailants and faced with a seemingly smaller and weaker adversary, lashed out at her opponent's head several times but could not cope with the masked man who had just entered the vehicle. Eventually she was bound and gagged.

The smaller form raised a clenched hand to pay back with interest the blows Aurelia had inflicted upon it. The other individual intervened on Lady Courtenay's behalf, however, and she remained unharmed.

Helpless now, Aurelia ceased her struggles and peered frantically about the carriage, trying to discern some clue to her abductors' identities.

She felt the coach jerk violently as the driver raced from the scene of her kidnapping. In the distance she could hear Elva barking, the sound gradually fading away.

The shades were drawn, and Aurelia had not the faintest idea where they were headed. The man she had thought was Philip sat across from her, a smile that was half a sneer prominent on the visible portion of his face.

Unexpectedly the smaller being spoke.

"Well, Lady Courtenay, how do you feel?"

The tone was taunting and unpleasant.

It was a distinctly feminine voice, one that Aurelia remembered but could not immediately place.

Then she knew, and with the knowledge came the absolute certainty of who her abductors were. Almost as if in confirmation of her thoughts, both persons removed their masks. Even in the dim light Aurelia could make out the depraved features of Lord Chandler and the menacing visage of Marie Manton.

"Let us see now whether Philip values his revenge more than he does your life, Lady Courtenay," Chandler gloated. "I have him where I want him at last, and there is no way he can possibly link your disappearance to me."

Aurelia knew that there was truth in his words, and her heart and soul cried out to Philip, hoping beyond hope that he would somehow sense the danger she was in. She realized full well that Lord Chandler had no intention of releasing her, regardless of what was offered him in exchange. The very fact that he had exposed his identity proved to her, irrevocably, that he had no reservations about adding her name to his list of victims.

The coach seemed to travel for an eternity before finally coming to a halt. Aurelia was aware that she must be somewhere outside London now, since the sounds of the city had been absent for some time.

Motioning the driver to assist him, Lord Chandler carried Lady Courtenay into a small ramshackle cottage. Taking up more rope, he lashed her to a wooden support in the back of the structure, untying her feet to enable her to stand.

"I believe the cords are enough to hold her, Marie," Chandler said, moving toward the door. "Untie her hands. We wouldn't want her circulation impaired. We may yet have need of her."

Mounting a horse from the team that the coachman had saddled for him, Lord Chandler rode off in the direction of London. Now that he had the advantage, he was determined that his stepson be made to forfeit not only the documents but also his estates. He was not an extremely perceptive man, but he did know that because of Philip's nature, Aurelia was probably the only woman his stepson would ever love. Therefore, there was no doubt in his mind that Philip would willingly give up all he possessed for Lady Courtenay's return.

He had no fear of retribution from Philip Dalton, because he intended to arrange, with considerably more care this time, for him to be eliminated soon.

He arrived in good time at his London home and prepared to make an appearance at White's.

It had been less than three hours since the kidnapping of Lady Courtenay, but all of London was already agog with the news. Everyone knew of it, everyone, that is, except Lord Dalton, who had spent the majority of the morning with one of his numerous agents who was assisting him with the complex planning of an elaborate wedding ceremony.

"I'm sure I can leave the rest of the details to you, Mr. Dearman," Philip said at last, donning his hat and caped coat. "I want this to be perfect down to the last item, and I shall depend heavily upon you. As I have little knowledge of these matters, it shall no doubt be up to my betrothed and her mother to decide on the guest list."

Mr. Dearman looked up from the huge pile of papers on his desk. "If you will excuse me, Lord Dalton, might I ask how you can be so positive that the lady will accept your proposal? She might refuse your offer, you know."

Lord Dalton replied, "Then I suppose we shall simply have to make arrangements for my funeral instead, for I most certainly would not survive without her."

These words were said in deadly earnest, and Mr. Dearman was left in a state of astonishment as Philip strolled from the room.

Stepping into his carriage, he ordered his man to take him to White's; he felt in need of those restoratives for which that establishment was so well known, after spending well over four hours within the somber confines of Mr. Dearman's offices.

Upon entering White's, Lord Dalton was puzzled by the covert look with which the footman at the door greeted him. The look was echoed by several members of the club when he entered the main salon. The buzz of activity gradually subsided, and all eyes turned to stare at Philip.

"Gentlemen, is there some reason why I have become the center of your combined attentions? Is my cravat askew? My features unusual in some way? Pray tell, what it is that fascinates all of you so?" Lord Dalton asked, a touch of irony in his voice.

Several members glanced at one another, and Philip could see that none of the gentlemen present wanted to assume the responsibility of informing him of what was indeed the matter.

Just as he would have inquired more pointedly, Chandler walked into the room. Upon seeing Lord Dalton and the way in which the assembly stared at him, Lord Chandler deduced that his stepson did not yet know of Lady Courtenay's disappearance.

Philip had noticed Chandler's entrance and turned to face his adversary. Lord Dalton immediately had the strange feeling that his stepfather no longer regarded him in the same light. The situation seemed to be reversed, but Philip could think of nothing that might have caused this effect.

"Tell me, Lord Chandler," Lord Dalton questioned languidly, belying his inner tension, "why have these gentlemen suddenly taken such an immense interest in me?"

Chandler smiled slightly and said, "It would seem, Lord Dalton, that you have not heard. In which case, I present you with my most sincere *condolences*. Lady Aurelia Courtenay, who I believe is an acquaintance of yours, has reportedly been missing since early this morning. The authorities suspect an abduction by some faction or another."

The blood instantly drained from Lord Dalton's face. His features remained immobile for a fraction of a second longer; then gradually the other club members became aware of a subtle difference in his expression. Although he still looked calm in general, his eyes appeared to blaze with intense heat, seemingly burning through to his stepfather's very soul and finding there the answer to some unasked question.

He took a step toward Lord Chandler, his intent threatening to result in a brawl had not Brett Sheringham entered the portals of the club at that very moment.

Brett quickly stepped between his friend and the cringing Chandler.

"I see you've heard," Brett said, holding Philip back with a restraining hand.

"Yes," Lord Dalton answered through his frozen expression and clenched teeth. "I have been informed of the facts by Lord Chandler."

Brett shook his head. "Not all the facts. The man who drove Aurelia to the place where she was abducted has regained consciousness, and there are several interesting aspects to this crime that you will want to hear."

"Let us go, then." Philip took up his hat and cloak from a footman. He looked directly at Chandler once more and said, "Whoever the instigator of this misdeed may be, I vow that if Lady Courtenay is harmed in any way, I shall personally hunt him down and see to it that retribution is paid in full. I don't intend to leave the fiend's capture and punishment to the authorities, and I swear that I shall not be half so merciful as they would be."

Lord Dalton then allowed himself to be pulled away by his friend's persistent tugging.

Entering Lord Sheringham's coach, Philip said tightly, "He has her, Brett! I know it, and she is suffering only because she became involved with my affairs."

"You couldn't know that Chandler would attack you through Aurelia, Philip," Brett countered. "In any case, he can't have harmed her. He went through too much trouble to steal her away alive, to have killed her so quickly. After you talk to the coachman, we can decide what to do next."

They soon arrived at the Courtenay residence, Lord Sheringham supplying Lord Dalton with the facts of the incident on the way. Gabrielle hurried out to greet them, worry showing plainly on her face.

"Lord Dalton, has Brett told you . . . ?" she asked in a strained voice.

"Yes, Lady Standen," Philip answered. "Why did Aurelia go off to the park like that? Brett told me that the coachman was found unconscious by the stone benches."

Gabrielle nodded. "I questioned the servants, and Aurelia's maid showed me this letter that she received this morning. It bears your signature and it asks Aurelia to meet you alone." She handed it to him.

Philip read the note.

"Already read it when I came to see Gabrielle today. Must have been forged," Brett commented.

"What are you talking about? Do you know who has done this?" Gabrielle demanded.

"We only suspect. We don't have any proof. We think that Lord Chandler may have had Aurelia kidnapped so he could get the evidence from Philip."

"Lord Chandler!" Gabrielle cried bitterly. "So he's struck at Aurelia because of you!" Almost immediately she was ashamed of her words. "I didn't mean that, Lord Dalton, believe me. I am just overwrought."

Philip waved her words aside. "You are right. I am responsible to a degree, but I will find a way to save her." His voice rang with conviction. "Now, where is that coachman? I want to talk to him."

Gabrielle led the way to the servants' quarters, where Lord Dalton found Antoine prostrate upon his bed, recovering from his ordeal. Several colorful bruises decorated his face. He attempted to sit up when Lord Dalton and Lady Standen entered the room, but winced with pain at the effort.

"Lie still," Gabrielle ordered. "Lord Dalton is here to ask you a few questions."

Sitting on a chair by the bed, Philip gazed intently at the man, as was his habit.

"Did you recognize any of the people who took your mistress?" he asked.

"None of them, my lord," Antoine answered. "They were all masked and there were no markings on the coach. They came upon us à l'improviste."

Philip suspected that this had been the case.

"I see you put up a game fight. How many of them were there?"

Antoine thought a moment before replying, "I think there were four or five, my lord. We were outnumbered, but, *envrai*, my mistress did not go quietly, I can tell you that. If there had only been one or two less, I think we might have bested them."

"I've no doubt you would have. Is there anything else you can tell me?"

The footman shook his head; then a thought struck him.

"The dog," he said.

Philip looked at the man in a way that implied that the blows to his head had done more than simply bruise the surface.

"What dog?"

"Lady Courtenay's little dog. The animal was with us when my lady was taken. It must be lost now."

Rising to leave, Lord Dalton said, "I see. You must mean Elva. You rest now. I will try to find the dog later."

He was met by Brett outside Scarron's room.

"We will have to give in to his demands if there is no other way, but I am not sure that we have completely exhausted all avenues open to us," Philip mused.

Brett did not want to say what he was thinking, but felt compelled to.

"You know, Philip, that man hates you. He probably will not return Aurelia no matter what you give him. You would not be able to prove it, and he would have a perfect opportunity for his revenge."

Brett saw no reaction to his words except for the flashing of his friend's blue eyes and a slight movement of his jaw, suggesting the grinding of teeth.

Abruptly Philip turned and with a determined stride left the house, Lord Sheringham following in his wake.

Lord Dalton and Lord Sheringham spent the remainder of the day with the authorities investigating Lady Courtenay's disappearance. They were fruitless hours, however, for no clues had come to light regarding Aurelia's whereabouts or the identities of the culprits.

After examining the abduction site, Philip and Brett entered their waiting coach and gave the driver instructions to convey them to Chandler's home, for Lord Dalton knew that his stepfather would be expecting him.

As the carriage pulled up before Chandler's residence, Philip turned to his friend and said, "I have to do this alone, Brett. Besides, he won't want any witnesses."

"Good luck."

Philip had never been in Lord Chandler's home before, and as he looked upon it now, he received a fair idea as to the financial state in which his stepfather was placed. There were silhouettes on the walls where paintings had once hung, the furniture was sparse, and the rugs were stained and threadbare.

What was more, the slovenly servant who led him to the library would never have been able to enter his own service, as he could afford to be more discriminating about the help he employed.

"Lord Chandler is awaiting you within," the manservant muttered, leaving Philip to announce himself.

Pushing open the library door, Lord Dalton stepped slowly inside and saw Chandler sitting by the fireplace, glass in hand. His stepfather had partaken of the spirits in great quantity, and looked up at the earl through an alcoholic haze. As always, Philip was moved to revulsion at the sight of Chandler, whether he was in a drunken state or not.

"Lord Dalton," his stepfather said, making no attempt to rise from his sprawled position. "I have been waiting for you." Looking about the room, he added, his speech slurred, "But where is Lord Sheringham? Surely you have brought him along—"

"No," Philip broke in brusquely, "he is not here. Let us get on with this. I know what you have done, and I am prepared to concede to any of your demands for the safe return of Lady Courtenay. However, there are certain conditions to which you must adhere. No doubt you want the documents and my estates, and there is also no doubt that you are in desperate need of money."

Lord Chandler made a motion of protest at these words, but Philip ignored him and continued rapidly, for every moment he spent in Chandler's home made him feel soiled:

"I am willing to give you both the incriminating evidence I have gleaned and a signed document transferring my estates to you on the night of the ball. In return, you must bring Lady Courtenay to the fete unharmed. We will make the exchange in the library at the south corner of my house. If you refuse to cooperate in a direct exchange, I shall assume that Lady Courtenay is unable to appear because she is dead. And if this is so, your own life shall pay the forfeit, that I guarantee!"

These last words were declared with a ferocity that struck cold fear into Chandler's heart. Philip had come with the intention of remaining calm on the exterior in order to give his opponent no sign of the inner agony he felt, but it was becoming increasingly difficult to keep up the façade.

Regaining his composure, Philip asked, "Do you agree?"

"I agree to the exchange, but you must be perfectly alone. I shall be holding a gun on Lady Courtenay, and one false move on your part will insure her death. It would be a shame and a pity to destroy such beauty." Chandler's face bore a sensuous expression. "She is a lovely woman. Doubtless she is worth all that you—"

Chandler could not complete his words, for Lord Dalton had grasped him violently by the neck and was shaking him as he would a rag doll.

"If you have laid hands upon her, I will kill you!" Philip roared, the thought of Aurelia's possible outrage superseding his common sense.

Lord Chandler could not speak, but shook his head to indicate his innocence.

Lord Dalton looked down at this wreckage of a man and saw that the only forces sustaining him were his greed and his lechery. He considered for a moment putting a period to Chandler's existence. It would be so easy, but there was Aurelia's safety to consider. Keeping the thought of her in mind, Philip released his hold on his stepfather, then turned to leave.

"Wait," Chandler croaked, rubbing his sore and bruised neck. "If you have any notion of following me to find Lady Courtenay and play the hero, I assure you I will know. If I even suspect that you or anyone else is watching my movements, your little lady love will die," he sneered.

Philip's hands itched to throttle the man again, so it was with the utmost of willpower that he jerked himself around and left.

"We shall see, Lord Dalton, who gets the better of whom," Chandler muttered. Yes, he would bring a woman to be exchanged for the documents, but it would not be Lady Courtenay. Instead, it would be Marie in costume, and she would be supplied with a gun.

"After Marie kills that savage, I shall be able to enjoy my wealth completely."

Lord Chandler attempted to laugh but choked on the effort, his bruised throat being unable to cope with the impulse.

He would go to the cottage in the morning to dispose of Lady Courtenay, and to prepare Marie for the masquerade that evening.

Lord Chandler poured himself another glass of claret to keep him company during the night, and reeling up from his seat, he stumbled toward his bedroom.

His would be a sleep through which nothing could penetrate, while Lord Dalton would spend the night in mental anguish, never relaxing until exhaustion compelled him into a fitful half slumber in the early hours of the morning.

CHAPTER 9

THE MORNING PASSED slowly at the Courtenay residence, Lady Standen and the duchess having spent most of the previous night pacing about their rooms.

Davis could attest to this since his sleeping quarters were situated directly beneath Gabrielle's. Needless to say, his night's rest had been less than complete, so it was with extraordinary forbearance that he responded to a sudden commotion created by an excitable lackey early that morning. Davis discovered the man on the front steps, practically leaping up and down in his flurry.

"Look, Mr. Davis! I came out here to sweep the steps when I found it!"

Davis was astonished to see Lady Courtenay's missing dog lying there, exhausted and injured.

Whisking the dachshund off to the kitchen, Davis instructed the lackey to inform Lady Standen of Elva's return.

Lady Standen hurried down to the kitchen to preside over the reparation of the little dog. Upon seeing Gabrielle's face, Elva managed a small wag of her tail and perked up considerably.

The cook had warmed a saucer of milk for the invalid, and placing it before her, anxiously waited to see if the animal would drink it.

Sniffing at the saucer, the dachshund gradually realized that the contents were edible. She attempted to rise to her feet but was unable to, and squealed with pain as she held up one of her paws. It was examined closely by Davis and was found to be sprained.

"Poor Elva," Gabrielle said sympathetically. "Davis, I want you to feed the dog by hand if you must, but make sure that she eats something. Also, I want her leg tended to immediately."

So saying, Gabrielle went upstairs to inform Lady Faye that Aurelia's pet had returned.

Would that it had been Aurelia, Gabrielle thought miserably.

Lady Aurelia Courtenay was far from capable of returning home at that moment. Tied to a post in the cottage, she had remained bound the entire night. Marie had deemed it unnecessary to remove her gag and enjoyed making insulting remarks from time to time, knowing that her captive could not answer back. At one point Marie had asked Lady Courtenay if she desired a drink of water. Aurelia could tell that Marie wanted her to answer in the affirmative so that the dancer could sadistically withhold the liquid; therefore, Aurelia merely ignored the offer.

Eventually Marie had fallen asleep in the other room, content in the knowledge that the coachman was standing guard outside.

All through the night Aurelia had attempted to work her way out of her bonds. Earlier she had ached to free her hands in order to strike Marie several times, but the only thing on her mind now was escape, and in doing so, bringing both Miss Manton and Lord Chandler to grief.

She struggled for a long while before she felt the knots begin to give way. She was overjoyed with the thought of freedom and started to work more frenetically than ever, but was forced to cease her activities when the coachman came in to check on her early in the morning.

Seeing nothing amiss, the man left her alone, and after a moment she could hear him talking to Marie in the next room. Lady Courtenay strained every muscle to loosen the ropes enough so that she could turn. Then, when her hands were free, she would be able to untie the cords that bound her feet to the post.

Aurelia allowed her mind to wander briefly, recalling an incident that had occurred only hours ago. Miss Manton had taken the liberty of possessing herself of Aurelia's signet ring, telling her that she planned to sell it at some later date. Lady Courtenay remembered her rage when Marie had wrenched the ring from her finger, commenting that it would be a shame to bury Aurelia's body with the ring still on her person.

The thought of this particular event fired Lady Courtenay's blood once more, and giving a singularly violent twist, she found that she could now maneuver her frame. She could still hear Marie and the coachman talking, and by the tone of their voices, she discerned that their discussion had taken a turn toward the romantic. She divided her attention between the task of untying the remaining knots and listening to be sure the guards remained occupied. Only three more knots and she would be free. She worked feverishly at them, noting several bursts of raucous laughter and shrill giggles from the other room.

At last Aurelia was free. The voices beyond the dividing wall had been silent for the past few minutes, indicating that the coachman had no doubt succeeded in his amorous overtures.

She found herself to be drenched in perspiration from her efforts and removed her cloak to cool herself. Searching the room for some avenue of escape, she became aware of sunlight shining between the boards of the outer wall. She trod softly across the floor and examined the planks. The cottage was falling to ruin, and the nails holding the wood in place had long since rusted through. Picking up a spoon Marie had left, and using her cloak as a muffle, Aurelia pried the boards apart until there was enough room for her to slip between them.

She strained her ears. The only sound from the other room was the occasional creaking of the cot.

Bunching her cape in front of her, she began to crawl through the hole to freedom. She was blinded by the bright light and had to stop until she became accustomed to it. Then, crouching low, she moved stealthily toward the pasture where the carriage horses were grazing. Her breath came hard and fast as a mixture of fear and elation urged her forward.

Suddenly she heard the noise of nearing hoofbeats.

Regardless of what might happen, she could not bear to turn back, so she burst into a full run.

Had Aurelia looked behind her, she would have seen a sight to freeze her in her tracks: Lord Chandler, monstrous of visage, had arrived at the cottage in time to witness her flight and was now giving chase.

Leaping on the back of a chestnut stallion, she dug her heels into the surprised animal's flanks, spurring it into immediate action. Her only chance for escape was to lose the horseman in the woods to her left.

Chandler dogged her, his face almost maniacal from the intensity of his feelings. Drawing a pistol that he had loaded previously with the intention of using it on Lady Courtenay, Chandler aimed it at her retreating figure. He knew that if she reached the woods, she might very well elude him, and this he could not risk.

Just as she would have entered the protecting trees, Aurelia turned around to determine where her pursuer was. It was at that moment that Lord Chandler fired.

Her horse, frightened by the shot, dashed off with its rider into the dense forest, but not before Chandler saw his target jerk, and knew that his bullet had struck home.

He searched the woods, but he could find no trace of either Lady Courtenay or the stallion. His anger rose as his hunt proved futile, and he wrenched his mount back toward the cottage, intending to deal severely with both Marie and the coachman.

As he neared the ramshackle dwelling, Chandler perceived that two more horses were missing from the pasture and realized that Miss Manton and the coachman had fled, fearing retribution at his hands.

Entering the rotting structure, he noticed several articles of clothing that Marie and his driver had left behind in their haste, and deduced what activity they had been engaging in while Lady Courtenay escaped.

Falling heavily into a chair, Chandler seemed to see all his plans crumbling into dust. He had no doubt that Lady Courtenay was either dead or dying, but since Marie had gone off with her ill-chosen lover, he no longer had a decoy for Philip. He would have to formulate a plan to obtain the documents without Miss Manton's aid. It was imperative that he have those papers, for if he failed he would be forced to live the life of a fugitive; there would be no alternative except to face execution.

"But not," he mused aloud, "before I pay Dalton back. If I am to be ruined, I will see him dead first."

Rising from his chair, features set in an ugly sneer, Lord Chandler made haste to return to London to plan his next move. Mounting his horse, he rode off without a backward glance.

It was well for Aurelia that Chandler had made no further attempt to search her out, for she was indeed wounded. She was not as badly injured as she might have been, because she had turned at the exact moment the gun had been fired; thus the bullet, instead of lodging in her back, grazed her lower ribs, after tearing through the layers of the cloak she had been holding.

Her stallion had run through the woods for a considerable distance, until her persistent if weak tugging had halted its mad dash. Erelong, Aurelia had slipped from the animal's back, too tired to continue.

The bleeding had subsided for the most part, the cloak having staunched the flow. Aurelia made a crude dressing from the lining of her wrap, binding it in place with more strips torn from the edges. As she worked at the task, chills racked her body and she began to feel the effects of lost blood.

Although in great pain, she could not help but think

of Philip. She shuddered at the idea of Lord Chandler's using her abduction as a weapon against him.

I must get back to London, she resolved. I have to let Philip know I am safe.

She attempted to rise, but gasped at the excruciating pain. Lady Courtenay knew that she must rest before riding back to London, so she seated herself on the trunk of a fallen tree. She was unsure of her location but knew a road was nearby as she had caught a glimpse of one during her horse's wild run.

While she sat there, Aurelia gradually became aware of a faint gurgling. Rising slowly from her seat, she stumbled toward the sound and soon reached the bank of a small river. It was not until she had drunk her fill of the clear water that Lady Courtenay realized she was still clutching her much-abused cloak. Feeling feverish now, she dipped a corner of the garment into the river and wiped her neck and brow. She then abandoned the cape as she moved slowly back to the spot where her horse stood.

Leaning against the stallion, she gritted her teeth and with one supreme effort hoisted herself onto its bare back. She pulled up the animal's head and directed it to where she determined the road should be. She decided to travel close to the woods in order to conceal herself in case Lord Chandler was riding on that byway.

She spotted a rough signpost indicating the direction toward town, and started her long, lonely journey home.

Lady Courtenay's departure was as timely as her delay, for only moments after she had left the riverbank, another weary traveler stopped at the very same spot to refresh herself.

Dismounting awkwardly from her horse, a small female figure, disheveled in appearance, bent to drink of the water. Seeing her reflection, Marie was disgusted by the sight. She had had little opportunity to make herself presentable, since she had left the cottage in rather a haste.

Brushing back stray hairs, she drank, cursing her bad luck and the coachman, who had not been able to find his pistol amidst the disarray in time to fire at Aurelia Courtenay.

She had known Chandler would return, and after the manner in which she had bungled her responsibility, she decided that it was best to hasten away while she could. Still, she bitterly regretted that she would not now be able to collect the monies owed her. She had nothing to show for her efforts and had even suffered the loss of several articles of clothing.

Rising, she kicked viciously at a small plant, uprooting the loose weed and sending clods of compacted soil flying. Almost like an act of revenge, several clumps rained down on Marie, spattering her dress and matting her hair as they burst atop her head.

This was the last straw for Miss Manton, and a stream of obscenities flowed from her lips startling her horse. The animal, familiar with the tone of voice, shied away from the woman, expecting the accustomed crack of the whip that usually accompanied such outbursts.

Marie, seeing that her only form of transportation was about to be lost, spoke soothingly to the beast while she approached it slowly. As she moved forward, she became aware of some object becoming entangled about her ankle and dragging behind her. Looking down, she discovered it was a wrap. Upon closer inspection she recognized it as the cloak that Lady Courtenay had been wearing when she was captured.

From the condition of the cape Marie deduced that Aurelia had fallen victim to Chandler's murderous propensities. She noted the bloodstains and counted several holes through which bullets must have passed.

She could not know that Lady Courtenay had not been wearing the cloak at the time of impact, and that because the cape had been bunched up, what appeared to be numerous holes had been created by only one bullet.

Looking from the garment to the river, Marie imagined Lady Courtenay floating downstream or perhaps lodged between rocks with the water pulling at her lifeless body.

She smiled as she suddenly hit on a plan to gain a profit from the circumstances. Gathering up the cape and making sure that she still possessed Aurelia's ring, Miss Manton hastily mounted her horse.

There is one person who I am sure will pay me well for this information, Marie thought as she urged the animal forward, taking a shorter, faster route to London than had been taken by Aurelia.

It was almost dark when Marie reached the Theater of Delights. Her mount had nearly been ridden to the point of collapse, so anxious was she to arrive at her destination. Dismounting quickly, she left the horse to shift for itself and hurried into the theater to change her clothes. She wanted to look her best, for she was about to pay a visit to Lord Dalton.

Philip had spent the greater part of the day discussing his strategy with Brett. His plan was to station his friend nearby, perhaps at the window of his library, when the exchange between him and Chandler took place. Lord Dalton had no intention of allowing Chandler to extort his property from him, since he was sure that his stepfather did not mean to leave either Aurelia or himself alive after the exchange.

The rest of the day had been spent reassuring Lady Faye of his efforts to rescue her daughter.

Gabrielle had been calm but reserved. She had little reason to put much faith in Lord Dalton's words, though she did hope he would be successful, since Aurelia's life depended on him.

Lord Innane's four friends, who had just moved in with Philip and Brett, had already begun to grate on the former's nerves, and he had sent them off to a card party. Even under normal circumstances Lord Dalton would have found them irritating, but with Aurelia missing they had become totally unbearable to his jarred sensibilities.

Now while he rested in the paneled library, his servants decorating the vast rooms for the ball, he allowed his mind to dwell on the fear he had tried to hide from others. He winced as he tortured himself with the idea of never seeing Aurelia again. It was too painful a thought, and he shook it from his mind. Picking up a decanter, he poured a glass of port for himself and Brett, who watched his friend silently.

"Philip," Brett said, taking the glass from Lord Dalton's hand, "it will work. You'll see. We'll get her back."

Philip managed a strained smile.

"I just don't want to lose her, Brett. I couldn't bear it if I did." His voice shook, and he began to pace the length of the room. "We have had so little time together. I couldn't live if she should be taken from me."

Lord Dalton tried to imagine his existence without Aurelia. Even in the small space of time they had shared, he knew that life without her would stretch out cold and desolate before him. He would not be able to endure it.

"It will work. It has got to work!" he raved.

The library door opened at that instant, and Simpson, the butler, entered.

"What is it?" Lord Dalton demanded, irritation coloring his words.

His butler was quite accustomed to the short manner in which Lord Dalton dealt with his servants, but was surprised by the master's appearance: he looked haggard and almost violent.

Clearing his throat, Simpson said, "A Miss Manton to see you, my lord."

"Manton?" Philip repeated blankly. "I don't know any Miss Manton."

"She insists upon seeing you, my lord." The servant fidgeted uncomfortably, then added, "She asked me to show you this."

Simpson produced a small object and placed it in Lord Dalton's hand. For a moment Philip stared at it in astonishment. It was Aurelia's signet ring.

"Send her to me at once," he ordered.

The butler showed Marie to the library and left her.

She had dressed in her finest clothes for Philip, but it was obvious that he had no interest in her personality, for he did not ask her to remove her cape or to sit down.

He strode menacingly over to her, his face grim, and demanded, "How did you come by this ring?"

Marie was taken aback by the vehemence in his voice and began to have second thoughts about dealing with the ill-natured Lord Dalton.

"I have information to sell," she replied, trying to brazen out the situation. "For a price I will tell you what I know."

Philip considered her words for a moment. "What price?"

Marie took courage from the fact that he was willing to discuss the cost.

"Five thousand pounds."

"Done."

Miss Manton was surprised by the swiftness of his decision. The sum had been only a tentative one, and she had expected an objection to her proposed amount.

"Now, what do you know?" Philip prodded, his tone causing Marie to shiver slightly.

She did not answer him; instead, she pulled out a wrapped object from her cape.

"This is her—Lady Courtenay's—cloak," Marie said, her voice uncertain as she watched for his reaction.

Slowly taking the package from her, Philip opened it and beheld the grisly prize that Miss Manton had found.

Brett gasped when he saw the light shine through several holes in the garment, making the red stains all the more visible on the pale material.

Lord Dalton did not move. He stood there staring with unseeing eyes at the blood-drenched cloak.

"I found it by the river. She escaped and Lord

Chandler must have killed her," Marie continued nervously. "She must have been carried downstream. I—"

Marie did not finish the sentence, for her words had shattered the last remnant of Lord Dalton's restraint. With a cry of rage Philip turned on the cowering girl, grabbed her by the neck, and shook her violently.

"You helped him do this!" he shouted, his face mottled and contorted.

Lord Sheringham was sure that if he did not intercede, Philip would be capable of murdering this woman, so he leaped upon his friend, who seemed to have gone mad at last.

"Philip!" Brett yelled, attempting to drag him away from the gagging woman. "Stop! You'll kill her!"

Lord Dalton did not appear to heed this warning, and Brett could see that Miss Manton's efforts were becoming more feeble. Though he used all his strength to pull Philip back, his endeavors were less than nothing against Lord Dalton's fury.

In desperation, Lord Sheringham attempted to pry Philip's fingers from the dancer's throat. The earl's grip was like a steel vice, but Brett finally succeeded in breaking the murderous hold.

Marie was hurled to the floor. As she lay there, her breath coming in ragged gasps, Brett wondered if he had been too late.

Philip paid no further attention to the woman, staring down at his empty hands in disbelief.

Although her breathing was still labored and harsh, Marie stumbled to her feet, her eyes wild with fear. Brett did not attempt to stop her as she staggered out the door.

Touching his friend on the shoulder, Brett realized there was nothing he could say that would comfort Philip now.

"She's dead," Lord Dalton whispered, mesmerized by the ring on the table.

Then, shaking himself, he walked to the chair on which he had dropped the cloak, his footsteps heavy, his legs dragging as if in quicksand. He picked up the cape and clutched the stained fabric tightly in his hands.

"Chandler did this!" he cried savagely. He did not have to speak the words; Brett could see the wrath in his eyes and knew what he meant to do.

Lord Sheringham was ready this time for the manifestations of Philip's violent nature, and barred the exit.

Attempting to push past his friend, Philip discovered that Brett would not allow him even this gratification. He had never before threatened Brett, but found himself on the verge of doing so now.

"Aurelia would not want you to be hung for killing Chandler," Brett said quietly.

Lord Sheringham's words only took effect because he had used Aurelia's name. Philip slowly unclenched his fists, and after a long moment he spoke.

"You had best go and tell Gabrielle."

Although Philip no longer appeared to be in a rage, Brett was hesitant to leave, for he had been fooled more than once by his friend's outer façade.

"You will not seek out Chandler?"

"No. I will wait until tonight at the ball for my—our—revenge. Leave me now."

Brett looked once more at Lord Dalton. He saw that sorrow was at last starting to penetrate Philip's anger, and he left his friend to mourn in his own manner, solitary and in silence.

Hearing the door close behind Brett, Philip slowly sank into a chair by the fire, the cape and the ring in his hands. He was oblivious to the noise made by the servants still preparing the house for the party; to the clock on the mantel that struck the hour; to the fire that failed to warm the numbing coldness in his heart. His whole world had ceased to have meaning owing to the words "she's dead".

Now, in the deserted room, alone as he had always been, Philip had nothing to cling to. No promise of a bright future urged him on. All that remained were her ring and a bloody scrap of cloth.

Her ring . . . His mind wandered, and he began to remember, to think of Aurelia, of her face, her mannerisms; and with the thoughts came the grief, almost suffocating in its intensity, and he could not stay the flow of tears as he buried his face in her cloak.

CHAPTER 10

TRISTAN CULPEPPER HAD succeeded in descending from the family carriage without the aid of one of Lord Dalton's overzealous footmen.

"I am far from being totally incapacitated, I assure you," he uttered with irritation.

"Of course, my lord," the young man said, backing away.

"Really, Tristan, my love," Lady Culpepper admonished as he turned to assist her from the coach, "I am sure the man meant well. He simply is not used to serving at such a large affair."

"Still, my dear," he insisted, "I do not appreciate being treated as if I were subject to the vagaries of old age."

"There, there, my dear," his wife murmured in her most soothing tones. "Don't let the incident put you in a foul humor. After all, it is not every day that we are invited to an event as unusual as this."

As the couple moved toward the entrance, they could see the crests on various coaches that were being moved by a veritable horde of servants.

"I must say that when Philip decides to provide an entertainment, he does it in grand style," Lord Culpepper observed. "It looks as if he has issued invitations to every important member of the ton."

There was truth in this statement, for as Lord and Lady Culpepper handed their outerwear to Simpson, Lady Culpepper was positive she had seen an individual who looked remarkably like the prince donning a mask before entering the already crowded ballroom. Important guests indeed!

"Come now, Tristan, put on your mask. We don't want to be recognized," Lady Culpepper said, putting her own mask in place.

Lord Culpepper complied with his wife's wishes, and, now sufficiently disguised, they entered the ballroom. Lady Culpepper was amazed at the change in the house since she had last seen its interior some twenty years ago. At that time it had been going to ruin, Lord Chandler little caring about the deterioration of the late Lord Dalton's London home. She had thought it a shame, but now the house was more than simply restored. The splendor that had always imbued a Dalton residence with a special aura had been regenerated in full force.

The orchestra was playing a waltz, and the swirling couples seemed to charge the ballroom itself with movement and sound. The chatter of the crowd, the laughter and sparkle that only the ton could provide, brought back memories of previous balls over which Lady Dalton had presided when her husband was alive.

Lady Culpepper reflected how sad it was that the present Lord Dalton had no charming wife to preside over his ball, nor would he be likely to have one unless Aurelia were rescued from her abductors. Lady Culpepper had been most distressed when she had heard of the kidnapping, and would have shunned this evening's entertainment had it not been for the irresistible lure of hearing Lord Chandler, whom she fully suspected of instigating the abominable crime, denounced before his peers.

Lady Culpepper then attempted to recognize her

friends beneath their costumes and soon succeeded in spotting two of them.

"There are Lady Chatalot and Lady Ianthe!" she exclaimed. "I know it is they because where Louisa goes, so goes Catherina, and Catherina has always had the most shocking taste in colors. She is the one in the green and red mantua."

So saying, she left her husband to his own devices and joined her friends. Lord Culpepper continually felt out of place at such fetes, and it was his wont to search out his male companions and spend the evening discussing the races or other subjects of interest. He only wished he could find them. The array of capes and masks interspersed with gaudy costumes was dazzling, encompassing the entire spectrum of colors and styles. It was rather difficult to tell who was who in the crowd. There had not been one refusal to Lord Dalton's invitations, of that Tristan Culpepper was sure.

Out of the corner of his eye he became aware of a particularly flamboyant figure dressed as the Roman emperor Nero, making the typical gestures he tended to associate with Lord Innane. The gentleman beside him, though wearing a staid domino of indeterminate color, was easily earmarked as Lord James, for the form underneath the costume was singularly obese.

Lord Culpepper made his way across the room toward the gentlemen. He was not terribly eager to spend the evening in discussion with Innane, but he had always enjoyed the company of Lord James and would not have forgiven himself if he left that jolly fellow alone in the clutches of Lord Innane's maddeningly grating vocalizations.

As he neared them, Innane's voice rang out above the playing of the orchestra:

"I mean, really," he rasped, "the very idea of keeping four mistresses at once. It is positively indecent."

James winced visibly at the sound and turned toward Culpepper as a drowning man to a rope.

"Lord James, Innane," Lord Culpepper greeted.

"How did you know?" Lord Innane squeaked in astonishment.

"A lucky guess," he replied dryly, then addressed Lord James. "Have you seen our host yet?"

"Not yet, Tristan," the rotund gentleman answered. "I have heard he will make the announcement at midnight. It's only eleven o'clock now."

"Do you think he will really reveal the man's name?" Innane's tone revealed his incredulity. "After all, why should he do it publicly? It's all a sham, if you ask me."

"What is a sham?" a voice inquired from behind Lord Innane.

Turning almost in unison, the three men faced a figure clothed in an elegantly cut black velvet domino.

For a few seconds Innane went pale under his mask. Then, suspicion creeping into his voice, he asked, "Is that you, Royer?"

Seeing the familiar grin beneath the disguise, he let out a sigh of relief.

"Good Lord, for a moment I thought you were Philip."

Lord Royer laughed loudly.

"You would have had cause to regret your words just now if I had been," he said archly.

Looking narrowly at him through the slits in his mask, Innane commented, "You are worse than Dalton in your way, Royer."

"Perhaps," Lord Royer admitted. "In any case, I doubt very much that Lord Dalton is shamming. Although I don't know him well, I dare say he is not the type to make up a tale such as that to amuse or fool the ton. He has no interest in either."

The last statement was pronounced with such flippancy as to be insulting.

"I think I see Chandler over there in the gray domino," Lord James remarked, pointing toward the doorway.

All heads swiveled, and they perceived it was indeed

Lord Chandler, who was in the process of donning his mask.

"Obviously he does not relish being in the home of his enemy, but I see he could not resist attending," Lord Innane commented, following the gray domino's progress across the ballroom floor.

"I imagine he has to know who Lord Dalton will name," Royer said, "considering a guilty conscience must constantly fear exposure; and Lord Chandler has, unless I am very much mistaken, a good deal to feel guilty about."

Lord James hardly heard these remarks, for he was intent on watching Chandler.

"He seems to be looking for someone," he announced to no one in particular.

Lord Innane, whose attention span was not the lengthiest, soon grew disinterested in Chandler. Digging down into the depths of his outlandish toga, he produced a small gold snuffbox embossed in an intricate design. With a flourish, he offered each man in turn a pinch of snuff. Innane had become much addicted to the habit of taking snuff, but none of his close acquaintances shared his propensity, and they all refused his offer, Royer going so far as to wonder aloud at the displaying of such a preposterous activity.

Just as Lord Innane would have taken exception to this, Lord Royer's attention was diverted from his sputteringly unworthy prey to something of more interest.

Emitting a low whistle, he said, "Lord Chandler makes his move early."

Tristan Culpepper looked in the same direction, trying to put meaning to Royer's cryptic words. He saw Chandler's gray domino advancing on a gentleman in black, almost an exact duplicate of Lord Royer's costume.

"Lord Dalton?" Culpepper asked.

"Indeed; who else?" Royer replied.

All four men watched intently as the spectacle took shape before them. Chandler was unaware of the eyes that followed him, his concentration being centered on the person in black. He felt sure that it was Philip, discounting Lord Royer, whom he had recognized by the company he was keeping.

Philip turned when Lord Chandler neared, as if he sensed the presence of an enemy. Chandler stared into Philip's eyes and was once again subjected to the deathly gaze that could be associated with no other human being. One might have expected that time would inure him to this look, but, if anything, Lord Chandler had felt the hatred and fear grow stronger within himself as the years had passed. Now, tonight, he sensed that his stepson's power was at its apex, and if necessity had not motivated him into this situation, he would never have confronted Philip.

Lord Dalton was alone at the moment. He was unused to the role of host, and he had matters of far greater importance on his mind than the endless chatter of his guests. After his initial violent outburst, he had managed to bring his emotions under a semblance of control. It had taken an enormous effort, but, as disciplined as he was, he was still unable to hide his grief entirely. His torment simmered just below the surface, and at odd, unprotected moments his control would lapse, his face contorted by misery. It was during one of these moments that Philip had taken himself off to this corner of the ballroom and now faced the cause of his suffering.

For a time, anger and loathing prevented Philip from speaking, and Chandler pressed forward before the animalistic terror that his stepson inspired within him made him turn and flee.

"Lord Dalton," he began, controlling as best he could the desperation in his voice, "there will be a change in plans."

Philip remained silent, waiting to hear what his stepfather would say.

Seeing that his words did not seem to have an adverse effect on Lord Dalton's temperament, Chandler continued:

"You will give me the documents you hold, and I

shall make arrangements to exchange Lady Courtenay for the deeds of ownership at a later date. The papers can be considered a gesture of good faith, insuring the safe return of Lady Courtenay."

Philip still did not speak, and appeared to be pondering the proposition, but the silence that Chandler interpreted as consideration of the proposal was actually stemming from the irascible young earl's attempt to restrain himself. The sheer audacity of his stepfather's move enraged him even more than he had been previously. In his fury he almost gave way to his most basic impulse, that of attacking Lord Chandler on the spot.

The crowd, the music, everything had vanished for Philip the moment Chandler arrived, but gradually he became aware of his surroundings again, and the purpose of his elaborate plans. He would not give in to the compulsion to eliminate this worthless man himself. No; instead, he would make his announcement at midnight. Aurelia would have wanted it that way.

In a voice as chilling as a cold hand reaching out from the grave, Philip said, "I know that Lady Aurelia Courtenay is dead."

The last word had the same effect as a blow, and Lord Chandler shrank back slightly.

"I will expose the murderer at midnight, as I planned. Until then, I would suggest you do not attempt to escape my 'hospitality.' You may have noticed that Lord Sheringham is not in evidence. He has been busy checking on the security. We have posted guards at all the doors and windows."

Philip stalked away, leaving his stepfather to suffer out the next hour as he himself had done earlier in the evening.

Brett Sheringham was not the only person who was not in evidence at the ball. Lady Standen could not bring herself to witness the final outcome of Lord Dalton's plans. She had been overcome by anguish when her beau had told her of Aurelia's death, and Philip's revenge held no consolation for her.

It had been Brett's bad luck to have to carry the news to Gabrielle, and as is often the case with bearers of bad tidings, the messenger was, if not killed, at least banished from sight.

He had gone quietly, but Gabrielle had been bitterly certain he would be with Philip that evening. She knew enough about Lord Sheringham's nature to realize that he would not desert his friend at this point, even though she felt that Philip Dalton was responsible in part for Aurelia's death.

Brett's reply to Gabrielle's accusation had been fore-seeable, but it had enraged her nonetheless:

"You shouldn't cut at Philip so. He couldn't know what would happen to Aurelia. He loved her, too, and your attitude won't make his grief any easier to bear."

These remarks, so solicitous of Lord Dalton's feelings and so blind to Gabrielle's loss, had shattered the last of her reserve. She had screamed at him to leave and added a threat if he did not do as ordered, posthaste. He had done as he was bidden, sadly and without a word.

She had contained her desolation for the most part, not wanting to tell Lady Faye the terrible news until after the fate of Lord Chandler had been sealed.

She had managed to maintain the calm façade until the time when the mantua maker had arrived with Aurelia's costume. Upon seeing it, Gabrielle had dissolved into tears, throwing the poor woman into a state of shock. Lady Standen had regained control erelong and sent the woman off with a handsome sum for her trouble.

The garment had been laid on Aurelia's bed, out of Gabrielle's sight.

The afternoon had worn on, and Gabrielle had nothing to occupy her time with, except for paying a good deal of attention to the little dog that had belonged to her friend. But seeing that Elva was pining for her mistress, Lady Standen left her with Davis and Crane, charging them with her care before retiring to her room. Gabrielle could not sleep, however, and remained wide awake, watching the clock as the time drew nearer and nearer to midnight.

Meanwhile, belowstairs Davis was playing a game of faro with Crane. The Standen butler would glance down at the dachshund at his feet from time to time as he continually lost to Crane. As Crane shuffled the cards he smiled with satisfaction, for every time Davis had a winning hand, he would give himself away by looking down at the dog.

Crane smiled. "Well, Davis, another go?"

Davis was reluctant to accept another challenge and was considering retiring for the night when he suddenly noticed Elva prick up her ears.

"Why, look at that, would you!" he cried out in surprise. "That is the most life this dog has shown all day. Wonder what she hears?"

He reached down to reassure Elva but found that she was of a different mind. Bolting for the door, barking loudly, the small brown form eluded both butlers' attempts to stay her.

"Quick, after her!" Davis shouted, chasing her to the hallway.

Davis saw the dog scuttle across the polished marble floor to the front doors. He ignored the curses Crane was emitting from behind him—having tripped over his own feet—and hurried to retrieve the animal. Davis was puzzled by Elva's behavior as she whined and pawed at the double doors.

"Poor little begger," the butler said sympathetically. "You think your mistress is out there, don't you? Well, I'll let you have a look."

He started to unbolt the door when he heard the unmistakable sound of skirts brushing against the floor.

"Davis," Lady Standen demanded, "what is the matter? I heard Elva from upstairs."

Gabrielle thought she saw the butler go red, but years of service held Davis in good stead, and he regained his composure. He explained the dog's odd behavior and his intention of showing the beast that there was indeed nothing outside.

Elva started to whine and paw at the door again, and the sight was so pitiful that Gabrielle could barely suppress the tears in her eyes.

"Open the door, Davis," she requested as she saw Crane limp to her side with as much dignity as possible.

Drawing back the final bolt, Davis pulled the double doors toward him. For a moment there was absolute silence as Lady Standen and the two butlers stared down in disbelief at a familiar figure who, half kneeling, leaned on the archway of the doors for support.

The small dog at their feet rocketed into action, leaping on the outspent form of Lady Aurelia Courtenay, profuse in her greetings.

Elva's exuberant barking roused the trio from their trance, and three pairs of arms quickly reached out to assist Aurelia into the drawing room.

After the initial shock of seeing her friend alive, Gabrielle was all efficiency.

"Hurry, Davis, fetch sherry. She is as cold as ice," she said, feeling Aurelia's frozen hands.

Lady Courtenay tried to speak but was unable to find the strength, so she lay back on the lounge in exhaustion.

"Light more lamps," Gabrielle ordered, sending Crane about the room.

Davis was sent to the kitchen to boil water and make bandages while Lady Standen helped Lady Courtenay drink a glass of sherry.

"Thank you. That is better," Aurelia murmured weakly as Gabrielle placed a cushion beneath her head.

Lady Standen began to examine the wound. With a sigh of relief, she said, "It looks superficial, but it is rather large. Who did this to you?" she asked, washing the injury with the water the butler had just brought.

Wincing, Aurelia answered through clenched teeth, "Lord Chandler. Did you not guess it?"

"Of course," her friend replied, placing a compress

on the lacerated flesh. "Philip knew immediately. Chandler tried to extort the evidence and his estates from him, but when he found out that you were . . ."

The strange look on Gabrielle's face did not escape Aurelia.

"Found out that I was what, Gabrielle?"

Lady Standen was having trouble formulating her words and finally blurted out, "That you were dead. Aurelia, Philip thinks you're dead. That little ballet dancer, Marie Manton, said you were. She gave Philip your bloody cloak and your ring and said that Lord Chandler had killed you."

Lady Courtenay was confounded.

"My mother!" she exclaimed at last. "You haven't told my mother that, have you? She couldn't bear the strain."

Gabrielle assured her friend of the duchess's ignorance on that subject. No sooner had she told Aurelia this than Lady Faye appeared at the doorway, having been awakened by all the activity.

With an exclamation of joy, she ran to her daughter's side.

"Aurelia, my baby, are you all right?"

Seeing the bloody dress and the remains of the bandages, she blanched, but was quickly reassured by Gabrielle that Aurelia would definitely survive. Nonetheless, her Grace continued to fuss over her daughter as Lady Standen completed the bandaging.

"Gabrielle," Aurelia said, trying to rise from the lounge, "I must go to Philip."

The Duchess squeaked and howled at this, trying to deter her impetuous daughter.

"You are not yet strong enough to travel. At least wait until I can send for a doctor."

"Nonsense, Mama, I must go."

Gabrielle tried to convince her friend of the inadvisability of such a move, but Aurelia would have none of it.

"You know how reckless Philip is," Lady Courtenay

insisted. "He may do something rash. What time is it?"

Gabrielle looked at the clock.

"It is almost eleven, but really, you can't be seriously contemplating traveling in your condition."

"I most certainly am serious. Now, help me to my room, please. I must change. I can't go to Philip looking like this. He probably has over half the ton at his home," she giggled, her whimsy getting the better of her.

Lady Standen would have made another protest, but she knew the obstinate look on Aurelia's face all too well.

"Oh, all right," Gabrielle sighed.

Giving in to the inevitable, she helped Aurelia to her chamber, Crane supporting her other arm, while Lady Faye fluttered about them like a mad hen.

"If we hurry, we will arrive before Philip makes the announcement at midnight," Lady Standen said.

The duchess, seeing that her daughter was indeed intent on killing herself, rang for Renée to assist the girls.

"Well, Gabrielle, if you must go, there is no reason to let the entirety of fashionable society see you in your night clothes. Do put on a gown," Lady Faye admonished. "Renée will assist you, Aurelia, while Gabrielle is changing."

Gabrielle did as she was bidden, and Aurelia, with the maid's help, donned the costume that had been delivered earlier, all the while feverishly conscious of the minutes passing by.

CHAPTER 11

AT THE DALTON residence, the ball was reaching a crescendo as the guests reveled in the pleasures provided by their host.

Lord Royer was more caught up in the mini-drama he had just witnessed, however, than in the entertainments. As he watched the unmistakable form of Lord Dalton walk away from Lord Chandler, he had to admit that his curiosity was intensely sharpened.

"I wonder what Philip said to him," Lord Innane wheezed. "He certainly looks to be in a state."

"That is an understatement," Tristan Culpepper observed. "Near the end there, Philip seemed nearly willing to ignore his surroundings in favor of venting his wrath on Chandler."

"Good God! Will you look at what is coming?"

The voice of Lord Innane drew Lord Culpepper's attention away from the solitary figure in gray. Glancing around, he saw a singularly astonishing apparition: a personage decked out in purple and yellow was approaching the group.

"Gentlemen, how are you?" the buffoon asked, bowing.

The Spanish accent was plain, and Lord Culpepper returned the salute.

"Lord Torres, I am surprised to see you here. I thought you would be on your way back to Spain by now."

Diego Torres's face fell beneath his bright yellow mask, but he perked up almost immediately.

"I could not miss this affair, Lord Culpepper," he explained. "Lord Dalton will be making his announcement shortly."

Lord James said, "And I am sure all our curiosity will be satisfied then."

"Indeed," a voice behind James responded.

Turning his attention to the newcomer, Royer found himself being appraised by none other than Philip Dalton.

Royer made a leg.

"Lord Royer," Philip said, "your attire seems vaguely familiar."

A smile hovered about Royer's lips as he replied, "I hope it finds favor in your eyes, Lord Dalton. I would not for the world wish to offend such a formidable host."

The earl simply raised one brow in answer to this remark. Royer noticed the noncharacteristic tolerance on Philip's part and was surprised.

Perhaps he is storing his thunderbolts for midnight, he mused.

"Gentlemen," Lord Dalton announced, "may I present Constable Morgan."

All heads turned toward a hitherto unnoticed individual dressed as a harlequin. Tall, topping six feet, this thin and lank man made an awkward bow, his upper and lower extremities making an uncoordinated attempt at unity.

"Constable Morgan is here at my request," Philip explained. "I will hand over my evidence to him on the spot after the announcement."

His pointed look at Torres was not lost on the gentlemen assembled, and there was an obvious pause as smiles and snickers were suppressed. Diego was uncomfortably aware that he was being singled out for ridicule by Lord Dalton, and decided that he would do best to absent himself from his host's presence.

Lord Torres made as dignified an exit as was possible under the circumstances. He could hear laughter as he walked away from the group, but he did not let this affect his mood unduly. This was to be his last night in England, and he had every intention of enjoying himself.

Circulating among the guests, the former Spanish diplomat suddenly became aware of someone dressed in a gray domino motioning to him from the doors leading to the garden. He could not tell who it was, and curiosity compelled him to uncover the person's identity.

"Good evening, Lord Torres," the man said as he drew Torres into the garden.

Diego instantly recognized the voice.

"Lord Chandler, I hope your luck in cards has improved."

Chandler made a gesture of indifference with his hand.

"It is of no importance. One loses one night, wins the next."

"It is all up to fate," the Spaniard responded.

"Not entirely," Chandler countered.

"I am a fatalist. Everything in life is up to fate."

"I believe somewhat in fate, but I also feel that one must take an active role in altering one's destiny," Chandler said as they continued to walk.

Lord Torres found these words, delivered with a good deal of intensity, quite perturbing. The glitter in Lord Chandler's hardened eyes made Diego's throat constrict involuntarily. For a moment he felt somewhat foolish for his seemingly unaccountable wish to run away from his present companion, but when he saw something that looked suspiciously like a foil protruding from Chandler's domino, he felt foolish no longer and looked about desperately for some avenue of escape. As he gazed around him, he suddenly realized that he and Lord Chandler had walked rather far from the ballroom and that there were no milling couples in this part of the garden.

If anyone had been in the vicinity at that moment,

he might have heard a faint cry, a thud as if a sack had been dropped, and the sound of something being dragged across the ground.

Innane had detached himself from Lord James's company, seeing that his wife was approaching him, and endeavored to lose himself in the assembly. He made his way toward the open garden doors in the hope of attaining sanctuary from his wife's eternal nagging. At the threshold someone brushed past him.

"Lord Torres!" he called out as the person in purple and yellow moved away. "Odd fish," Innane mumbled to himself. "Rude fellow not to answer me."

Walking out the doors, he reflected on the lack of manners of foreigners.

While Lord Innane made good his escape, it was left to Royer and the others to smooth Lady Innane's ruffled sensibilities. Her husband's unseemly flight at her approach would be the subject of the men's conversation for the next three weeks, she knew, but she covered her irritation well.

"Lord Royer, I have heard so much about you from my husband," Lady Innane gushed, making her way toward the table laden with refreshments, Lord Culpepper her unwilling escort and Lord Royer following close behind.

"I did not realize that Lord Dalton was an acquaintance of yours," she added, accepting a glass of punch from Tristan Culpepper.

"I am acquainted with Lord Dalton as much as it is possible for any mere mortal to be," Royer replied.

"Then I am to assume that Lord Sheringham is no mere mortal, Lord Royer," Lady Innane tittered.

Royer tilted his head by way of reply, his face expressing his doubts about that matter.

"Where is Lord Sheringham, anyway? I have not seen him all evening, and I am positive that Lord Dalton could not have neglected to invite him," the lady observed.

"I am sure he will be present at midnight, which will be in another ten minutes," Royer noted, replacing his watch in his waistcoat. "It would be more appropriate to ask where Lady Standen is. I should think she would be here, considering her attachment to Lord Sheringham."

Lady Innane shot him a look of surprise.

"Surely you cannot expect the girl to come to a party when her friend Lady Courtenay has just been abducted! I am astonished that Lord Dalton is even giving this affair," she commented with disapproval.

Little did she know that at that very moment both Lady Courtenay and Lady Standen were in a coach speeding through the streets of London toward Philip's house.

"Hurry, driver!" Aurelia urged as the coachman cracked the whip once again.

"He is going as fast as he can," Gabrielle observed, smoothing the creases from her costume. She was strikingly attired in the guise of a fairy, complete with gossamer wings, but the outfit was somewhat wrinkled because she had not thought to hang it out.

Lady Courtenay fidgeted in a corner of the coach, barely able to contain her overwhelming agitation.

"What time is it, Gabrielle?" she demanded for the tenth time.

With a sigh, Lady Standen bore her friend's constant inquiries.

"It is five minutes to midnight," she answered, "and we are almost there."

Aurelia looked out the window to see that they were indeed very near Lord Dalton's residence, and for the first time that evening she let herself worry about less important things than Philip's life.

"Gabrielle, do you think I look all right?" she asked as she pulled a small reflecting glass from her reticule and began to arrange the stray curls on her white powdered wig.

Lady Standen looked at Aurelia, who was dressed as

an aristocrat of the eighteenth century, and could find no fault with her appearance.

"You are stunning," she declared. "Philip will not believe his eyes."

The truth in this statement was so obvious that both women broke into laughter of the type created by tension.

"I am sure you have nothing to worry about. Philip can take care of himself, Aurelia," Gabrielle said as she gasped to regain her breath.

"Yes, I suppose so," Lady Courtenay replied breathlessly, pressing one hand to her well-trussed wound.

In her heart and mind she was already with Philip; it only remained to link the emotions with the physical reality.

Back at Lord Dalton's residence, the guests were beginning to gather in the ballroom for the announcement. No one wished to miss the event that had induced nearly all of fashionable society to attend.

"It would appear that Lord Dalton is about to make his disclosure," Lady Innane commented.

Royer glanced about him and saw that this must be the case. The orchestra was being cleared from the platform, no doubt to make way for their host.

"There are still five minutes left," Lord Culpepper said.

Those five minutes were being put to constructive use by Lord Sheringham, who had been occupied for the most part with security.

"Brett," Philip asked while checking the guards with his friend, "have all the guards been warned to keep an eye out for a gray domino?"

Brett looked dubiously at Lord Dalton.

"Yes, they have, but there are at least half a dozen men here wearing gray dominoes. You are taking a risk going up there. Even if Chandler makes a move, you will probably be dead, and I don't like the idea of exchanging your life for his overmuch."

Philip did not seem to be paying any heed to his

friend's words, for he was preoccupied with checking the guards once more.

"Brett," he said at length, "I am sure that our guards—over twenty of them in the ballroom alone—can keep an eye on six men in gray adequately enough to give me due warning of his location. And as for the danger—"

His speech was cut off by a catch of his breath, accompanied by a look of such utter despair that Brett knew of whom Philip was thinking and, subsequently, why he chose to be so negligent as to his safety.

Lord Dalton recovered himself forthwith, and glancing over to the area where he was to make his declaration, noted that there was but a single guard at the doors to the garden.

"Why is only one man there, Brett?"

"I have six men posted outside the garden walls. If Chandler should try to escape by that route, he will have nowhere to go in any case."

This explanation did not satisfy the earl very much, seeing that he would rather Chandler did not have the opportunity to leave the vicinity of his house, but, he reasoned, perhaps he was being irrationally cautious.

"It is time, Philip," Brett said ruefully. "Good luck."

Lord Dalton nodded at his friend and started toward the far wall. The guests, all waiting eagerly for his announcement, parted to form a path for him. He took his time, neither hurrying nor appearing hesitant, for he knew the tension he was building was important to his plan.

As he reached the platform, he could hear the clock striking twelve. A taut silence had fallen over the still assembly, making it seem suspended in time.

Pulling several sheets of paper from the depths of his domino, Philip Dalton took a deep breath and faced the crowd. Along the periphery of his senses he heard the grinding of a coach's wheels on gravel and caught the movement of a purple and yellow form, but he heeded neither. Clearing his throat, he began.

"I have asked you all here because I wish to reveal

publicly the name of a murderer. Publicly, because you all know this man though he hides behind a façade of respectability."

While Lord Dalton continued to speak, tantalizing the audience with bits of information, he was unaware that two new guests had just arrived.

Aurelia could barely restrain her impatience as she waited for Philip's butler to finish his examination of her invitation. She could hear Lord Dalton's voice faintly, drifting to her through the door to the ball-room, and she longed to be near him.

Finally Simpson concluded his perusal of Gabrielle's invitation and handed it back to her. He led the ladies to the ballroom, which they entered masked so as not to cause a sensation.

Gabrielle, who supported Aurelia in her weakened condition, felt her friend stiffen and catch her breath as she beheld Lord Dalton at last.

The scene was unreal. Philip, clothed in funereal black, was looking over the crowd of gaudily dressed men and women from his elevated position, holding them in thrall with his words as Lucifer might the souls of the damned.

After viewing this spectacle, Gabrielle was suddenly very relieved to see Brett's gentle face in a corner off to Philip's side. She forgot her previous anger and wanted very much to go to him.

Motioning to Aurelia, she did not have to speak. Lady Courtenay had seen Lord Sheringham, and nodded for Lady Standen to join him. She went thankfully, and Lady Courtenay drew nearer to Philip.

She did not really listen to what he was saying, for she was too mesmerized by the mere sight of him, but she was vaguely aware that he must be nearing the moment of truth when Lord Chandler would surely make his move.

The danger she had pushed to the back of her mind hung, suddenly, in the air about her. All the people present became a possible threat to Lord Dalton, and because she was wary of everyone, she saw the peril to which Philip was oblivious—the man in the purple and yellow costume.

The figure inched steadily along the wall, drawing closer to the platform, and a feeling of horror grew within Aurelia as she realized that Philip was not aware of him. He was not six feet from the spot where Lord Dalton stood, directly in front of the open doors to the garden. The guard was also unmindful of the man, his attention being claimed otherwise. Only Aurelia saw the glint of the barrel as the assailant raised his pistol and took aim. She was too far away to reach Philip, and seconds before the trigger would be pulled, she knew that there was only one hope.

Tearing the mask violently from her face, Aurelia screamed out, "Philip!"

Lord Dalton, on hearing his name and the cherished voice, moved slightly forward, unable to believe his senses.

It was enough. The shot rang out a split second later, missing Philip's head by a fraction of an inch.

The would-be killer fled into the garden. The guard at the door had attempted to restrain him but was unequal to the task, managing only to wrest the gun from his hand.

Instant bedlam followed. Guards rushed about; women fainted, their escorts trying feebly to restore them to their senses with ineffective massaging of their hands.

Aurelia's and Philip's eyes were riveted on each other, their two minds concerned with but a single desire: to be together. Lord Dalton struggled against the crowd for what seemed like an eternity before he finally reached her.

The two were conscious only of each other as Philip clasped Aurelia to him, the intensity of their feelings creating an impenetrable barrier separating them from the throng.

Aurelia gasped as the violence of his embrace placed an almost unbearable pressure on her wound. Philip drew back at the sound. He saw her go pale as death, and for a moment he feared he had lost her again.

"I am all right, Philip. It is a slight wound, I assure you." Reaching up, she smoothed the worry from his brow.

He looked into her large eyes, a mixture of wonderment and joy mingling with his overpowering love for her. Her appearance had, naturally, been a shock to him. He had half believed that it was her spirit that stood before him, but now that he was holding her and knew the reality of a tangible form, a sweet sensation, almost like drowning, enveloped him.

"My life, my love," he whispered, his eyes drinking in the sight of her.

Aurelia would have liked to gaze into Philip's blue eyes forever, but the hardships she had endured were starting to take their toll, and she felt her knees growing weak. She sank slightly and Philip lifted her in his arms.

The worry reappeared on his face, and Aurelia was determined to erase it.

"I am all right; I am just tired. But you must not let Lord Chandler escape us, love," she said, reminding Philip of his unfinished duty.

She is brave almost to the point of folly. There has never been a woman like her, he thought.

Philip looked about him and saw that Brett and several guards were already busy searching the garden.

Gabrielle was suddenly beside the couple, having managed to push her way through the crowd to assist Aurelia again.

The din was deafening by now as inquiries sounded from all directions about the pair. First an attempt on Lord Dalton's life, then the reappearance of Lady Courtenay—it was all too incredible. The questions would have to be answered much later, however, for their host had more important business to attend to.

Tearing himself away from Aurelia, Philip reluctantly relinquished her to Gabrielle's care, with whispered instructions to a footman to send for a physician.

Aurelia wanted to go with him to help search for Lord Chandler, but she was afraid she might lose consciousness and sat down to rest first.

Lord Dalton hurried into the garden, where Brett and several guards endeavored to control the throng that had poured out into said area. The constable was also among them, having by now guessed the purpose of the charade.

"Have the guards along the wall been alerted?" Philip asked.

Brett nodded vigorously.

"There is no way he can escape us," he replied, "but I am having a dashed difficult time controlling all these people."

Lord Sheringham saw his friend speak to a guard, who left momentarily, then returned bearing a sword. Lord Dalton took it from him as he faced Brett.

"You had best herd our guests back into the ballroom. Make sure they stay there. We don't want any of them getting hurt. Besides," he added, "I want Chandler to myself."

Lord Sheringham would have protested, but he saw the sense in his friend's words as several people began to poke about in the shrubbery.

As Philip turned to go, Brett called out, "Take care, he may yet be armed! I'll follow as soon as I can."

Lord Sheringham focused his attention on the wandering guests, indicating to the guards to escort them inside while gently pushing toward the door one crusty dowager who was prodding a bush with the toe of her shoe.

Just as he thought he had succeeded in containing everyone, two costumed women pushed their way toward him. He barred the way until he saw that they were Aurelia and Gabrielle. By the set expression on Lady Courtenay's face, he knew that she was more than he could handle at this time.

"Brett," she gasped, "where is Philip?"

Before he could utter a word, another unmistakable voice joined Aurelia's in inquiry.

"Yes, Lord Sheringham," Innane rasped, "never tell us that the man has gone off after the killer alone!"

The look Brett shot at Lord Innane conveyed perfectly his wish to consign said lord to perdition.

Innane, impervious to the severe countenance Lord Sheringham exhibited, continued undaunted:

"If that killer should happen to be Chandler, then Dalton is in deep waters indeed. I saw him leave with a sword, and Chandler, as I recall, used to be ever a deuce of a swordsman. I have seen Dalton fence, and"—he paused for effect—"I have my doubts that he is a match for Chandler."

Gabrielle looked daggers at the man, but the damage was done.

"Let me pass, Brett," Aurelia said. There was no sign of fear, just a quiet determination.

Brett considered restraining her, but Gabrielle shook her head.

"I have to agree with her, Brett."

"There seems to be nothing I can say to deter you," he admitted resignedly, stepping aside. "Whatever you do, be careful! Here, take this pistol. If you should meet Chandler first, don't hesitate to use it; I know full well you are able enough," he added wryly.

The two women stepped out into the darkness, Aurelia leaning heavily on Gabrielle's arm for support.

In the interim, Philip was searching along the perimeter of the grounds. He was sure that Chandler would be somewhere near the stone wall that surrounded the garden, trying to elude the guards posted just outside it. He too had seen Chandler leave with a sword, and so he had armed himself accordingly.

Walking stealthily, he heard only the slight crackling of the leaves and debris that he ground beneath his heel. Using his foil, he probed the bushes ahead of him. At times the moonlight was obscured by clouds, and he was forced to feel his way along, his hand brushing the cool, rough stones of the wall for guidance.

He had almost reached the opposite end of the garden and was about to retrace his path when he heard the sound of pebbles falling, and a scratching noise as if someone were struggling to climb the wall. Parting the foliage with his sword, he saw a small open space by the far end of the wall. There, the moon illuminating the stage, stood his stepfather.

Hearing the leaves that had rustled when Philip parted them, Chandler turned fearfully to meet the eyes of his persistent foe. For a moment Chandler lost all hope; then, seeing the foil Philip held, he experienced both relief and elation. It was not that long ago when he had been one of the finest swordsmen in all of England. Surely his ability was not so diminished that he could not make short work of his stepson; yet as he looked into Philip's coruscating eyes, he read the hatred that had been spawned so long ago, and he could not help but feel afraid.

"There is nothing for it, I suppose," Chandler said, his mouth so dry that he had difficulty in forming the words.

Philip did not reply, but had his glance been his foil, Lord Chandler would have been transfixed on the spot. Philip had waited overlong to bring his stepfather to justice, and it had almost cost him his one love. He did not intend to allow the cause of so much grief to escape retribution now.

Motioning Chandler to take his position, Philip stood at the ready, waiting for his stepfather to make his first move. He watched as Lord Chandler removed his gaudy disguise, his own domino having been discarded long ago.

Presenting the tip of his foil to his enemy, Lord Dalton saluted him, a mocking expression on his face. The blades glittered together in the moonlight for a few seconds while Chandler searched his opponent's face for any sign of fear or weakness.

There was none.

Then, tensing his muscles, Lord Chandler lunged swiftly at his adversary. The move, easily thwarted by

Philip, set the tone for the entire duel. Again and again Chandler lunged, and again and again Lord Dalton's blade countered and confounded each effort. Philip was aware of his stepfather's famed abilities, but years of overindulgence and debauchery had ruined Lord Chandler's constitution, dulling his once acute senses. Still, with all his failings, he was no easy mark.

So engrossed were both men that neither realized the presence of a pair of spectators. Aurelia and Gabrielle had followed Philip's trail, their own logic running along the same lines as his, and arrived just as the fight was reaching its peak.

The pistol so thoughtfully provided by Brett was virtually useless, for the opponents moved so swiftly that there was too great a chance of hitting Lord Dalton. The women could only watch as the battle grew fiercer, the shadows cast by the men forming a ghastly parody of the duel on the ground at their feet. Present was the same quality that imbues nightmares with their terror, and Aurelia could not bear to simply stand by impotently and watch as her love faced danger. Stooping painfully, she possessed herself of a large rock, determined that, should the tide turn against Philip, she would fling the stone, disrupting the fighters' concentration, and fire the gun.

Fortunately, as the duel progressed, it became evident to her discerning eye that her intervention would not be necessary. Though the proof of Chandler's skill was before her, she could see that he was growing weaker as Philip was closing in for the kill.

Gasping, his face ashen, Lord Chandler found himself backed to the wall, his moves from side to side blocked each in turn by the steel of Lord Dalton's blade. He was trapped, and Aurelia could sense his indecision. He could save his life if he threw down his sword now.

With a final, lightning-fast lunge, Chandler chose his fate. Parrying the move, Lord Dalton slid his blade along the length of his stepfather's foil, hitting the center of the older man's heart.

The figures seemed to hang in time, the silence deepening over them until slowly, noiselessly, Lord Chandler's body slumped to the ground, a dark red patch spreading over the front of his shirt.

Turning from the body, Philip felt no pleasure or sense of victory; it was more like the conclusion of a chapter in his life, and he was merely relieved.

He was suddenly aware of Aurelia standing a few feet from him. Letting the stone slip from her hand, she opened her arms to him. All at once she was in his embrace, both finally knowing complete happiness.

To Philip, Aurelia personified his hopes for a different kind of life, the joy in living he had thought would never be his before meeting her. Everything was possible now with her by his side.

"My most cherished love," he said passionately, kissing her with all the ardor and intensity of his being. His caress was repaid with interest by Aurelia, who reveled in his embrace.

As is usually the case with such intimate interludes, their moment of bliss was interrupted most rudely by several individuals crashing through the dense foliage into the clearing. Brett was the first to emerge. Seeing Aurelia in his friend's arms and the body of Lord Chandler on the ground, all he could do was walk over to the lifeless form and cover it with the discarded domino.

Thereupon, Lord Innane, who had insisted on coming along, much to Lord Sheringham's dismay, and Torres, whom Brett had discovered wandering aimlessly about the garden, a nasty lump on his head, presented themselves.

Lord Torres, upon seeing that Chandler had been finished off, bemoaned that he had not at least witnessed his demise, having had a strong desire to perform that particular task himself.

Innane, true to his rather fastidious nature, merely inspected the body through his raised quizzing glass.

"Well, Dalton," he said, "it would appear that you are the better swordsman."

"There was never any doubt," Aurelia emphasized, looking lovingly into Philip's eyes.

Lord Innane, quite put off by her remark as well as by her seemingly shameless behavior toward Lord Dalton, cleared his throat and asked, a note of disapproval evident in his tone, "Don't you think it is time you returned to your guests, Dalton?"

Tearing his eyes from Aurelia's, Philip Dalton, that most somber and reserved of individuals, winked at Innane, took Lady Courtenay once more into his arms, and displayed great skill in kissing her before the other gentleman's astonished orbs.

"Well, I never!" Innane ejaculated, raising his quizzing glass to the spectacle.

"Sheringham," he began, turning to look at him, "have you ever—"

His words were cut short when he found that Brett, having apparently lost all sense of propriety himself, was engaging in the same behavior with Lady Standen.

"Really!" he brayed, but he was ignored for the most part by both couples, and entirely by an embarrassed Lord Torres. And rightly so.

◈◈◈ EPILOGUE

Reported in *The Gazette*:

The most dazzling of wedding ceremonies occurred last Sunday at St. Paul's Cathedral as
Philip Lancelot, Earl of Dalton, and Viscount
Brett Montague Sheringham of Lockwood wed, in
a double ceremony, Lady Aurelia Jewel Courtenay and Lady Gabrielle Lettice Standen, respec-
tively. A singularly unusual procedure, that of
allowing Lady Courtenay's lap dog to hold the
position of ring bearer, was the talk of London.
All in all, a glittering and extraordinary affair, one
that has not been equaled or excelled within the
memory of this reporter.

Alice Chetwynd Ley...
The First Lady of Romance

_____THE BEAU AND THE BLUESTOCKING   25613—1.50
Alethea's sheltered life could never have prepared her for the
outrageous Beau Devenish or London in 1780!

_____THE GEORGIAN RAKE   25810 1.50
In England of 1750, one did not defy the social code...but Amanda would
do *anything* to prevent her sister's marriage to hellrake Charles Barsett.

_____THE MASTER AND THE MAIDEN   25560 1.25
Amid the violence of Yorkshire's Industrial Revolution, a young governess
risks her future by clashing with the iron-willed master of Liversedge.

_____THE JEWELLED SNUFF BOX   25809 1.25
Set against the backdrop of Georgian England, lovely and innocent Jane
Spencer falls in love with a nameless stranger who holds the key to her
destiny.

_____THE TOAST OF THE TOWN   25308 1.25
Georgiana Eversley—admired and pursued by all the men around her,
except one. Vowing to change this Buckinghamshire doctor's mind—she
ignores propriety and eventually must pay the price.

_____THE CLANDESTINE BETROTHAL   25726 1.25
In Regency England an unspoken vow awakens young Susan to woman-
hood when she finds herself trapped in a lie and engaged in name only to
Beau Eversley.

_____A SEASON AT BRIGHTON   24940 1.25
Reckless, impetuous Catherine Denham was too anxious to become a
woman to remember to be a lady...something one never forgot in
Regency England.

_____THE COURTING OF JOANNA   25149 1.50
While England is threatened by Napoleon's invasion, romance blooms
between daring, spirited Joanna Feniton and a man who could destroy her
future...and the future of England!

BB **Ballantine Mail Sales**
Dept. LE, 201 E. 50th Street
New York, New York 10022

Please send me the books I have checked above. I am enclosing
$....................... (please add 50¢ to cover postage and handling)
Send check or money order—no cash or C.O.D.'s please.

Name_____

Address_____

City_____State_____Zip_____
Please allow 4 weeks for delivery.   L-28

Available at your bookstore or use this coupon.

We know you don't read just one kind of book. | That's why we've got all kinds of bestsellers.

Available at your bookstore or use this coupon.

___**THE SEVEN PER-CENT SOLUTION, Nicholas Meyer**   24550 1.95
Sherlock Holmes meets Sigmund Freud in this, his most incredible case. At stake are Holmes's mental health and the political future of the Balkans. This #1 Bestseller is "a pure delight!"—CHICAGO NEWS

___**SOMETHING HAPPENED, Joseph Heller**   27538 2.50
The number-one bestseller by the author of "Catch-22" is about greed, ambition, love, lust, hate and fear, marriage and adultery. It is about the life we all lead today — and you will never be able to look at that life in the same way again. "Brilliant."—SATURDAY REVIEW/WORLD

___**HOW TO BE YOUR OWN BEST FRIEND,**
Mildred Newman and Bernard Berkowitz with Jean Owen   27462 1.75
This highly-praised book by practicing psychoanalysts tells you how to make yourself a little bit happier . . . just enough to make a difference.

___**THE SENTINEL, Jeffrey Konvitz**   25641 1.95
A novel that takes you to the very boundaries of belief — and one shattering step beyond.

___**THE WIND CHILL FACTOR, Thomas Gifford**   27575 2.25
Icy tension and hard-hitting action uncover a sinister network of key men in high places plotting the birth of a Fourth Reich — and only one man can stop it.

___**PRAISE THE HUMAN SEASON, Don Robertson**   24526 1.95
An old-fashioned panoramic story of two people who shared a lifetime overflowing with warmth and wisdom, people and events. It will make you believe in love again. "Magnificent."—SAN FRANCISCO CHRONICLE

___**THE SAVE YOUR LIFE DIET, David Reuben, M.D.**   25350 1.95
The doctor who told you everything you always wanted to know about sex now reveals the most important diet discovery of our times — high fiber protection from six of the most serious diseases of American life.

BB **Ballantine Mail Sales**
Dept. LE, 201 E. 50th Street
New York, New York 10022

Please send me the books I have checked above. I am enclosing
$......................... (please add 50¢ to cover postage and handling).
Send check or money order—no cash or C.O.D.'s please.

Name_____

Address_____

City_____State_____ Zip_____

Please allow 4 weeks for delivery.
                                                          L-7

NEW FROM BALLANTINE!

FALCONER, John Cheever   27300 $2.25

The unforgettable story of a substantial, middle-class man and the passions that propel him into murder, prison, and an undreamed-of liberation. "CHEEVER'S TRIUMPH . . . A GREAT AMERICAN NOVEL."—*Newsweek*

GOODBYE, W. H. Manville   27118 $2.25

What happens when a woman turns a sexual fantasy into a fatal reality? The erotic thriller of the year! "Powerful."— *Village Voice.* "Hypnotic."—*Cosmopolitan.*

THE CAMERA NEVER BLINKS, Dan Rather
with Mickey Herskowitz   27423 $2.25

In this candid book, the co-editor of "60 Minutes" sketches vivid portraits of numerous personalities including JFK, LBJ and Nixon, and discusses his famous colleagues.

THE DRAGONS OF EDEN, Carl Sagan 26031 $2.25

An exciting and witty exploration of mankind's intelligence from pre-recorded time to the fantasy of a future race, by America's most appealing scientific spokesman.

VALENTINA, Fern Michaels   26011 $1.95

Sold into slavery in the Third Crusade, Valentina becomes a queen, only to find herself a slave to love.

THE BLACK DEATH, Gwyneth Cravens
and John S. Marr   27155 $2.50

A totally plausible novel of the panic that strikes when the bubonic plague devastates New York.

THE FLOWER OF THE STORM,
Beatrice Coogan   27368 $2.50

Love, pride and high drama set against the turbulent background of 19th century Ireland as a beautiful young woman fights for her inheritance and the man she loves.

THE JUDGMENT OF DEKE HUNTER,
George V. Higgins   25862 $1.95

Tough, dirty, shrewd, telling! "The best novel Higgins has written. Deke Hunter should have as many friends as Eddie Coyle."—*Kirkus Reviews*

LG-2